PRAISE FOR DANGER'S EBB

"If you would like to clearly understand life both at sea and ashore in the Pacific during the height of WWII read Danger's Ebb!

In 1943 my mother worked as a Navy Nurse on both New Caledonia and Guadalcanal and my Dad on the Battleship Washington during multiple actions in the Solomons Islands and the Slot. Danger's Ebb *not only authentically reflects the crucial events that changed the course of the war but captures the heroic and often tragic moments that effected the lives of the men and women who asked for no more than to serve their country.*

Likewise the leadership examples of Adm Nimitz and Cdr Dudley "Mush" Morton and the feel for life in Hawaii and at the Pacific Fleet headquarters provides an accurate sense of the challenges, decisions and emotions of War in the Pacific.

If you enjoy history and a great story you will really enjoy Danger's Ebb."

— ADMIRAL THOMAS B FARGO, FORMER COMMANDER IN CHIEF US PACIFIC FLEET, FORMER COMMANDER IN CHIEF US PACIFIC COMMAND

"John Gobbell brings his Naval hero, Todd Ingram, back for a rollicking cross-Pacific tale that deftly mixes history with story telling at its best! From Vichy France to a hard aground destroyer to Pearl Harbor, Hollywood and eventually Vella LaVella, he weaves a tale full of interesting characters, real and imagined. Full of action that will stir the hearts of naval history and fiction enthusiasts, Danger's Ebb *is the latest installment in this current series of tales of WW II war in the Pacific! Carry on, Commander Ingram!"*

— RADM PETER L. ANDRUS SHCE/MC USN (RET)

"Who would have known a World War II novel about the naval battles in the Solomon Islands would begin with the perfume business in 1943 Paris, France. German occupied Paris, that is. In Danger's Ebb, we meet Coco Chanel and learn of her desperate efforts to prop up Chanel's sagging European sales. She starts a subsidiary six thousand miles away in Noumea, New Caledonia, a French Provence in the war-torn South Pacific. Chanel chooses the LaPresse family, Andre, his wife Charlotte, and their daughter Lolli, all master parfumers, to go there and get things started. Meanwhile, Todd Ingram is given temporary command of a destroyer grounded nearby off Espiritu Santo. Soon, he is thrown against the Japanese as they roar down The Slot trying to recover what they can out of the Solomon Islands. Character development and plotting are excellent as they are in the entire Todd Ingram series. Uncanny is seeing real-life characters such as Coco Chanel, Arthur Lamar, Chester Nimitz' flag lieutenant, and sub skipper "Mush Morton." Gobbell also throws in actors Cary Grant and John Garfield for good measure. This is an excellent work of historical fiction and will keep the reader up until the wee hours."

— DAVID L. SNOWDEN, CHIEF OF POLICE (RETIRED)
BEVERLY HILLS, CALIFORNIA

"Written like only someone who has served on one of these ships can, John Gobbell takes you inside a combat ship as she goes in harm's way. Fans of military machines will enjoy the accuracy and technical aspects while fans of World War II history will enjoy the closer look at some of the less studied parts of the conflict. Regardless of why you pick this up you will feel like you are on the bridge in this fast-paced installment in the Todd Ingram series."

— RYAN SZIMANSKI, EXECUTIVE DIRECTOR HISTORIC
NAVAL SHIPS ASSOCIATION

"DANGER'S EBB *delivers explosive action in the South Pacific during WWII as LCDR Todd Ingram takes on an overwhelming challenge. Not only must he go toe-to-toe with a Japanese naval force that outnumbers his by over two to one, he must do so with a patched-up destroyer, the USS Dunagan, and a crew that had lost its discipline. Gobbell's description of the Dunagan's sea battle in the Solomon Islands will leave you breathless.*"

— H. W. "BUZZ" BERNARD, AUTHOR OF THE PRIZE-
WINNING SERIES WHEN HEROES FLEW

DANGER'S EBB

JOHN J. GOBBELL

SEVERN RIVER
PUBLISHING

Severn River Publishing
www.SevernRiverBooks.com

This is a work of fiction. Names, characters, businesses, places, events and incidents are either the products of the author's imagination or used in a fictitious manner. Any resemblance to actual persons, living or dead, or actual events is purely coincidental.

Registered WGAW : 2132921

ISBN: 978-1-64875-593-4 (Paperback)

ALSO BY JOHN J. GOBBELL

The Todd Ingram Series

The Last Lieutenant

A Code For Tomorrow

When Duty Whispers Low

The Neptune Strategy

Edge of Valor

Dead Man Launch

Somewhere in the South Pacific

Danger's Ebb

Other Books

A Call to Colors

The Brutus Lie

Never miss a new release! Sign up to receive exclusive updates from author John J. Gobbell.

severnriverbooks.com

This novel is dedicated to my wonderful friends over many fine breakfasts. Staunch, loyal, patriots all; amazing first responders some; you all kept me going and, as in the past, provided a strong impetus to complete this work. My Thanks and Bravo Zulu to You.

And to Janine
My wife and love and one fine copy editor. All these marvelous years, I'm so blessed to have you with me.

PREFACE

Todd Ingram is a "Tin Can" man, as was yours truly having learned early on from my father who was a destroyer squadron doctor in the early 1930s. They were a gallant force in those days and on into the 1940s and 1950s.

Destroyermen did crazy and marvelous things, perhaps best evidenced by the men of Taffy 3 at the Battle of Leyte Gulf - Battle off Samar on 25 October 1944. Initially, there were just three American destroyers and four destroyer escorts against a Japanese battle force of over thirty capital ships, including four battleships, ten cruisers, two light cruisers and fifteen destroyers. Our naval air did an outstanding job at the same time. Often without ammunition, they made heroic dummy runs on enemy ships to draw fire, allowing armed planes to swoop in and drop their ordnance.

Without hesitation, these tin can sailors and airmen obeyed the order to immediately advance on the enemy force, fire torpedoes and create mayhem. And that they did. They had a job to do. And they did it.

A few of these fine men were left in the fleet when I went on active duty. By that time, most were near retirement and didn't want to talk about it other than to say, "*we did our job*."

I did hear commentary, though, by listening directly to whomever was left. But my rock has always been Samuel Eliot Morison and his fifteen volume *History of United States Naval Operations in World War II*. Thus we turn to Morison's *Breaking the Bismarks Barrier*, Volume VI. Also for this work, the wings have been perhaps Theodore Roscoe's *United States Submarine Operations in World War II* and his later work, *United States Destroyer Operations in World War II*. Elsewhere, Mush Morton and his USS *Wahoo* have always been heroic figures to me. And I was happy to have a chance to touch on him in this work. See him in the photographic section on my website.

People always ask which of my novels they should start with. My answer is, of course, at the beginning with *The Last Lieutenant*. After that, my recommendation is to read them in chronological order as you see in the opening front papers: *Novels by John J. Gobbell*. Please recall each novel has a pictorial section on my website with photos of locations, ships, and real-life characters portrayed, e.g., Mush Morton, Cary Grant, and Coco Chanel in this work. The charts (maps) also help to orient us across a worldwide stage.

Once again, many thanks to those of you who take the time to write. I've made some great friends through this process and am constantly amazed at your experiences and capabilities. Long may it continue.

Great Health to You and Your Families.

    John J. Gobbell
    Newport Beach, California
    www.johnjgobbell.com
    john@johnjgobbell.com

CAST OF CHARACTERS

Alton C. Ingram (Todd), lieutenant commander, Interim commanding officer, *U.S.S. Dunagan* (DD 504)

Tyler Childers, lieutenant, executive officer, U.S.S. *Dunagan* (DD 504)

Ronald S. Keating, commander, former skipper, U.S.S. *Dunagan* (DD 504)

Jonathon J. Grout, lieutenant, Operations Officer, U.S.S. *Dunagan* (DD 504)

Guy S. Huber, lieutenant, Gunnery Officer, U.S.S. *Dunagan* (DD 504)

Clinton T. Shorter, lieutenant, Engineering Officer, U.S.S. *Dunagan* (DD 504)

Gary T. Olea, lieutenant (j.g.), Supply Officer, U.S.S. *Dunagan* (DD 504)

Norman (n) Lutz, yeoman, first class, captain's talker, U.S.S. *Dunagan* (DD 504)

Theodore R. Myszynski, captain, commodore, DESRON 11, U.S.S. *Whitney* (AD 4)

Jerimiah T. Landa (Boom Boom), captain, commodore DESRON 6, Long Beach Naval Station

Arthur Lamar, flag lieutenant to admiral Chester Nimitz, Pearl Harbor Naval Station

Robert V. O'Connor, commander, U.S. Naval Torpedo Factory, Alexandria, Virginia

James Blackshear, captain, CinCPac staff, Pearl Harbor Naval Station. Presides over mark 14 hearings

Dudley W. Morton, commander, commanding officer, U.S.S. *Wahoo* (SS 238)

Verne l. Skjonsby, lieutenant Commander, executive officer, U.S.S. *Wahoo* (SS 238)

UNITED STATES MARINE CORPS

Gilroy (n) Hitchcock, Gunnery Sergeant, 1st Marines aviation logistics support squadron 13

Victor Harold Krulak, lieutenant colonel. 2nd parachute battalion, Guadalcanal-Choiseul

Alexander A. Vandergrift, general, 1st Marine Division, Guadalcanal

UNITED STATES ARMY

Helen Duran Ingram, Captain, Nursing Corps, Fort Macarthur, San Pedro California – Todd Ingram's wife

UNITED STATES – CIVILIANS

Cary Grant, internationally famous film actor, lead role, *Destination Tokyo*

Delmer Daves, Warner Brothers Studios, Director, *Destination Tokyo*

FRENCH

Coco Chanel – Born into poverty as Gabrielle Chasnel. Raised by Catholic nuns. Boot-strapped her fragrance and fashion business into a major international conglomerate

Andre Gerard Lapresse – Currently master perfumer at Royal Marquis Ltd in Grasse, France. Accepts position with Chanel Pacific in Noumea, New Caledonia

Charlotte Marie Eglantine (nee Duffet), Lapresse – Wife of Andre Lapresse - Currently master perfumer at Royal Marquis Ltd in Grasse, France. Accepts position with Chanel Pacific in Noumea, New Caledonia

Charlotte Marie Carleen (Lolli) Lapresse - Daughter of Andre and Charlotte. Currently master perfumer at Royal Marquis Ltd in Grasse, France. Accepts position with Chanel Pacific in Noumea, New Caledonia

GERMAN
Baron Hans Günther von Dincklage, Coco Chanel's Pomeranian courtesan, member of the German Abwehr

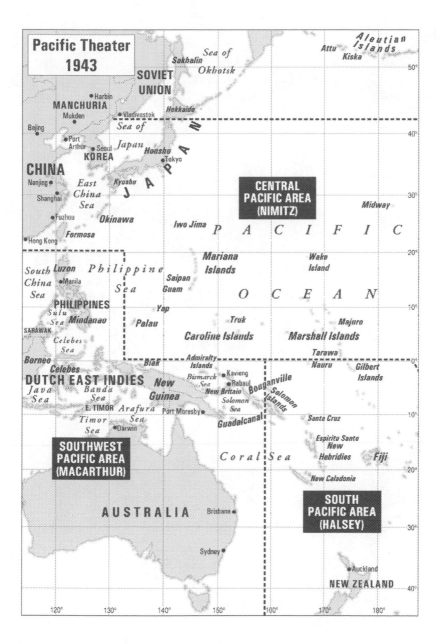

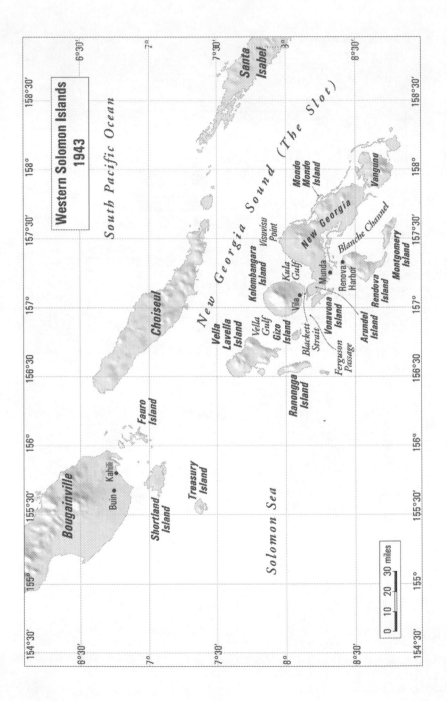

Western Solomon Islands
1943

South Pacific Ocean

New Georgia Sound (The Slot)

Santa Isabel

Mondo Mondo Island

Visuvisu Point

New Georgia

Yanguru

Blanche Channel

Kolombangara Island

Kula Gulf

Munda

Renova Harbor

Montgomery Island

Vella Gulf

Vila

Rendova Island

Vella Lavella Island

Gizo Island

Blackett Strait

Vonavona Island

Arundel Island

Choiseul

Ferguson Passage

Ranongga Island

Fauro Island

Bougainville

Buin

Kahili

Shortland Island

Treasury Island

Solomon Sea

0 10 20 30 miles

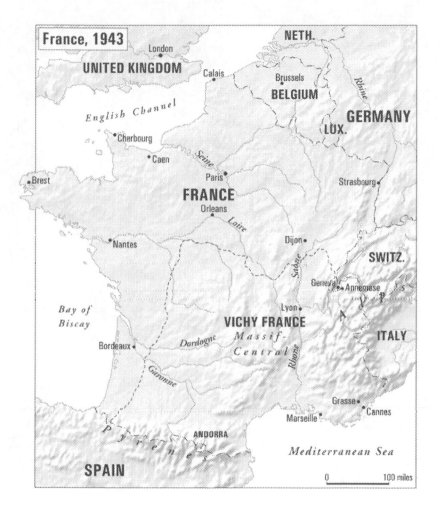

France, 1943

London

UNITED KINGDOM

Calais

NETH.

Brussels

BELGIUM

English Channel

Rhine

GERMANY

LUX.

Cherbourg

Seine

Caen

Strasbourg

Brest

Paris

FRANCE

Orleans

Loire

Dijon

Saône

SWITZ.

Nantes

Geneva

Annemase

*Bay of
Biscay*

Lyon

Bordeaux

Dordogne

VICHY FRANCE

*Massif-
Central*

Rhône

ITALY

Garonne

ANDORRA

Grasse

Cannes

P y r e n e e s

Marseille

SPAIN

Mediterranean Sea

0   100 miles

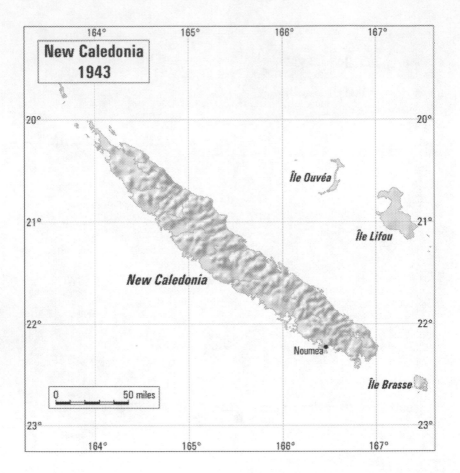

New Caledonia
1943

Île Ouvéa

Île Lifou

New Caledonia

Noumea

Île Brasse

0   50 miles

PART I

Character is like a tree, and reputation is like its shadow.
—Abraham Lincoln

PROLOGUE

21 February 1943
Ritz Hotel
15 Pl. Vendôme
Paris, France

Three figures sat huddled on a marble bench on the vast first floor mezzanine. The entire floor, done in marble, was cold this time of year as the sun remained hidden behind clouds, allowing rain to pelt Paris, day after day. Sitting close together helped keep the trio warm and buffer the fear they felt from the desk before them where a German officer worked tirelessly.

Or so it seemed. The man, Schiller, a Sturmbannführer (major) of the SS, was flanked by two armed guards in shiny jackboots standing at attention with their Karabiner 98k rifles at port arms.

On the bench was Andre Lapresse with two women seated to his right. The woman in the middle was his daughter Charlotte (Lolli) Marie Carleen Lapresse, born in Chartres, France in 1906. Lolli was followed by two still-born children when her namesake mother, Charlotte Marie Eglantine (nee Duffet), sitting to Lolli's right, gave up having more children and doted on their only one surviving, darling little Lolli, now a complete single adult at age thirty-seven.

Andre and his wife Charlotte were master perfumers at Royal Marquis Ltd., founded 237 years ago in Grasse in the South of France just sixteen kilometers north of Cannes on the French Riviera. Beginning in the 18th century, Grasse had become the perfume capital of the world with natural resources in great abundance such as lavender, jasmine, and roses. Later on, Grasse evolved into a major center for fashion, especially women's.

Andre's and Charlotte's families went back generations in the perfume business. Incredibly, they were unknown to one another until they met on the job. There, they fell in love and then later were successful in their careers and at raising their little Lolli to evolve in the business and become a master perfumer, an esteemed classification she reached at the age of twenty-nine.

In a way, inter-marriage, although not widespread, was fairly common at Royal Marquis, a company of 1,300 employees worldwide. Currently, there were six active families in the Marquis organization. Four of them worked at the main processing plant in Grasse. Another pair worked in the main retail store in Paris, and another pair worked in their newly founded subsidiary halfway around the world in Noumea, New Caledonia, a French protectorate. Technically, since the fall of Paris on June 14, 1940, France and its 'protectorates' were to be governed by the German puppet government, the Vichy government.

As it worked out, the Vichy government, with major problems from their Nazi occupiers, did not have the means to defend Noumea on the opposite side of the globe.

Without a whimper, Noumea was summarily occupied on November 8,1942, by the U.S. Army. This was an ominous date since, halfway around the world, the U.S. Army also landed on the North African Coasts in Algeria and Morocco, also Vichy-French protectorates. Thus began the Allies concentrated thrust to throw Rommel out of Africa while at the same time converting Noumea to a major U.S. Navy base for operations in the Southwest Pacific.

But now, in the Ritz Hotel, the Lapresses felt nervous as Schiller went about his exquisite rubber stamping. The Germans were clean-cut. Their uniforms, officer and enlisted, were well pressed. And yet, to Lolli, they were stiff, macabre, and unnatural wearing the SS black uniform. They were certainly handsome men; most were blond and two meters or more in height. The man at the desk, Sturmbannführer Schiller, was typical of this near-Hollywood appearance.

At his desk, Schiller spoke in crisp, unaccented French. Away from his desk, he predictably rattled in his native tongue as if the hotel was afire. Anyone who approached his tidy desk, military or otherwise, was to stand at attention while Schiller went about business.

The trio had arrived as scheduled at 1315 in the afternoon. And now, they had been waiting for two and a half hours. Their bench was near the head of the stairway and exposed to draughts of all kinds. The trio shivered and their teeth chattered, while Schiller sat nonchalantly, pounding away. His uniform kept him warm enough even though little wisps of condensation escaped his mouth and nostrils from time to time. When nobody stood before Schiller, he whistled as he stamped. But no tune escaped his lips. Just condensation and an occasional sneeze followed by a ceremonious display of a spectacular white handkerchief. He dabbed at his nose, then folded and carefully returned it to his top pocket.

Not so with Charlotte or her mother or her father. Their breathing was an effort, nearly forced. Their clothing was enough for the South of France. But not here. From time to time, Andre risked a glance at Schiller. Fortunately, there was no eye contact.

The phone rang. Loud. Strident.

Schiller planted his fists on his hips and looked down at the instrument as if it was going to run away.

Finally, he lifted the handset. "*Schiller.*"

He pulled himself erect. "*Ja, ja.*" He cast a glance over to the threesome. "*Jawohl, Herr General. Zu befehl.*" He stood and clicked his heels. Carefully, he leaned over and hung up the handset. Looking up to them, he said in French. "Yes, she will see all three of you." He scribbled on a small sheet of scratch paper and held it out.

Schiller pointed to a bank of elevators. "They are expecting you."

It was hard getting up. His joints seemed frozen. But Andre rose without, he hoped, displaying pain. Then he walked over and squeaked out, "Thank you." He accepted the paper.

Schiller had written precisely:

Baron von Dincklage
Room 302

Andre turned and gathered his family. Without looking back, they moved over to the ornate elevator bank where he jabbed the number three.

An internal bell located in the shaft rang stridently.

The elevator car descended to pick them up. As a piston in a cylinder, its passage forced air out the door cracks washing them with a soft burst of cold air.

"Brrrrr," said young Lolli.

In a low tone, Andre said, "Easy, dear one. I believe you'll find it a lot warmer where we're going."

Andre was right. Room 302 was a well-heated, two-bedroom suite overlooking the Ritz' main courtyard. Complete with two full bathrooms, a commodious drawing room, kitchen, and library. The Ritz, known world-wide, did not cut corners. The rooms were well maintained and staffed by a group of appreciative long-time employees. And the Baron was attended by a butler-batman as was Madame attended by a maid.

In this case, Madame was Gabrielle Chanel, later known as Coco Chanel. Born into poverty in 1883, her mother died when Coco was twelve years old. Her father gave Coco and her two sisters to the Aubazine convent-orphanage in the Corrèze region of central France where they became wards of Catholic nuns of the Etienne d'Aubazine, an order dating back to the twelfth century.

Lolli was amazed. From the moment she stood, Coco Chanel, a dark brunette with a simple pulled back hairdo, was everything and more than Lolli had imagined. Everything Chanel did exuded grace and elegance. No doubt, she was the master of so many things. Overall, Lolli, decided, she definitely was a beautiful woman, and yet her face was overshadowed with severity, as were all true Parisians in this horrible time of Nazi occupation.

Chanel was seated at a ten-foot couch situated in front of a fireplace where a comfortable set of flames burned. Chanel carried herself in a way that revealed none of her early years. She was her own person, Lolli decided, as she shook hands and offered tea. She wore a simple black skirt and white short-sleeved blouse. The only touch of jewelry was a rhinestone broach on the left side with a matching rhinestone clip in her black hair. She waved to three chairs arranged before the couch. "Please."

As they sat, she said, "I'm sorry we were late. Something came up that took more time than we thought." She was surrounded by folders and documents. She picked one up and then looked at Andre Lapresse. "Georges Devoe thinks highly of you. How did you meet him?"

Andre looked at his two girls then sputtered, "In Grasse, Madame. He showed up at our house."

"Indeed?"

"During dinner. But it was raining. We had him in. Very nice fellow. He stayed for dinner. And...then...and then he brought up this situation around the world in Noumea."

"And your response was to say yes?"

"Madame, when Georges Devoe comes calling, I stand on my head. It was an honor that he was there. In our own house. He is one of the finest in the business. And then the purpose of his visit became more apparent. But it was a great surprise to us."

"Well, I'm glad you followed up." Her smile was genuine.

Andre nodded. It had taken a while. Initially, they'd dodged Devoe's letters. Two months went by. "Yes, he called one evening and suggested we come to Paris." He shrugged. "He is very convincing. How could we refuse?" He spread his hands. "And here we are."

Lolli watched all this. Coco Chanel really is a queen, she thought. Like Papa, she speaks with the royal *we*.

Chanel picked up another folder and began flipping through documents. Silence descended as she read, glanced up to them, and then continued her perusal. Like Schiller in a way.

She looked up and said, "Well, things seem to have gone your way. Doctor Blais thinks highly of you also."

Doctor Neville Blais was the leading scientist at Chanel. They had met yesterday, and he had led them through a technical wringer. Andre was surprised to learn this morning that they were still under consideration. Apparently, Doctor Blais had blessed their candidacy for the position.

Andre replied, "That's nice to hear, madame."

She looked up to Andre. "And you have been spearheading this formula for Royale Hommes."

Andre nodded. "Yes, it is mine. It's the leader into our men's line."

"I see, and how is it doing?"

"Well enough, madame. But..." He shrugged. "Chanel is outdoing me. I can't seem to catch up."

She laughed, deep from within. "You are too humble. We are doing everything we can to beat away your marketers, but I'm afraid you're beginning to prevail."

Lapresse gave a quick bow. "Thank you, madame. But I owe all that to my wife," he nodded to Charlotte, "who has discovered some, ah, lucrative inroads."

"Lucrative," exclaimed Chanel. "They're downright genius. You are leaving us in the dust." With a broad smile, Coco Chanel leaned over and tapped Charlotte on her knee.

"I only wish," said Charlotte, the paragon of humility.

A deep baritone voice echoed from the foyer. "*Wiedersehen, schatze.*" A tall man stepped into the hallway. He was medium height, fair complected, and with a broad smile stretched to reveal a strong row of teeth. "*Ah. Mein Gott.*" He stood straight and bowed and said in French this time. "My apologies. I didn't realize you had guests."

The Lapresse family shot to their feet.

Coco sat back and casually introduced each one to Baron Hans Günther von Dincklage, her Pomeranian courtesan and high-ranking member of the Abwehr, the German military-intelligence service.

Still smiling, Von Dincklage waved them back to their chairs where small talk lasted about twelve and a half seconds. Then the Baron said. "Ahem. Please excuse me. Back to the office. Very nice to meet you."

He directed his gaze to Lapresse. "Madame Chanel is very interested in this project. I hope you give it serious consideration. Au revoir." Von Dincklage gave a bow and clicked his heels with a precision Schiller could barely mimic. And he was gone.

Lollie watched him walk. Normally, not like an arrogant strutting Nazi. Coco picked them well. This one was a true Pomeranian. And raised as a royal. And of course, he was the reason for the two-and-a-half-hour delay. *Rank hath its privileges.*

"Yes, sit, please," Coco repeated. She turned to Lolli. "And, my sweet. You have been a master perfumer for...how long?"

"Eight years, madame."

"Where did you attend?"

Lolli gulped. She was nervous. She couldn't help it. "I apprenticed at the Mane Institute full time for three years. After that, I came back to Royal and started all over as an understudy. Later, I apprenticed to Mama and Papa. They were the hardest."

Charlotte senior elbowed her daughter in the ribs.

Lolli squeaked.

They all laughed with Coco saying, "You have a beautiful smile."

"Thank you, madame."

"And have you had any projects?" Coco asked.

"Well..." She looked right and left. Both parents nodded in the affirmative.

"I am assigned to Le Fond."

"Yes, we know about that. What about *le Bâti?*"

Mother and daughter both gave a sharp intake of breath. Le Bati was a company secret at Royal Marquis Ltd.

Lolli found a voice. "Madame, I'm not supposed to—"

Chanel smiled and waved her off. "That's quite all right. We have good reports about le Bati. It is your project, is it not, dear one?"

Lollie looked from side to side. Both parents spent about ten seconds studying the ornate ceiling before nodding.

Lolli nodded. "Yes."

Coco Chanel whipped off her glasses and checked her watch. "Ah!" Looking back at them, she said, "Very well. I have your applications. You have excellent backgrounds, and we would like to have you join the New Caledonia branch of Chanel Limited, Pacific. It is a Swiss company which will open a lot of doors for you. You are citizens, yes?"

"Yes, madame," they answered. Andre's mother had been Swiss which conveyed citizenship to his direct family.

"Good. We can pay each of you the equivalent of two hundred dollars a month in U.S. dollars. It makes it easy that way. Plus there will be handsome bonuses based upon company performance." She pointed to Charlotte. "We're going after what will be an enormous market, a major flood of U.S. soldiers and sailors in Noumea and possibly throughout French Polynesia. Do you think you can do that?"

"Oui, madame."

"And you, Lolli. We would expect big things from you in new fragrances. New Caledonia abounds with flowers and plants with amazing potential for new exotic perfumes of the tropics. We see the surge coming and would like you to be at the forefront."

"Oui, madame."

Chanel clicked her teeth. Her gaze turned to Andre. "You do have a wonderful record with Royal Marquis Ltd. We could go with that but there may be some difficulty."

"Madame?" he asked.

She scanned a page. "I'm told that you were a member of the FFI. Is this true?"

Lapresse felt as if he'd just been shoved out of a ten-story window. "I... I..."

She said, "Please. Tell me. It won't go beyond this room. But I can't cut corners here."

The FFI was initially the French Forces of the Interior, established in 1940 by Charles de Gaul. Financed by the British and later the American governments, the FFI had become a very powerful resistance group in Southern France and now its tentacles reached north with assassinations, gruesome trainwrecks, blowing up of bridges and ammunition dumps. It was rumored that they were key to the Allied forces in the upcoming invasion of Hitler's Northern Wall, his *Festung Europa*.

Quietly, she asked, "Yes, or no?"

Andre sat straight. "I went to some meetings. But I never signed up formally," he lied. "And that was only for a month or two back in 1940."

Coco Chanel stroked her chin. "And that's it?"

"That is it, Madame."

At length, she said. "Very well. I'm going to endorse the three of you. Consider yourselves hired. Upon leaving here, you will pack your things for shipment to Noumea. This we will coordinate through our Swiss facilities. From Grasse, you bus to Geneva. From there, we fly you to Lisbon. And from there, we will book the three of you on Pan American through to Miami, to San Francisco, Hawaii, Fiji, then Noumea." She smiled and clapped her hands. "A lot of time in the air, but overall, a beautiful trip, don't you think?"

"Oui, Madame," they said.

Calmly, she folded her hands. "Are these terms acceptable?" Her dark eyes darted among them.

Andre looked over to his two Charlottes. They had discussed this over and over. It was unanimous. "Oui, madame," he said with conviction.

Coco Chanel gave a broad smile and a hand clap. "Wonderful. Welcome to Chanel International, AG. In Noumea, you will work with Pryor Benoit, our representative in charge." She tore off a sheet of paper and handed it over. "Either me or my representative can be reached here with questions. But for now, go home to Grasse, pack, and get ready to leave."

She stood and beckoned to Andre.

He rose and stepped to her side where she took his shoulders and hugged him. With the women gasping, she kissed him on the cheek.

Andre gave a sheepish bow. "Thank you, madame."

"Of course." Coco Chanel took Andre Lapresse by the elbow and started him to the foyer. The women followed as she said, "I'm so happy you all responded. In unison, no less. What a marvelous team you make. There are so few who meet all your magnificent qualifications. Thank you for coming."

Seeing them out the front door, Coco Chanel hugged each of the women, pecked them on the cheek, and, without a further word, walked back inside, the door-lock clicking into place behind her.

1

7 March 1943
Royal Marquis Ltd
79, rue Porte d'Orange
Grasse, France

The afternoon was warm, and Harbin Lamare sat in the backyard on an ancient wooden bench beneath a pepper tree overlooking Grasse. And this was unusual, for Lamare was normally seen in his office/laboratory, reading thick manuals, and fussing with beakers and Erlenmeyer flasks.

Harbin Lamare was an associate managing director to Doctor Prewitt Chassé, owner of Royal Marquis, a leading perfume company founded in 1706. And right now, Dr. Chassé was in Marseille checking a load of spices on the docks from Dakar.

So, the coast was clear.

At the age of seventy-four, Harbin Lamare was in excellent condition and rode his bicycle everywhere, especially now with strict fuel rationing. He had been through two marriages, neither one producing children, which suited him. In other words, Harbin Lamare, a balding man with a pencil thin moustache, was devoted to his job.

The day was hot. He was ready to walk inside when Andre Lapresse walked up. Lamare reached and took Andre's hand. The bench squeaked as he sat. Lamare said, "Finally. Glad you could make it. So this is the third day you've said so. Now, you're really saying goodbye. For real this time. And my beautiful Charlottes, will I ever see them again?" For seven years, Harbin Lamare had been Andre's boss.

"When the war is over, my friend. For now, they are at home with last-minute details. And the place is rented."

"Really?"

"Yes. And the bus comes in an hour." He took a deep breath.

Lamare knit his eyebrows. "What is it?"

"This is nice out here. But I rarely see you away from your desk."

Lamare looked from side to side.

"What is it?" asked Andre.

"I found a bug in my office this morning."

Andre stiffened.

"A daily sweep. It can only mean they are on to us. At least on to me, maybe you, too."

"Maybe I should stay. I'd be glad to shoot it out with the bastards."

"Don't be a hothead." Lamare took a deep breath. "This Coco. Why would she do such a thing? I mean she's French, through and through. Isn't that enough?"

"Coco?"

"Yes, Coco. Why would she turn you in?"

Andre rubbed his chin. "I don't think it's her."

"I don't believe it. You have fallen in love, you dog."

"No. She has too much at risk. The three of us have a major commit-ment. They've packed all our household goods. Their company truck is now on its way to Toulon. And tonight, we're on a Swiss Air charter for Lisbon[1]. We share a load of jasmine and roses. Maybe gardenias, too. They really want to go after this Pacific market. You watch, twelve, eighteen months from now, we'll have girls worldwide wearing Chanel Pacific fragrance behind their ear."

"Is that what you call it, 'Chanel Pacific'?"

"Well, I think so. We're just getting started."

"Horse piss."

Andre stared.

"It's a horrible name. Who are you selling to? A bunch of fourteen-year-old juvenile delinquents?"

"It's not set in concrete. We keep searching."

"And you have the formula already?"

"Yes." He smiled.

Lamare closed his eyes and smiled. "Can you tell me?"

"Company secret. Only Lolli knows."

"A blabbermouth. I'll asked her myself."

"All right, all right." Lapresse said softly. "The scent is what you find in the men's locker room."

"What?"

"Before the showers."

Lamare reached over and punched Lapresse's arm.

Lapresse lowered his voice and mimicked a radio announcer. "Horrible. We'll just have to go back to selling deodorant." They laughed.

Shaking his head, Lapresse said, "No, I think it has to be that clown she is shacked up with. Baron von Dincklage. He's top level Abwehr and smooth as silk. He could get anybody to spill the beans. But the issue here is you, not me. You should be the one getting out. Your footprints are all over La Tour-de-Calvagny." Two weeks previously Lamare and three others had blown a bridge over a deep gorge, taking with it two trucks of a five-truck convoy loaded with soldiers.

Lamare's eyes narrowed. "The gestapo is still sniffing around. That's why I am—" he said softly.

"What?"

"Tonight. And yes, that's why we're sitting out here, my friend. Listening devices inside. They're on to me like they might be on to you. So, my friends are sending a boat. A fast one like the Boche have...like those e-boats. I think I'll be in Gibraltar for a while. Maybe I'll see de Gaul. He could help. I'm sure he's noticed your work as well. So, is there anything you need?"

"We'll need lots of deodorant to get started."

The three of them were seated among seven other passengers on a 1923 Olympus bus built to hold fourteen. It was an ancient wood-gas burning bus that rattled its way north on A51 and then over to A41 and on to Geneva. It was a 290-kilometer trip which normally would have taken six hours or so. But this trip would take eight. After more delays, they left about midnight. The weather was not kind to them either, forcing several stops for snow and slides.

The worst part was Madame Marleau, a greying thin woman in her mid-sixties with a dark moustache. She had a shrill voice and was tethered to a little white terrier, constantly yipping.

The dog made so much noise that people complained louder and louder. Finally, just outside of Grenoble, the bus driver stopped, calmly set the emergency brake and walked back and sat beside Madame Marleau.

He leaned over and talked to her.

Gently.

He put an arm around her seat back and spoke. Madame Marleau slid close to him and after about five minutes, they were laughing and smiling.

Madame Marleau reached into a copious purse and produced two treats. The dog, she called him Bruno, slopped them up and soon was asleep beside Madame Marleau. The peace brokered, the bus driver marched forward and got them moving again.

Finally, they rolled into the little border town of Annamese. Andre checked his watch. O832. Geneva, beloved Swiss territory, was just across the street. They had counted on breakfast there. But now...

"Hungry," whispered Charlotte.

"Hot cakes and sweet rolls waiting for you over there." Andre pointed across the street.

But a large guard house was in the way with concrete ramming barriers, barbed wire, and a thick wooden barricade that swung over the road. They were still in France. Vichy controlled France.

The bus driver dutifully switched off the engine and gathered the passports in a pile. The double doors protested loudly. The driver growled and kicked at them. The doors groaned open to the cold. His feet crunched in snow as he walked across the road to the German control house.

Bruno started yipping. People groaned. They waited in hopes that

Madame Marleau would have more dog treats. She didn't. Twelve minutes passed. People stirred restlessly.

Charlotte rose to Andre's ear and whispered, "I don't like this."

He looked over to Lolli. Asleep. "Ummmm."

"What if we get separated?"

"If that happens, keep going. Run if you must."

"I won't leave you."

He looked up. The bus driver was returning, the passports clutched in a thick gloved hand.

"If something happens, leave me. You two are the most important."

"I won't."

"Two out of three isn't bad if it comes to that. Do what I say. I can handle these pigs. But I don't want them near you."

"But—"

"Do it," he ordered.

She looked at him wide-eyed.

He kissed her on the nose. "Do it," he pleaded. "Please. I live for you."

The doors protested as the driver swung in. He looked up to the passengers. With a wave of his hand he called, "*Allez.*"

Little Bruno yipped and spun in circles. Madame Marleau reached for treats. Gone.

People groaned.

Amazing, thought Andre. *We're clear to go.* "That's for me," he said. He swung out and to his feet. "Come on, before Hitler changes his mind."

He looked over and realized Lolli had been awake. And then they knew she had overheard. With her mother, she stood saying, "Papa. Don't you think—"

"Go!" Andre ordered. "No time now. Get going."

"Go," repeated her mother.

Lolli turned and shuffled down the aisle.

Bruno yipped. He didn't want to go and dug in his paws. Madame Marleau gritted her teeth and dragged him the rest of the way and toward the door.

He piddled on the front doorstep.

Madame Marleau screamed at him.

After Bruno and Madame Marleau, the Lapresses were the last ones off the bus. One by one, the driver handed back their passports, and with a thin smile, pointed to the luggage compartment beneath the passenger deck. To conserve fuel, each passenger had been allotted just one suitcase. Madame Duval, Coco Chanel's assistant, had warned them of this so they were prepared. The Lapresse family each had worked hours getting the right things packed.

Moving ahead of Madame Marleau and Bruno, Andre grabbed two suitcases: one Charlotte's, the other his. Lolli walked on ahead with hers in hand. The line moved quickly. Soon, they were up to two German guards and an officer, a young *Leutnante* (lieutenant).

The officer held up a hand and asked in well accented French, "A moment please."

"Oui." Lolli stood right up to the officer.

"Passport, please."

"Of course." Lolli handed over her passport and looked him in the eye.

He was taken with her. He hardly read the passport. The others looking on made him nervous. At length, he handed it back, "*Ja, Ja.*" He waved her through.

Lolli crossed over a few meters in Swiss territory and looked back.

Charlotte was next. She was better than her daughter. Her hazel-green eyes skewered the German. He actually stumbled as he handed back her passport. He managed, "*Danke.*"

"*Keine Ursache.*" She rattled at him. And stepped over to join her daughter in Switzerland.

It was now Andre's turn with little Bruno right behind barking and yapping.

Handing the passport to the *leutnante* Andre leaned back and said to Madame Marleau, "He's hungry."

She looked at him, her face flushed and screwed up in irritation. "You don't think I know it?" She kicked at one of the guards. "Look at these fat Boche. They confiscated all my food, including my dog food at the last stop."

The guard had neatly parried her kick and jumped away.

Unaware, the *leutnante* looked at Andre and nodded toward the guard house. "Can you come with me, please?" He raised the passport in the air and tapped it against his cap brim.

With a growl, Bruno jumped on the guard's foot and bit his ankle. With the protection of the guard's boot, the dog bite wasn't too powerful. Yet it was enough to throw the guard off balance. "*Scheise*."

The guard stumbled into the other guard, both men cursing.

The *leutnante* looked down on Bruno. "*Was ist...?*

The passport was still held high as the *leutnante* took in Bruno and the guards.

Andre reached up and snatched it. "Thank you." Suitcase in hand, he ducked under the barrier and ran into Switzerland.

"*Halt*," shouted the *leutnante*. He pulled a pistol from his holster, a 9-millimeter Luger P08, and leveled it.

But Andre had, by this time, scrambled about five meters into Swiss territory,

dragging his suitcase.

"*Komm zurück.*" (Come back) ordered the lieutenant.

Andre stood to his full height and bit his lip. Then he spun on his heel and began walking backwards, holding his suitcase chest high.

It became quiet. The bus passengers began to back away. The bus driver too, on the French side.

"*Was*?" Two Swiss guards ambled out of their hut about ten meters distant and began walking toward them.

Andre kept moving, backwards, deeper into Switzerland.

The lieutenant racked the Luger's slide. The sound ripped among them as a round was chambered. "*Jetzt*," (now) he shouted.

"You can't do that," Charlotte shouted across the barrier. "He's a Swiss citizen. Look." She pointed to the Swiss guards who began unlimbering their rifles.

Andre shuffled past the women. And kept going.

"*Bleib stehen, oder ich schieße*," Screamed the *leutnante*. (Stop or I shoot). He leveled the Luger on Andre.

"He's Swiss, I tell you," screeched Charlotte.

"Papa," wailed Lolli.

"*Nein!*" shouted one of the Swiss.

A growling Bruno clamped down on the *leutnante's* ankle and yanked back and forth.

"Verdammt." The German officer snarled and kicked the dog. The dog squealed in pain. But the *leutnante* stumbled and lost his balance.

The Luger fired. The bullet hit the pavement and ricocheted into the distance.

Andre ran and disappeared behind a car.

The Swiss guards watched him go. One turned and began following Andre, the other stared at the *leutnante* and unlimbered his rifle.

The open-mouthed *leutnante* shifted his gaze to the Swiss. "Ach." He dropped his hand, the pistol hanging loosely. "Scheise."

2

For the first time in years, since the Germans had occupied Paris, the Lapresses enjoyed themselves as simple tourists. They slept soundly and took long walks. And they enjoyed food that had been completely forgotten in France.

And the coffee. From all over the world they had any coffee that suited them. Charlotte and Andre settled on *Casa Nova*, a Brazilian coffee while Lolli enjoyed the bean harvested in the South Pacific, the Solomons. It was the sunshine, she claimed. Her beans got more sunshine, more vitamin D.

Two days ago, they had taken a train to Sintra, a trip of about thirty kilometers, and marveled at the architecture and beauty of the restored castles. One, for example, was the Varzea de Sintra where they toured the Quinta da Regaleira, a beautiful 16th century castle brought up to Renaissance standards. Everything, they agreed, was simply gorgeous and looked move-in ready.

. . .

But after five days, anxiety began to set in. The real part of their excursion would start tomorrow when they were to board a Pan American Boeing B-314 clipper for the Azores and then on to Miami.

They worried about German fighters who were on the prowl from airbases on France's Southwestern coast. So much so, that American or British fighters escorted the U.S. inbound and outbound flights for 150 miles west of Portugal.

And now, they had vowed to have just a simple dinner, turn in early and then get down to the Pan American Airline sea plane ramp for their flight across the Atlantic; first to Horta in the Azores to refuel and then on to Miami. It was the second time their Swiss citizenship had come in handy. This time, it had translated to direct acceptance aboard the Boeing, an American airliner, and flight 12A to Miami.

It all went so smoothly in Portugal with no black-suited SS agents popping out of bushes and reaching to arrest anything in sight and drag them to gestapo headquarters.

Andre and Charlotte got up at 6:00 a.m. the next morning and walked across the hall to wake Lolli. She refused to get out of bed, but Charlotte, foreseeing this, had her own key and they burst in. A pillow fight followed with everybody laughing and the parents dragging their daughter out of bed. It took the two of them to shove Lolli into the shower, bed clothes and all. They left her there, spewing and sputtering.

They had breakfast at 7:00 a.m. After that, Andre sent Mme Duval, Coco Chanel's assistant, a progress report, as promised, via telegram.

Next, a cab whisked them to the Cabo Ruivo seaplane base by 7:50. They were inside by 8:00 a.m. But Andre's heart jumped when the ticket clerk held up his hand. Something was wrong. It was their passports. The officious little man ordered them to step out of line and wait. He said the problem was their Swiss citizenships. While Andre and the two Charlottes stood aside and looked about nervously, the clerk picked up the phone and dialed a three-digit number. A rumbling male voice at the other end screeched at the clerk that the United States was not at war with Switzerland and therefore, the Lapresses were to be admitted aboard the aircraft.

The clerk was Portuguese and indifferent. He didn't care if he had just scared the daylights out of the Lapresse family. He stamped their passports and then their tickets. After that, he ceremoniously removed his stubs, and nodded over his shoulder to a door to the seaplane ramp: their gate to freedom which they tried to approach very nonchalantly, even though they wanted to bolt.

Pan American had vowed to keep its commercial routes open during the war and was able to book freight and passenger service, although expensive, on the surviving clipper routes. Their B 314 was painted in U.S. Navy livery: Mediterranean blue with a large three by four national ensign under the pilot and co-pilot's windows. The plane held seventy-four in great comfort, but for this trip, it was only booked for half.

Once aboard, the Lapresse family learned they were assigned to the last of the B 314's six main compartments.

It was quiet as the crew filtered aboard along with flight attendants to take care of the passengers. People settled in their seats and buckled up.

Their trip through the fourth compartment was somewhat sobering. There were Americans in this compartment. Army, it looked to Andre. There were two bunk beds and four chairs. One of the chairs was occupied by a man in ill-fitting civilian clothes who just looked straight ahead, his face expressionless. But at the same time, it screamed with emotion, Andre saw. It was the *one-thousand-yard stare*. Very unnerving. He didn't know what to do except shift his gaze elsewhere.

Lolli, in particular, became subdued and quiet, unlike her normal bubbly self.

A man in the lower berth was hooked up like a hospital patient. Most of his body was heavily bandaged. He had a full head of dark red hair. His face and his shoulders were unscathed. But the rest of him, including his arms, were all covered.

A tall, thin, sparrow-headed woman leaned over him with a hypodermic. Her name tag read **SHEILA THOMPSON, RN**. She found a place in his arm.

The red head grimaced as she jabbed it in. Then he saw Lolli. "Hi ya, Toots," he called.

Lolli beamed. She bent over. "Hello, Joe."

"It's George," he said. He held up a bandaged hand.

She took it gently. "Okay, George."

Andre stood behind them for the two or three minutes they talked. Finally an attendant came up, "Sir, could you please clear the aisle and take your seat? We're getting ready to take off."

"Of course."

Andre wrapped an arm around Lolli. "Time to go, sweetheart. We must get in and buckle up."

Lolli stood straight. "That means me, George. See you later." She tapped George on the nose.

"Whew!" he said. "Glory be. I'm in love."

They walked on with Andre leading his smiling daughter to the last compartment. There were three chairs, two berths, and a mirrored table for cosmetics. A small writing desk and chair was off to the right. Their luggage was already aboard and arranged on separate stands.

He nodded to one of the berths and looked at Charlotte. "Do you mind?"

She arched an eyebrow and said softly, "I think we can fit in that one quite nicely." She looked at Lolli who pretended to blush.

They were buckling up when the flight engineer started rolling the four Wright GR-2600 Twin Cyclone, 14-cylinder radial engines. The ground crew shoved the sea plane away from the dock and the Boeing taxied out to the fairway. Seven minutes later, the pilot fire-walled the throttles with Andre finding himself leaning forward against his seat belt, urging the giant Boeing into the sky.

They climbed to eight thousand feet and, within minutes, two American P-38s slid into formation on each of the Boeing's wings. The twin-engine lightnings remained in place for an hour and a half, their pilots constantly scanning the skies behind and ahead. Then, they each threw a salute and peeled off to return to Gibraltar, leaving the B-314A alone on a smooth, clear blue day.

While Andre read, his wife and daughter played parcheesi until they landed in Horta Bay in the Azores, around 1:00. The B-314A was refueled while the passengers took lunch ashore.

Two hours later, the giant seaplane lunged into the air for the longest leg of her journey; twenty hours to Dinner Key in Miami, Florida. It would be an overnight trip with the seaplane scheduled to arrive at 11:00 the following morning.

Andre settled down with a book while Charlotte and Lolli walked forward to mingle.

It was dark in the fourth compartment . The thousand-yard-stare man was asleep as was the man in the upper bunk.

But the lower bunk. Charlotte looked closer. The man on the lower berth was covered head to toe with a blanket. She looked sharply at the nurse.

Nurse Thompson nodded. "Gone." She whispered. "A half hour ago. The doctor tried everything, but he...he..."

Charlotte looked at Lolli.

Lolli's hand was to her mouth. The shock evident. She had heard. "Was he the red-headed guy?"

"Well, yes," said the nurse.

"He smiled at me when we first came through. And then...and then he winked.He called me Toots."

"Yes, that was George."

Lolli continued, "I know, and we spoke. He knew French. And he knew something about perfuming. He was..."

"Lolli," said Charlotte. She took her hand and squeezed gently.

Lolli looked at the nurse, "Really? His name was George?"

Sheila replied, "That's right. George. But he just didn't want to live. He was in a lot of pain. Burn victim. He hated morphine. Made him sick. We tried to give it to him but he said no." Sheila eased an arm around Lolli. "It's okay, sweet one. George is in a better place now."

A tear ran down Lolli's cheek. "I don't understand."

Sheila said, "It was his heart, hon. It just gave out. Too much. Always on the edge since I met him four days ago."

"Argh!" she wailed.

"It happens," added Sheila.

"Shhhhhhhh." Charlotte wiped away the tear with a forefinger. She bent low and asked, "You still want to go and mix?"

Charlotte whispered back, "I guess so."

She looked at Sheila. "Okay if we go up there?"

She shrugged. "Fine with me, I hear them singing."

"Singing?"

Sheila smiled. "It's Agnes. One of us. She's pretty good with a guitar." She nodded toward Lolli. "Probably get her mind off of it, too."

Charlotte added quietly, "You see, the Boche came to our company and grabbed one of our perfumers. A brilliant red-headed, young man. He was up and coming. On track to become a master perfumer."

Sheila crossed her arms. "Let me guess. His name is George."

Charlotte said, "Yes, his name was George."

Sheila said slowly, "Another guess. You said His name *was* George?" she repeated. "Yes?"

"That's right." Past tense.

"What happened?"

"The Boche shot him. Right out in our courtyard."

"My God."

"Bad for Lolli. She went blind for a week. Wouldn't eat a bite for three weeks. Hysterical blindness, the doctor said. We took her to this top-notch ophthalmologist in Lyon. He said hysteria reduces or cuts off the blood supply to the optic nerve. So it stops sending images to the brain. And that's it. Sometimes your vision comes back. Sometimes it doesn't."

The nurse turned to Charlotte and hugged her. "You and your husband have done a magnificent job with your little Lolli. Keep loving her."

"Thank you." Charlotte pecked Sheila on her cheek and took Lolli's hand.

They nodded to Sheila and stepped forward.

From the moment they opened the hatch, it was all different. The lights were bright.

A nurse, a short-haired brunette, was playing the guitar and singing *Home on the Range*. Her name tag read **AGNES WHITMAN, RN**. She was sitting on a table beside a grinning passenger with a long moustache. His knees were drawn up in his seat and he was singing along in a duet.

His baritone was as good as Agnes' alto.

The two of them were pretty good. But for now, most of the eyes in the compartment passed over Charlotte, then over to Lolli. And stayed there.

The seaplane hit some chop. Things jumped around. Thermometers fell. Glass rattled. An ashtray fell on the floor as more than one passenger cursed. Charlotte reached and grabbed a chairback. Lolli tried the same thing. But both hands missed. Charlotte grabbed her arm with her left hand and got her steadied. "You okay, sweetheart?"

"Uh-huh."

The air smoothed. The big Boeing droned on.

"Maybe we should go back," offered Charlotte.

"I'm okay, mama. Any time you want to go."

Agnes hit some chords then came up with *In the Evening by the Moonlight*. Everyone jumped into that one. The cabin resonated with their harmonizing. Their mainland-USA-bound voices thundered.

And then Charlotte saw it. They were passing a bottle of booze. Their voices were well lubricated.

Ba Ba Black sheep was next. Fred Waring never had it so good, as the passengers crooned and harmonized and sang their hearts out. It was deep.

And then the aft hatch opened. A man stepped through. Andre! Charlotte spread her mouth in a wide grin and ran into his arms. People clapped and cheered thunderously as the two kissed.

The song was over. But then Agnes got them going with *Auld Lang Syne*. People who had never met before were arm in arm as they sang the universal words. They cheered and Agnes started it again. The bottle got to Andre. He tipped it up and drank, then passed it to an elderly couple beside him.

Near the end, a man, a blond kid with long hair, reached for Lolli. But she twisted away. The youngster grabbed her arm but again, she pulled away, this time growling. She backed away. Looking from side to side like a cornered dog.

With slight nods, Charlotte and Andre looked at one another for confirmation. They'd seen it before. When the German SS shot George Descoteaux in the courtyard of Royal Marquis Ltd., in Grasse, France. His crime? Being Jewish.

Their daughter had once again gone blind.

3

15 March 1943
Phillipe Auberge Hotel
Baie des Citrons (Lemon Bay)
Noumea, New Caledonia

Gunnery sergeant (flying) Gilroy Hitchcock was in Noumea to pick up a new TBF, or as he discovered later, a seriously reworked TBF with several bullet holes nicely patched. Three bullets had entered the cockpit and exited the other side without doing too much damage, he hoped, to the pilot or to the equipment. She had been reworked and painted and was ready to go. Until...Hitchcock discovered the sparkplugs hadn't been changed after 400 hours of rugged use.

So, he didn't make friends when he insisted on a new set of plugs. It went all the way up to the base executive officer, a lieutenant colonel named Jon McGovern. He'd been a TBF pilot as well, They'd known one another in Pensacola, when both were learning to fly. Once or twice they had gone out and painted the town.

Hitchcock came close to yelling at a superior officer insisting on a plug change. The XO's shoulders sagged in agreement. Not only did he authorize the spark plug change, but he gave Hitchcock an overnight pass to enjoy a good meal somewhere in a good hotel without bedbugs.

McGovern found the cheapest room in a very nice hotel. A tiny room next to the elevator with a bath across the hall at the Phillipe Auberge, a top-grade hotel on the *Baie des Citrons* (Lemon Bay). After checking in, Hitchcock changed into shorts, a t-shirt and walked across the *Rue du Captaine Desmier,* an expansive boulevard. The sun was bright, the sand a soft powder, something he could dig his feet into; the whole setting was something that would give Waikiki a run for its money. It was early afternoon and he sat on a towel, looking out into the near mirror-smooth bay.

Gorgeous. The water was clear; and once in, one could see thirty, forty feet under water along the shallow bottom. Little orange and silver fish darted about in large schools, here, there, and then zap! Gone.

He sighed. It was wartime. The beach was empty, except for a trio on the boulevard. A man in street clothes stood beside two women, also in street attire, sitting on a park bench under a palm, fanning themselves. They were hot. The man sorted through a folder of slick brochures.

They were a family, he guessed. Maybe French. The man, a stalwart fireplug with salt and pepper hair and a solid chin. Early sixties, maybe.

The woman, gorgeous, but foreign looking. Also sixties yet very attractive with shoulder-length reddish brown hair and blue eyes. Very fetching. Most likely she was the wife. Beside her was a similar edition in her mid to late thirties. Same features, much younger. A daughter, probably. The sun caught flashing white teeth. Spectacular.

Hitchcock, you fall in love too easily.

It was the way she talked to her mother. She shrugged in the most provocative way. Bare arms in a sun dress only emphasized it.

Another couple sauntered toward them, a man and a woman in beach clothes. He was short, maybe five seven, with a five o'clock shadow. She was about the same height and her hair was tied back in a bun. She twirled an umbrella over her shoulder. She walked right up to the man in street clothes and the next thing Hitchcock heard was a squeal. The man was stumbling in place, the other man walking close behind.

Hitchcock saw it. The little bastard's hand flashed. That was it. The two men smiled and apologized for apparent clumsiness. Then the couple were on their way along the *Rue du Captaine Desmier*.

Hitchcock stood and rubbed his chin. The couple walked faster.

What the hell? he decided. "Hey, you!"

The man broke into a run.

The man in street clothes didn't understand what had happed. Nor did the two women. All three looked on, puzzled.

Shiiiit. Hitchcock broke into a run after the little guy. By this time, he had a one-hundred-meter lead. But Hitchcock was in good shape. The little guy wasn't. Soon, Hitchcock had him cornered in a parking lot. He was backed up against a car, a Renault.

"Hand it over, dipshit." Hitchcock beckoned with his fingers.

The man's face turned to that of a black adder. Dangerous. His eyes like slits. His tongue flicked over his teeth. He whipped out a long-handled knife. "Click." A stiletto. His tongue flicked again.

"Come on, Pierre." Hitchcock stepped close.

The man slashed at Hitchcock. But Hitchcock jumped back far enough to let the knife pass. Then he grabbed the man's wrist. And twisted. Heard a crack.

The man screamed horribly. The knife dropped. With his free hand the man reached to pick it up. Hitchcock kicked him in the balls.

The man screamed horribly again and dropped to his knees. With both hands, Hitchcock clapped the man hard over his ears. The little man fell to his side groaning, nearly unconscious.

Hitchcock rolled the man to his back and patted him down. There. He pulled it out. The man's wallet, loaded with U.S. dollars.

The pickpocket's girlfriend, or whatever she was, stood about ten feet away. Hitchcock called over, "His wrist is broken, maybe an eardrum or two busted. You better start taking care of him." He picked up the stiletto, folded and locked the blade, and dropped it in his pocket.

The other man was there also, the one in the street clothes. He walked over to Hitchcock, his hand out to shake. Hitchcock lightly slapped the wallet in the man's hand. "Welcome to Noumea, Mr. ...ahhhhhh..."

Andre Lapresse," he bowed.

Hitchcock replied, "Gilroy Hitchcock, United States Marine Corps at your service."

They shook and walked on back to the women.

"Marine Corps?" Andre asked.

"Yessir."

Andre waved a hand. "Ah, that explains it. I've never known a gendarme quite so accomplished."

Hitchcock pulled out the stiletto and showed it. "That was his undoing. Didn't know how to handle a knife. Here, you want this?" He held it out.

Andre took it and turned it over. "A CZ Swingard, not bad. But no thank you, monsieur." He handed it back.

Interesting. This guy knows his stuff. "Okay," Hitchcock tossed it into a garbage can.

They came up to the women and Andre introduced the two Charlottes. He shook hands and studied the younger. Something was not right. The elder Charlotte caught his glance and waved her hand over her eyes. *Blind,* she mouthed.

They talked under the sun, then moved into the shade, enjoying each other's company. Hitchcock was amazed these cultured French were letting him join them. They were delightful, especially young Charlotte. They called her *Lolli* and she responded with *Papa* and *Mama*. Her voice was low, her English excellent. All three displayed that compelling European sense of humor even though they were thousands of miles from home. Andre explained their business purpose in Noumea but did not discuss wartime Europe. For the same reason, Hitchcock did not bring up the war in the Pacific.

A waiter walked across the boulevard and took drink orders. Later, Hitchcock tried to pay, but Andre grabbed the check and took care of it.

They talked and relaxed in the mild sun. Eventually, the sun fell over the palms and headed toward the horizon. Andre invited Hitchcock to dine with them. Of course he accepted graciously.

They were at the same hotel, so they met downstairs in the restaurant. He wore class A khakis; the only dress uniform he had in the South Pacific. He wasn't parade ground presentable, but he still looked like a Marine.

After they sat, Andre focused on his wings. He pointed, "Ah, you are a pilot?"

Hitchcock bowed, "Guilty as charged, Andre."

"Fighters?"

"No sir. I sort of fly people and parts and supplies and medicine around the zone. That's why I'm here. To check out my new plane."

"Is it a good airplane?"

"Sure, a TBF. One of the best, This one is a little haggard. Seen its day, so they took it off the line for combat. I just fly it around to deliver parts, medicines, and supplies." He winked, "You know, scotch, bourbon, gin, critical stuff like that."

Andre grinned.

"Tell you what," he said. "Tomorrow, I check my plane out. Just got a new set of spark plugs. I can take all three of you up tomorrow on a check ride, ten or twenty minutes. Then I return to my duty station up at Guadalcanal."

Andre and Charlotte looked at one another and nodded. Andre leaned over to his daughter, "Okay with you sweetheart?"

"Sounds exciting. Yes, okay."

The menu was limited: Hitchcock chose steak while the Lapresses picked

halibut. Wine was served and conversation swung all over the place. Over salads, Hitchcock was fascinated when they talked about perfuming and what they were doing in New Caledonia. Then they told him about all the products that must be included to make a successful perfume. And Noumea had great potential as a new source. For example, they explained Chanel No 5 had 83 different ingredients. The formula was locked in a vault in Grasse so impenetrable that even the Boche could not get in.

There was a five-piece band who played slow music during dinner. Later, coffee was served and Andre and Mama insisted Hitchcock and Lolli dance.

Lolli acted flustered and waved her hands. "No, no."

Hitchcock's chair squeaked as he stood and shoved it back. He bent over and took Lolli's hand, "Would you care to dance with me ma'am?"

She made a show of sputtering. "You see, I'm...I can't..."

Gently, Hitchcock pulled her to her feet. "Why don't we try?"

And they were on the floor. They began dancing and she followed him well. She was close and...her perfume. It was dynamite. In a way, it made him want to throw her over his shoulder and head for the nearest clump of bushes.

He decided to ask, "That scent, that perfume, what is it?"

"It's called *Je te défie.*"

"Wow! It's driving me nuts."

"Oui? Nuts?"

"Yes, nuts. Like in crazy. Can't you tell? I'm breathin' hard."

She gave a chuckle. "A little secret?"

He held her closer. "It's safe with me, Lolli."

"It's mine. It means *I dare you*. It's my formula."

"Wow! You did this?"

"Oui, monsieur."

He made a show of breathing deeply. "Mmmmmm. But how come we haven't seen it?"

"The Boche. They won't let it out of France. We must wait until the war is over."

"Let's hope that's sooner than later."

Early next morning, Hitchcock called the base and insisted on being put through to Lieutenant Colonel Jon McGovern, his executive officer friend.

He came on the line. "Yes, Gilroy, you have your stupid spark plugs. What is it now? You want a bathtub installed? Maybe a year's supply of beer?"

Hitchcock told him.

"No. French civilians? Definitely not."

They talked some more.

The cab pulled up to the main gate. Hitchcock talked to the sentry. After checking Hitchcock's ID, the sentry signaled. Three flight suits and three parachutes were brought out. A Jeep escort lead them to hardstand and the TBF. Hitchcock waited outside while they worked on the flight suits. Then they got out and walked around the avenger while Hitchcock explained about the airplane and then where they were going to be. With parachutes on, he first put Lolli into the radioman's compartment, just aft of the pilot. The turret gunner's compartment was too small and cramped so he got Andre and Charlotte into the bombardier's compartment down below. There were windows on each side and there was plenty of space. Then he hooked them all up with headsets. Once he climbed into the pilot's seat and donned his own headset, he found them all talking like jay birds.

He cranked up the big R-2600 engine. It sounded and looked okay to him, so he taxied to the runway and took instructions from the tower.

At length, he rumbled on the runway, lined up and asked, "All set, everybody?"

Andre said, "Gilroy. We are all yours. Charlotte?"

"I am with you, my love."

She sounded a bit nervous, so Hitchcock said, "Don't worry honey, you are aboard one of the safest airplanes in the U.S. Navy's inventory."

Andre asked, "Navy? I thought you were in the Marine Corps."

Hitchcock groaned, "We'll get into that later. How 'bout you, Lolli? You okay?"

"Weeeeeee."

"I take that as a yes."

"Oui, Monsieur."

Hitchcock flew them up the island's west side and back down the east side to return. Halfway down the east side he sensed a commotion over his left shoulder. He checked his rear-view mirror. It was Lolli smiling and waving, extending her hand. He reached back. She grabbed it and squeezed. For ten minutes, he held on until he needed both hands to land.

Hitchcock collected and returned the parachutes, but not the flight suits. The Lapresse family wore them with pride.

A cab waited just outside the fence as they stood near the guardhouse and hugged Hitchcock with lingering goodbyes. They watched him board his TBF, start up, line up on the runway, wave and take off.

Moments later, as they walked through the gate, one of the guards shouted, "Look out! Crazy son of a bitch!!"

At full throttle, the TBF thundered overhead, no more than thirty feet off the deck. It was a world of ear-ripping sound as people instinctively ducked. The guard shack windows rattled. The Marines cursed as papers scattered. Somebody knocked over a stool.

Rising to their feet, the guards bitched and moaned as the Lapresse family got up alongside. Andre grinned from ear to ear as if feeling for the first time complete freedom from Nazi bonds and oppression. He whooped and hollered, his fists in the air as did his wife and daughter beside him as they watched Hitchcock disappear to the west, his wings waggling.

He got up to 5,000 feet, set the course, flipped on the autopilot and sat back. He looked about the cockpit. A unit of the 1ˢᵗ Marines aviation logistics support squadron 13, it was his airplane, now. He could name it anything he wanted. He knew what this TBF's name would be:

Lolli

4

6 August 1943
USS *Dunagan* (DD 504)
14° 39 2"S, 166° 34'9.E
Espiritu Santo, New Hebrides

"Pssssst, sir. Wake up, please. Pssssst."

Ensign Arthur Hill blinked himself awake. A dark shape loomed before him. A face. He stammered, "Huh? What is it?"

"Sir, please. They need you on the bridge."

"Who are you?" Hill still blinked. The face looked familiar. He smelled spearmint gum. It was Darryl Pollard. A seaman in the deck division. The kid had an inexhaustible supply of gum. He clacked twenty-four hours a day jamming in a new stick every hour.

The man whispered, "I'm on the bridge. Messenger of the watch." He took a step back, his white hat clutched in both hands.

Hill's bunk was the top in one of the officer's three-man staterooms. He looked directly at the man. "Yes, I remember. Pollard. Is that right?"

The man straightened up. "Yes, sir."

"What's up?"

"They need you as JOOD, sir."

"The hell? I just stood my watch, the four to eight."

"They know that. But Mr. Eckert didn't make it. Don't know why. They need you, now."

Hill sighed and lay back for a moment. George or *Flaky George Eckert* didn't make it. Eckert disliked, no, hated to be awakened to take a late-night watch. And now, Hill checked the luminous dial on his Bulova: 2335. Hill had been made to stand three other watches when Eckert couldn't climb out of his rack. Somehow, Tyler Childers, the executive officer put up with it. But he had no choice.

It was quiet at this hour. The deck ventilators howled with clean, fresh air pumped from outside where the temperature was moderate this time of year at Espiritu Santo. It felt good.

He looked over. Pollard was scared. Nearly standing at attention. Winding his dixie cup in his hands. *Not his fault.* "Go on, Pollard. Give me time to get my pants on. Maybe some shoes and socks, too. I'll be along soon. And thank you."

"Thank you, sir," Pollard rushed out.

He sat up, sensing the ship's motion. For two seconds, he cocked an ear at the sound of the Pacific Ocean gushing along the hull right outside. Their stateroom was right at the waterline, and it was easy to hear. And now, it was still the same as when he'd turned in about three hours ago. Just a gentle rocking back and forth. He didn't need a knot meter. The gushing water told him the ship's speed would be fifteen knots. With practice, it was all so damned predictable, almost like being on a cruise ship.

Hill eased to the deck trying not to awaken the other two officers bunked in there. Lieutenant Jonathon Grout, the ship's operations officer, lay in the bottom bunk. Flat on his back, his mouth was wide open as he snored almost noiselessly. Lieutenant (j.g.) Leon Buckner, the main battery director officer, lay on his side, his head propped on his hand. He was awake. He smiled at Hill and gave him a thumbs up. Hill nodded back, eased to the deck and stepped to the mini-sink and ran water over his face and hair. Next, he pulled on his clothes, yanked a light foul weather jacket from the closet, pushed on his garrison cap, and stepped into the passageway.

He mounted three ladders, finding himself on the bridge's starboard side.

It was a beautiful night. A solid canopy of stars was suspended overhead. To starboard, he could make out the mainland of Espiritu Santo. To port, the stars glistened and blinked right down to the horizon. Otherwise, there were no lights showing.

Darkened ship.

With no lights showing, the *Dunagan* was like a phantom slipping through the night. Only the screeching of her ventilation blowers announced her presence to the outside world. Otherwise, it was silent.

He stepped into the pilot house finding two red lights glowing, one over the chart table, the other mounted to the aft bulkhead.

Hill stepped to the chart table finding the quartermaster of the watch. It was Edward Bond, a second-class quartermaster. Hunched over the table, he was running a dead reckoning plot. Beyond that, a glance around the pilot house told him something was weird. The men at the helm and lee helm stood straight up and down, their faces frozen, as if pasted to a book cover. Bond didn't look that engaging either.

Pollard was nowhere in sight.

"Who is OOD?" Hill asked.

Not looking up, Bond said, "Mr. Allred, sir."

"And..." Hill looked around, "He is..."

"In the after fireroom, sir," said Bond.

An imaginary puff of smoke flashed before Hill revealing a red flag. "Who has the conn?"

His eyes still glued to the chart, Bond said mechanically. "Mr. Childers has the conn, sir." Lieutenant Tyler Childers was the ship's executive officer. He was not normally on the watch schedule. The red flag grew brighter.

"Wait a minute." Ensign Hill, a ninety day wonder out of University of Georgia, looked at the chart. Good God! If Bond's plot was accurate, they were a mile off the beach and gradually getting closer. "Where's the Exec?" he demanded.

"Ahem." Bond nodded to the port bridge wing.

Peering through the porthole, Hill saw two figures in the gloom close together. They looked animated.

Hill made to walk outside. But the hatch to the port bridgewing was closed and dogged tight.

Bond put a hand on his elbow. "I wouldn't do that, sir."

"What are you talking about?"

"The skipper's out there with him."

"Yeah, so?"

"I think they are having an argument. A doozie."

Just then the ship jumped; there was a terrible howl. Then the *Dunagan* tilted to starboard and slid, and screeched, and bumped, and ground along for six agonizing seconds.

It stopped. Dead in the water. Aground.

In the pilot house they all looked at one another wild-eyed.

Ensign Arthur Hill found his voice. "All engines stop."

With that, he undogged the port bridgewing hatch and dashed outside. It was a macabre scene under a moonless night. Two men were splayed on the deck grating. On his knees and hunched over the other, the executive officer of the USS *Dunagan* (DD 504), lieutenant Tyler Childers had the captain's collar squeezed in his left hand. His right fist was clenched, his arm cocked and poised to punch the ship's captain, commander Ronald S. Keating in the face.

"Bastard," yelled Childers.

"No!" yelled Hill. He leaned into the pilot house, "You men, on the double, out here."

Childers yelled at Hill, "Back inside you little shit, or you'll be getting the same."

"Eyaaaaaaaaaah." Hill took two steps then leapt on Childers who easily parried the 165-pound ensign and threw him aside. Hill crashed against the bulwark, holding his head and moaning.

But then five others in the pilot house, including Pollard who had been hiding aft on the signal bridge, streamed through the hatch and jumped on Childers. It wasn't pretty, but with each man taking an arm and a leg and one sitting on Childers' chest, he finally gave in, growling.

With all that, Lieutenant (j.g.) Travis L. Allred, recently inspecting the after-fire room, dashed to the bridge and resumed duties as officer of the deck of the USS *Dunagan* (DD 504).

5

9 August 1943
PT 72 (Little Lulu)
Utility Docks, Henderson Field (CACTUS)
Guadalcanal, Solomon Islands

Little Lulu's engines growled as Lieutenant (j.g.) Tubby White, khaki shorts, shirtless, blond and jungle boots, reversed his Packards and backed down. The seventy-eight-foot Higgins boat kissed the dock softly and drew to a halt.

Lieutenant Commander Todd Ingram jumped onto the dock and under the welcoming shade of palm trees where a tinge of honeysuckle found its way to his nostrils. A sailor handed over his B-4 bag. Tubby White and Al Cluster stooped to lean over the rail and shake.

Lieutenant Commander Al Cluster, wearing clean khaki shorts, shirt and garrison cap, was PT Squadron 2 and 3 boss. After trying to talk Ingram into taking over one of his torpedo squadrons, he asked, "Promise you'll at least think about it?"

Ingram twirled a finger in his ear. The thunder of *Little Lulu*'s three Packard engines lingered in his ears. He grinned. "What?"

Just then, the engines shut down.Cluster tried again. "I said, promise you'll think about it?"

"Think? I can't do that anymore, let alone hear." He bumped a palm against his ear.

Tubby said, "Doesn't surprise me. A couple of ring knockers can't even keep up a civil conversation."

Ingram said, "To tell the truth, Al. I'm committed to the Tin Can Navy."

"Well," Cluster muttered, "At least stay in touch. Don't want to lose sight of you."

Ingram stood tall. "Tubby knows how to find me."

"That's the scary part," said Cluster. "Maybe he'll switch back to destroyers."

Ingram laughed, "Take away Tubby White? Anyone who does that to you is doing you a favor."

"Appreciate the vote of confidence." Tubby checked his watch. "Rendova calls. So long, Todd." He stood and walked to his conning platform. He called back, "Have fun stateside, you lucky bum." He twirled a finger over his head. The Packards, still warm, instantly rumbled into life.

Raising his voice, Ingram replied, "We need you out here, Tubby, to keep us all safe and sound back home."

All the lines were off except line two. Ingram bent to uncleat it and handed the tail up to a deckhand.

"Yeah, yeah." Checking the lines were free, Tubby dropped the shift levers into reverse. The boat shuddered for a moment and then gathered sternway.

Al Cluster bent down at the rail. He said softly, "He's a great kid, Todd. We'll take good care of him."

Ingram flashed a grin. "If you don't do that, he'll take care of you. It'll be the monkey running the zoo."

Cluster cackled. "Todd, he's good, but he ain't that good." Cluster rose and saluted Ingram as *PT 72* backed away, her gears grinding.

Ingram returned the salute while Tubby expertly pirouetted *Little Lulu* and got her headed onto the fairway and toward Iron Bottom Sound. Tubby was silhouetted as he called, "Adios, Todd."

Ingram shouted back, "Adios."

Tubby hit the throttles and *Little Lulu* roared out onto Iron Bottom Sound.

"Mr. Ingram?"

Ingram turned to find a young sailor standing beside him. "Yes?"

The kid, a third-class quartermaster, nodded. "I'm your ride to Camp Crocodile."

"Thank you, son, but I'm headed for the amphib dock and a connection to Noumea."

"That's not what they told me, Commander."

"Who are you looking for?"

The kid, with straw colored hair poking out from under his sailor's white hat, drew himself to a semblance of attention and said, "I am supposed to pick up Lieutenant Commander Todd Ingram and take him to Camp Crocodile."

A gelatinous feeling ran through Ingram. "Who precisely at Crocodile?"

"The OOD. Lieutenant Monday. He said I could tell you that your space on the PBY has been cancelled."

"Cancelled?" Ingram barked. "What the hell for?"

They were practically nose to nose.

The kid didn't blink. Instead, he shrugged and said, "They don't let me in on their secrets, Commander. I'm just supposed to pick you up and take you to Crocodile."

A long moment passed. Then Ingram said, "Crocodile." A statement.

"Yessir. Crocodile." A quick smile flashed over the kid's face.

"What's your name"

"Florentino, sir. Rudy Florentino."

Ingram sighed. "Very well." He reached for his B-4 Bag.

Florentino was quicker. He stooped and snatched up the bag. "Please, commander. Allow me. Jeep's right over here."

Ingram was being had, he knew. "Thank you, Florentino. Lead on." They jumped in the Jeep and headed toward the Tenaru River.

Camp Crocodile, was so named as the headquarters for General Alexander Vandergrift, commanding officer of the First Marine Division, victors who threw the Japanese from Guadalcanal. Basically, Crocodile was a series of three Quonset huts joined and tucked in a grove of palm trees, ingeniously assembled by Seabees. Their greatest achievement was inside, where a semblance of an air conditioning system occasionally blew semi-humid air in short spurts. Putrid swamp air blew on the door as they sweated inside as much as the others outside.

Florentino set the hand brake and jumped out. "Here, commander, let me show you where to go."

Ingram followed him through the main door into a room of buzzing fans, buzzing mosquitoes, clacking typewriters, and clanging telephones. He walked toward a placard that said **OOD**. It was piled high with papers, folders and books. Behind that stack sat an anemic staff sergeant stamping a stack of papers.

Florentino touched Ingram's elbow. "Excuse me commander, better you go to that one." He pointed to another desk, with the placard, **CHANGES**. Ingram glanced at Florentino.

"Hottest desk in the South Pacific, commander. Guys line up here to find a way out."

"And this is where I start?"

Florentino shrugged.

Ingram stepped up.

A dark-complected sergeant with eyes like slits looked him up and down. A Bakelite name tag announced: **HONEYKUTT**. "Sir?"

"Ingram, Alton C., Lieutenant Commander, United States Navy. I was told to start here."

"Serial number?"

"Six three eight two one seven."

There were three metal in-boxes stacked at the upper left-hand corner of Honeykutt's desk. Systematically and with staccato precision he started at the top.

Nothing.

Halfway through the middle box, "Ah!" Then, "No shit." Then, "Shit and shinola." He stood and handed over three envelopes. "Here you are commander."

"Thank you." Ingram walked over to the wall. A long 2X12 piece of rough lumber ran from end to end.

Two envelopes were official USN correspondence. The third was yellow. A Western Union telegram. He started there.

"Shit!"

Involuntary. He looked up to surprised faces looking at him. Shading his eyes, he leaned down and studied the telegram, a masterpiece of brevity

TODD X SORRY ABOUT THIS x MORE MALARIA x RON KEATING, SKIPPER OF THE DUNAGAN, CAME DOWN WTH A BAD CASE OF MALARIA x NEARLY DIED x OTHER GUYS TOO INCLUDING THE CMAA x ALL IN ALL SIX GUYS OFF THE SHIP x BETTER NOW x ENROUTE PEARL REHAB .x HENCEFORTH YOU ARE C/O DUNAGAN x NAV DEPT SEEKS PERMANENT REPLACEMNT x I NEED YOU HERE x YOU'LL BE HOME SOON x HELEN SENDS LOVE x JERRY

Quickly, he went through the other two envelopes. One contained orders as commanding officer of USS *Dunagan* (DD 504) . The other was travel orders with the myriad of documents and authorizations to get from where Ingram was to wherever the *Dunagan* was supposed to be. Ingram was guessing Noumea. He turned to Honeykutt: "Gunny?"

"Sir." His chair scraped.

"Location, please, USS *Dunagan,* DD 504, a destroyer."

"Stinking destroyers I know", muttered Honeykutt. Softly cursing, he thumbed messages, went through instruction manuals, reviewed clipboards, and spoke to other Marines. All shook their heads. At length, Honeykutt snapped his fingers, "Ah ha!"

He reached behind and pulled out a clipboard thick with messages. "Slush pile," he said, flipping through flimsies. He stood straight. "Right you are." He pointed to a message, then handed the clipboard to Ingram.

The message was dated two days ago. It said the USS *Dunagan* enroute to station MT.

"Gunny. Where is station MT?"

Honeykutt flipped more pages. Finally he said, "Station MT is Espiritu Santo, Commander."

Ingram grunted. "OK. Now we're getting someplace."

Honeykutt yelped. "Hold on, Commander. More stuff here. Another message was stuck to the original. This one dated early this morning." He scanned it. "Ah, this is really sweet. You're gonna love this."

"C'mon. Out with it."

"She's aground. Yesterday morning. Espiritu Santo. Aground."

9 August 1943
Camp Crocodile
Headquarters, First Marine Division
Henderson Field (CACTUS)
Guadalcanal, Solomon Islands

Luther Honeykutt said, "A fine how do ya do. Looks like they're giving you a turd in a tin cup."

The fact that he was getting a command had not sunk in. There had been no time for a feeling of euphoria. No jumping up and down. No singing and shouting at the 'O' Club. No popping of champagne corks. Instead they were giving him someone else's troubles to clean up. And aground at Espiritu Santo. That sounded awful.

What are they doing to me? "I have to get out there, Honeykutt. You have any ideas?"

"Well, we can find a rack for you tonight and ship you out tomorrow morning, 0800."

Ingram snatched back his orders. "I think these people need help. And Espiritu Santo is still getting occasional Jap air raids. These guys need help. Right now." He stared at Honeykutt. "Stranded. They're a sitting duck."

"Tin can, huh?"

"*Fletcher* class."

Honeykutt rubbed his chin. "My kid brother is on a Tin Can. The *Mugford*."

"He sounds like the more intelligent of you two."

The corners of Honeykutt's mouth turned up. "Tin can people are a bunch of...weenies."

"Weenies, huh? Tell you what, Honeykutt. You have just five seconds—."

Honeykutt didn't let him finish. He rose on tiptoes and called over Ingram's shoulder. "You, what's your name?"

"Florentino, Sarge."

"What's your ride?"

Florentino and Ingram traded glances.

Ingram shrugged.

"Jeep," said Florentino.

Honeykutt checked his watch and stepped from behind his desk, "C'mon. We can just make it. What's your name?"

"Florentino, I said."

Honeykutt held out his hand. "I drive. Gimme your keys, wop."

Now it was Florentino's turn for his face to turn red. His fists balled and he stepped up.

Ingram stood between them. "You idiots. Do I have to put you both on report?" He looked at Florentino. "I don't have time for this. Give him your keys."

"Why should I? He's a pile of dog s—."

"Easy, Florentino," said Ingram.

Honeykutt growled.

Ingram hissed, "Listen, you two. See that gunny in the back of the room? As his superior officer, I can order him to arrest you two and stuff you both down a hole. Now come on Florentino. Let's go!"

Florentino looked at Honeykutt who returned the stare. Then Florentino dug in his pocket and produced a set of keys. Tossing them in the air, he said, "You sure you know where the steering wheel is?"

With a flourish, Honeykutt caught them one-handed. "Where's his bag?" he demanded.

Florentino lifted it with a thin smile.

"Outta here. C'mon," shouted Honeykutt.

Ingram and Florentino followed Honeykutt to the Jeep and piled in; Honeykutt driving, Ingram in the passenger seat and Florentino in back, holding on tightly to straps. Honking the horn, Honeykutt roared down a couple of dirt pot-holed roads and onto a runway. "There," he pointed.

A faded old TBF sat just off the runway, running up its engine, and unfolding its wings.

"That's my ride?" yelled Ingram.

"Gilroy Hitchcock. He's a friend. He'll take you there."

"He a Marine?"

"Of course."

Ingram groaned. He looked over. Honeykutt had the Jeep cranked up to sixty-five miles per hour. Amazing.

Honeykutt yelled over the wind blast, "Tell Gil I'll revise the manifest. It'll be ready when he gets back."

"Thanks."

The TBF swung onto the runway. The pilot ran up the engine to full power.

Honking the Jeep's horn, a frantically waving Honeykutt caught up and pulled in front of the starboard wing.

The pilot jammed on the brakes. He had no choice. The TBF jumped in its oleos, pitched forward, then settled.

The Jeep jerked to a stop. Yanking the handbrake, Honeykutt yelled, "C'mon." He jumped out, climbed on the wing and dashed to the cockpit.

Two grown men argued over the low rumble of an R-2600 engine. It was almost comical, especially with the pilot strapped in. They waved their arms.

Honeykutt looked down to Ingram. The man pointed to the aft hatch and mouthed over the engine's growl, *Get the hell aboard*.

Honeykutt went back to arguing with the pilot, an older-ruddy-complected man, his arms folded against his chest, slowly shaking his head. He waved his arms again, this time yelling and yanking off his goggles and canvas helmet.

Honeykutt shot both fists in the air and bellowed something.

The pilot slumped back and nodded.

Honeykutt stood tall, cupped both hands around his mouth and yelled to Ingram, "Get back there, goddammit."

Ingram jumped out, grabbed his bag, and shook Florentino's hand. "Thanks for everything, wop."

Florentino's eyes jerked to him. Then he laughed although it was hard to hear over the TBF's rumble. He yelled, "Have a good trip, Commander. Hope you get your ship out of the mud."

"We'll give it a hell of a try." Ingram dashed off, bag in hand.

Honeykutt had jumped down and opened the fuselage hatch.

Ingram threw in his bag. "Thanks for everything, sergeant."

"Don't worry. This is for my kid brother. But next time you're through here, you owe me a beer." He nodded inside, "Set of phones in there. Put 'em on. Talk to Gilroy. He's a good guy. But give him a few minutes. He's pissed at me." He checked his watch. "This trip should take about three and a half hours."

Ingram patted him on the shoulder. "The beer is yours. Maybe a bottle of scotch, too."

"Now, you're talkin', sir. "

Ingram scrambled in. Instantly, the pilot hit the throttle, fully intending to whack Honeykutt with the horizontal stabilizer. Through the hatch window, Ingram watched Honeykutt, like a cat, leap out of the way. It was as if he were expecting it.

Yes, Honeykutt's fist was in the air, happily flipping the bird to Flying Sergeant Gilroy Hitchcock.

But Hitchcock kept the hammer down. Gathering speed, the TBF roared down the runway and wobbled into the air within seven seconds.

7

9 August 1943
1724 South Alma Street,
San Pedro California

The phone rang. Helen jerked awake. So did Fred, her gray tabby cat, nuzzled up against her legs, big eyes blinking as she flipped on the bed-side lamp.

"Ugggh." She reached, knocking the little wind-up alarm clock off the nightstand. But she saw the time as it toppled off: 1:47. It smacked the floor with a clang.

She grabbed the phone and jammed it to her ear. "Uhhh."

"Hello?" said a distant voice. She hung up the phone and then reached down and picked up the alarm clock. Fred rolled to his back and groaned, his feet in the air.

Helen scratched his belly.

The phone rang again. This time it seemed strident, jerked at her, louder than before. She couldn't get it off the hook fast enough. "Yes, Mom, what is it?"

"Captain Ingram?" It was a male voice.

"Who, er, yes. I'm Captain Ingram. Who...who...?"

"Yes, it's Lieutenant Lamar, U.S. Navy, out here in Hawaii."

She drummed her fingers on the nightstand and scratched Fred with her other hand. It hit her. "Out there. Three hours. Wow." She checked the clock. It was nearly eleven o'clock in Hawaii. "Up past your bedtime, Lieutenant."

"Well, yes, ma'am. The boss had a rough day."

Lamar, Lamar. The name. Jeeeez. Lieutenant Arthur Lamar, nicknamed "Hal," was flag lieutenant to Admiral Chester Nimitz. *Holy Cow.* "I'm sorry, Lieutenant. It didn't hit me until now that you are—"

"Please, Captain Ingram. We're on an open line here. On the other hand, I'm happy you figured it out."

"What can I do for you, Lieutenant?"

"We need you out here for a day and a half."

Hawaii? Nimitz? Lamar? It hit her what was coming. Torpedoes. Those damned torpedoes. Would they never stop? These people have no feelings. They don't care. Just as long as they fill their own agenda. She replied dryly, "Lieutenant Lamar, I'm under travel restriction to CONUS." Continental United States.

"My boss will arrange a waiver. We'll transport you via Navy air, only passenger aboard. And we'll put you up at his place where security is very tight. And if you're nice, we'll throw in free food. Good stuff, too."

Now she remembered Lamar. A decent fellow who would go to any length to get the job done for his boss. "Of course. I remember you, Lieutenant. You report to—"

"—open line, captain."

"They call you Hal?"

"Those close to me do."

"Okay. Why me? I'm just a lowly Army nurse."

"A meeting. An inquiry into how you obtained what you did."

"Who is inquiring?"

"The Navy, the Bureau of Ordnance."

"But I went into all that."

"Not with them. They want to hear it from you personally."

"With whoever it was, it was quite rigorous. Some of your Navy pals were very unfriendly."

"This time we'll have someone there if that happens. And I have to say, my boss does not want to let that happen."

This is real. I have to face these ghouls once more. She slumped in the bed, still scratching Fred. Just then, the cat licked the top of her wrist and rolled over, Helen absently scratching along his spine. "Okay. I don't have a choice, do I?"

Silence, except for static popping and clicking along what was a surprisingly good connection.

She waited another ten seconds. "All right, Lieutenant."

On the other end, she heard an exhale, "Thank you, captain. Okay. We will pick you up today at your home. Please expect a Lieutenant Holmes."

"Holmes."

"That's right, captain."

"What about my job here?"

"Oh, don't worry about that. That's been taken care of. You're taking the next few

days TAD to attend a burn seminar."

"I've been to enough of those."

"Holmes will have all the documentation you need. He will drive you to the Allen

Naval Air Station and board you on an R5D."

"Navy blither. What's an R5D? Will I have to get out and paddle?"

"No, captain. No paddling. An R5D is a DC 6, one of Douglas Aircraft's finest.You will have to suffer with me at the other end when you arrive. It will be my honor to drive you to the boss's place."

"Tomorrow, the next day?"

"Today. Four o'clock local time for you. The inquiry starts tomorrow. We have

spoken with your people. You're off the clock with them, so don't worry. Your section will be just tomorrow. Your today, actually. Then we'll fly you home."

"Four o'clock. Today? The ninth?"

"Yes. I'm afraid so. Just make sure you get plenty of sleep."

"Sleep. Do I have time to pack?"

"As of now you have about fourteen hours. That should do it don't you think?"

"I guess."

"Bring something to read."

8

9 August 1943
Enroute Bomber Field, Espiritu Santo
New Hebrides

Honeykutt was right. Gilroy Hitchcock was a good pilot. A flying sergeant, he nursed his TBF up to 7,500 feet, leaned out the carburetor to where the engine purred like a kitten and set her on a course for Bomber Field.

The TBF Avenger is a large, single-engine mid-wing airplane. A long compartment on top houses the pilot who sits solo over the wing with outstanding visibility. Behind the pilot is a compartment originally reserved for a radioman. But later on, BuAir deemed that superfluous and simply piled it full of radio and navigating equipment. Behind that was a gunner manning a .50 caliber machine gun in a powered rotating turret.

Beneath those three compartments was an internal weapons bay, with either a 2600 pound Mark VIII mod 8 torpedo packed with 500 pounds of TNT or four 500 pound bombs. Behind all that is the bombardier/radio man's compartment. When the bomb bay was open, the bombardier, using a panel of flight instruments right next to him, could view the target and guide the TBF to an accurate launch point.

Of interest was that this TBF had been personalized. A simple name was painted on each side of the cowl: *Lolli*. An exotic female face accompanied the name, a palm tree waved in the background.

Back aft, Ingram ran his eyes over the bombardier's panel. Yes, the plane chugged along at 1900 rpm, air speed 165 knots, course 130°. Yes, it all seemed about right. Ingram lay back among a bunch of canvas bags and crates, scrunching a nest for himself.

He donned earphones and was soon talking to Gilroy Hitchcock, an old China Marine. Hitchcock had escaped the Philippines long before it was surrendered to the Japanese, but still, he found himself in assignments overseas.

Hitchcock asked, "What brings you beneath the Southern Cross, Commander?"

Ingram played coy with, "...oh I just took a little cruise up in the Vella Gulf."

"For real? Seriously?"

"Well...yes."

"Just tin cans. Six of you?"

"You've been reading your Sunday paper. Yes, I was along for that one." Three nights ago, Ingram had ridden with Commander Frederick Moosbrugger aboard the USS *Dunlap* (DD 384). With the six destroyers of DESDIV 11 and 12. They had ambushed and sunk three out of four Japanese destroyers of the Tokyo Express in Vella Gulf.

Home. And a few days with Helen. He missed her so much. That glistening raven black ponytail. And her eyes. She always knew when to drill her husband with her eyes. She always sensed his most vulnerable moments. Then, she would just look at him, the corners of her mouth barely turned up. His knees would become like jelly and he would throw his arms around her and bury his face in the nape of her neck. He wondered if—

"I said her name is Lolli. Say Commander, where you been, sir?"

Still sleepy. Ingram shook cobwebs from his head. "I'm here, Gilroy. Lolli. That's a pretty name." The name on the cowl jumped in his head. And the face. Not bad...

"You bet. Lolli is French. Pure bred, actually. Exotic as all get out."

"Amazing."

"Lives in Noumea. Lives with her folks in a little bungalow near the beach." Once a month, Gilroy snagged a three-day pass and, quietly, they spent the weekend just watching the ocean. Sometimes with her parents, too. They were very nice.

"And here's the kicker," Hitchcock said.

Ingram did an eye-roll. "What is that?"

"She's blind."

Ingram sat upright. "Say again."

"Blind as a bat, they tell me. But here is this gorgeous woman saying *Je vous aime,* in my ear."

"What's that?"

"Yeah, I had to look it up. It means I love you."

"Jeeeez. And what did you say?"

"I love you back. And I mean it. She is really something."

"Ahem. And she's blind."

"Well, yes. But the docs have told her it's only temporary. But right now, she don't know what an ugly son-of-bitch I am. I got it made."

"Gilroy."

"Sir?"

"I have news for you."

"Lay it on me commander."

"You're underselling yourself."

"Huh?"

"I can see where any number of women would make a run for you."

"Maybe so. Lolli's mother has put in a pitch for me. Don't know why, but that seemed to be enough to tip over Lolli."

"See? I told you."

"Well, it gets worse."

"Yes, Gilroy. What is it now?"

"We've discussed marriage. But I have yet to tell her that I'm stilll married to not one, but to two women in the U.S."

"Two?" gasped Ingram.

"Well, yeah. Eva for two months. Lauren for five months. I learned the hard way."

"Hard way," Ingram repeated.

"They played some sort of game with my allotment. There was never any money in the bank. I didn't know what to do, so I walked."

A small detail. Gilroy had simply walked out. By walking out, Gilroy had shipped out, overseas, out of reach.

But both women had lawyers. Grizzled San Diego lawyers with vast experience representing women who suffered terribly from runaway husbands. Or at least played the game. It didn't matter that these women were predators who married for money. And made a living at it. They did their best to flog their unsuspecting husbands, people away from home for the first time, many in their late teens. Rapacious women like Eva and Lauren went after Marines knowing they had the best chance of getting killed out in the Pacific. When that happened, the lawyers were able to chop off something from the insurance policies for their clients, always taking the lion's share.

Two lawyers specialized in cases such as this, and it was inevitable they would discover one another. Now, they had joined up and pursued a unified hunt to track down Sergeant Gilroy Hitchcock, United States Marine Corp, age fifty-seven, and hang him out to dry.

But Ingram had heard the stories; some of these *lawyers* simply disappeared. Oftentimes their *clients* along with them. It was a dark time for police work. Especially with the international border only twelve miles to the south where bodies could be dumped.

Ingram picked up the mic and said, "Hitchcock, You ever think about this being a scam?"

"Maybe."

"So get a lawyer. A good one."

"Yes, sir. But I ain't got no money."

"Well, I know a guy who might be able to help you out."

"I appreciate that, but I have to say up front that I ain't one of them cowboys who whacks people and dumps their bodies over in Mexico,"

"No, no. This guy is a personal friend. I think he'd do it pro-bono. Besides, he's a Navy guy. "

"Pro which?"

"Bono. Free. Free of charge. He's extra good. Top of the list. Very trustworthy. We got out of Corregidor together."

"Jeeeez. You was on Corregidor?"

"I was one of the lucky ones who got out. So did this guy. Very brave. He saved my life. I trust him, implicitly."

"Implic...what?"

"He's the best there is. You can trust him with your life."

"What's he do now?"

'ONI[1]. Learning to be a spook.'

"ONI! Sheeeyyyat. Commander. I don't know if I could—"

The engine bucked and backfired.

"Awww shit."

The engine backfired again, louder.

"What?" said Ingram.

"Dirty bastards," he shouted.

"What?" demanded Ingram.

"Shitty gas, Commander," said Gilroy. "Some idiot doped off at the pump. Water in the gas. And now, you and I are getting screwed. Excuse me. I gotta get out a May Day. We may be goin' in." He clicked off.

Ingram looked wildly about. Good God. The man had said May Day. He wanted to sit up. Then he wanted to lay back. Hell. He didn't know what to do.

The engine kept seizing and back-firing. Then it would smooth out for twenty or thirty seconds. And start all over.

"Commander!"

"What?"

"Good news. There's a dumbo[2] in the area. I just spoke with him. Looks like we can join up in the next five minutes or so. So if we do go in, your dainty feet will only be wet for a minute or two."

"Oh, I'm so very pleased." The engine now ran smoothly. Ingram untensed a bit. "What's with your power plant? It seems to be working."

"Switched back to the left tank. We used almost all of it. Same with the center tank. It's dry. Only about ten gallons or so in the left. But at least it may be enough to keep us in the sky until dumbo shows up."

"I didn't think you were that smart."

"Semper Fi, Mac. Up yours."

They laughed.

Ingram asked, "Seriously, what have you done?"

"I pulled the throttle back a tad. That dropped our speed but *Lolli* ain't popping and farting as much. That's about it."

It was true. Except for occasionally back-firing outbursts, the engine was running smoother. Ingram checked the panel. They had dropped down to two thousand feet and their air speed was a hundred and five knots.

"We got company, Commander."

Ingram looked out the window to see the dark slender silhouette of a PBY edging up to their starboard side. The plane was in dark camouflage except for nose art of a young woman in a show-everything bathing suit. The name beneath her spelled out BLIND DATE.

"So I see," replied Ingram. "Nice."

"Bunch of rangy bastards. They're giving me shit about going swimming."

"Ignore them."

"They don't like Marines."

"There's something to be said about that," said Ingram

"Aww, c'mon." Gilroy protested. "But there's something else. The dumbo pilot told me the Seabees just finished an emergency runway a few miles closer on Espiritu Santo at a place called Olpoi. So we'll head there instead. Trouble is the beer is shitty."

"Any port in a storm."

"I wouldn't have it any other way."

"Yeah, maybe about thirty miles closer."

"Nice." Relief began to creep in. Ingram checked the gauges. He figured they had about 80 miles to go to Bomber Field on Espiritu Santo. And now, thirty miles closer to Olpoi. They just might make it.

Fifteen minutes passed in silence with *Lolli's* engine bucking and jumping. Finally, it quit all together. But Gilroy kept the prop windmilling. After thirty seconds and six hundred feet, it caught. And this time it purred for sixty whole seconds.

"What did you do?" asked Ingram.

"Damned if I know. I keep leaning it out to see if—"

The engine back-fired again. A really loud blast this time.

"Shit I gotta watch it."

"Then watch it. Between you and me, you're doing fine Gilroy." He looked ahead to see a thin strip of purple on the horizon. "Hey, is that what I think it is out there?"

"Yes, sir. Welcome to Espiritu Santo."

"Wow. What are you doing to keep it going?"

"Little bit of everything, Commander. Actually, I bin talking to the Navy puke on the PBY, the engineer up in the wing pylon. He ain't such a bad guy. He knows his engines. He's giving me some good tips."

"Great."

"They're a bunch of goldbricks."

The engine blasted again. The whole plane shuddered but the R-2600 kept chugging horribly as Hitchcock swore and yelled at the same time, a glorious stream of invectives making Ingram almost laugh.

He looked out. The mountains of Espiritu Santo stood out in detail. But the bad news was they had lost quite a bit of altitude. They were down to less than 1,000 feet. "Geez, Gilroy. You're doing it. Getting closer."

"Not bad, I must say"

"Anything I can do?"

"Do you have a right hand, commander?" Hitchcock asked solemnly.

"Yes. I do."

"And a left hand?"

"I have one of those also."

"Well, please put those together and pray like hell that we make these last few miles."

"I'll do that."

"And it is just up ahead about ten miles or so. The runway is right around that white bluff. A left turn and we're in. Sorry commander. Looks like there will be no swim call this afternoon."

But the poor R-2600 didn't seem to agree. It was bucking and jumping in its mount. *Lolli* shook horribly. "Shiiiit," muttered Hitchcock. "Here it comes." It seemed as if only eight of the engine's fourteen cylinders were firing.

"What?"

"The beach. Left turn. Only got about twenty seconds to get the gear down."

"Anything I can do?" asked Ingram again. He looked out. They were down to about fifty feet. A white gleaming beach, trees, jungle, flicked beneath.

"Pray, dammit." At close to stalling speed, Gilroy kicked in left rudder and eased left aileron. He found a hand to slap down the landing gear as—

The engine backfired loudly once and bucked to a stop.

"Shiiiit."

Three seconds of blessed silence. The wind whistled. Ever so gently, Hitchcock eased back on the stick. With her landing gear barely down and locked, *Lolli's* tail wheel snagged the top string of the barbed wire security fence. The wire snapped. *Lolli* surged on.

Two seconds later, she kissed the white, coral runway of Espiritu Santo's Olpoi Emergency Airfield.

Exhaling loudly, Hitchcock let her roll to a stop.

Blind Date blasted overhead, wagging her wings in victory.

"Commander?" called Hitchcock.

"Yes, Gilroy."

"Bad news all around."

"What is it now, Gilroy?"

"I was here about two months ago when them Seabees started."

Ingram expelled his own breath. "Yes, Gilroy."

"Beer is still shitty."

9

The sun beat down on the airfield's white bleached coral, making it seem hotter than it really was. The dazzling effect made one feel weary and tired. It was hard to focus clearly without sunglasses, hence one automatically stayed in the coconut palm's soothing shade whenever possible.

The airstrip was virtually unused. Nobody had landed there. Ingram and Hitchcock scrambled out of the TBF which, without power, just sat there like a dead whale, an intruder popping and clicking as parts expanded in protest to the heat of the day.

The field was protected by a security squad of Marines, four of whom roared up in a Jeep, demanding explanations. With his hands full, Hitchcock hadn't had time to radio ahead and request permission to land, let alone simply announce their presence. Now gathered in an awkward group about the Jeep, they were as puzzled as Hitchcock as to what to do with him. Finally they all piled in with their gear and the Marines took him to their bivouac at the other end of the field where the chow and fresh water were in reasonable supply.

That's when Ingram first saw Hitchcock physically. He was a big man. Almost too tall for *Lolli*. Ingram watched as Hitchcock sort of "unwound" himself, limb by limb, from his TBF and planted himself on the ground. He was a solid six feet five inches in height and looked to weigh about 205 with no evidence of body fat. A typical Marine with close-cropped blondish-gray hair and chiseled jaw, he had piercing blue eyes and looked to be about forty or so years of age. But the man took good care of himself. His skin was tight, his muscle tone that of a teenager. His shirt was unbuttoned and a scar, an old one, ran from his right shoulder down to his navel.

Their HQ was a twelve-by-twelve tent. Hitchcock made for that and got on their radio. He dialed up his boss back on Guadalcanal and explained the situation. He received orders to stick with the TBF for the next week or so. They had no use for him until a spare R-2600 could be flown in from Noumea. At which time he would, with the assistance of the Marines on Olpoi, exchange the engine and fly out. Until then, he was their headache.

That settled, it was close to noon when Ingram and Hitchcock languished in the shade of a palm grove, at what could be called an "operations shed." *Lolli* was tucked in another grove nearby, having been towed down the field by the jeep. Marines ambled about in shadows. They were simply dressed: shorts, pith helmets, and jungle boots. That was it. Three of them wore side arms: a duty belt with a .45 pistol.

Ingram smacked his lips. They sipped Olpoi's beer which wasn't that bad. But Hitchcock's grumbling made one feel as if it actually was terrible. He called it *Old Lizard Piss*. Ingram sighed. Listening to the flying sergeant made one really want the beer to taste awful just to satisfy Hitchcock's epithets.

But then Ingram came up with, "Any port in a storm."

Hitchcock nodded. "Can't argue with that."

They heard the whine of aircraft engines. Louder. They looked up through palm branches to see *Blind Date* flick overhead. This PBY, being the 5A variety, was fitted with landing gear which made her as comfortable on land as she was on water. She orbited the field once, then steadied up on final and landed easily, taking 350 yards to roll out. That done, she turned, waddled right up to what was called the operations center, and drew to a stop. Power was chopped, her propellor blades ceased twirling and she sat mutely, creaking and popping just like the TBF.

Without the noise, the stillness seemed louder than before. But then, the cockpit hatches popped open and both pilot and co-pilot rose up into the hot air. The mid-ship blister hatches rolled open and men vacated the PBY like rats leaving the ship, the temperature rising quickly inside.

The pilot climbed all the way out. Using handholds, he slid down the side, his boots lightly thumping onto the coral. He called, "Good morning, gentlemen. I am Lieutenant junior grade Homer Cogswell and understand Lieutenant Commander Todd Ingram could be here."

Ingram rose. "That would be me."

Seeking comfort from the shadow of the PBY's giant parasol wing, Cogswell walked beneath, his co-pilot close behind. "Very good, sir. We have orders to take you to the USS *Dunagan*. Before we go, I would like to gas up if possible. Is there a Captain—"

"Gant, Rudolph Gant, Homer. Welcome to Olpoi." Captain Gant was an enormous Marine. Larger than Hitchcock, he bulged in all directions and for some reason it actually looked good. This was complimented by a drooping handle-bar moustache that made him look comical, almost avuncular. But still, he carried his authority well.

Homer Cogswell walked up, drew to attention, and saluted. "Thank you, sir. And we're looking for—"

"Yes, Mr. Cogswell, your passenger is here." Gant nodded to Ingram who walked over. Gant twitched his handlebar. "He's all yours."

Cogswell faced Ingram and saluted. The two shook hands. "We'll get you to the *Dunagan*. She's up the coast about forty miles."

"Thank you," said Ingram.

Cogswell asked Gant, "Also, sir, do you have any gas?"

"About six thousand gallons."

"Oh, wow. Great. Could we have five hundred?"

"Sorry. No."

"Huh—er what, sir?"

"Somebody spiked it. All full of water. We don't get any new gas for another two days."

Under the glowering stares of Lt (j.g.) Homer Cogswell and Captain

Rudolph Gant, Flying Sergeant Gilroy Hitchcock laughed and spat on the brilliant white coral.

As far as Ingram was concerned, *Blind Date* was a hot date as everyone piled aboard. Anxious to get into the air, Cogswell was already on the intercom, working with Aviation Chief Machinist Mate Constantine Merriweather who sat up in the pylon to get the engines rolling. An amazingly thin man with a pencil thin moustache and slicked back salt and pepper hair on the sides, his vast knowledge of aircraft engines combined to earn him the nickname of "Duke."

By the time Ingram squeezed his way forward into the pilot's compartment, the Duke, had already boarded the PBY and wiggled up into the wing pylon getting the engines ready to start.

Standing beneath him was Gunnery Sergeant Gilroy Hitchcock who, over a period of twenty minutes, had come to know the Duke very well. Turns out they had a lot of mutual friends in the aviation business and shared a passion for Pratt and Whitney air cooled engines. So much so that Hitchcock begged a ride just to see what it was like in the tower and how the PBY's engines were coordinated. Merriweather asked Cogswell who nodded and said, "As long as he doesn't try to convert you to the corps."

Merriweather laughed. "Me a Jarhead? No worries there, skipper."

That earned a shrug from Hitchcock and the two went back to blabbing Pratt and Whitney.

At Cogswell's urging, Ingram donned a headset and sat in a jump seat in the back of the cockpit, in full view of the instrument panel. Gus Johnson, the red-headed co-pilot was last and began buckling up with everybody else.

"Whew, shit," someone muttered in the radio compartment. "Let's get going."

"Hey Duke? How 'bout it?" demanded Johnson.

Merriweather yelled from the pylon, "Almost there."

"Get it going, Duke," Cogswell snapped over his shoulder.

Merriweather shouted right back, "Roger, sir. Clear prop! Rolling two."

Sure enough. Ingram looked up to see the right engine's propellor ticking over right above them. Nine blades flashed past and the R 1830 twin wasp engine, still warm, rumbled easily into life, greasy black smoke blasting under her wing. Number one soon followed, the PBY coming fully awake.

Cogswell and Johnson did a quick preflight with Cogswell yelling over the intercom, "All set, Boys?"

A number of epithets ranged on the intercom, most downright filthy.

Exchanging grins with Johnson, the two pilots secured their cockpit windows. Cogswell yelped, "Ride 'em cowboy!" He grabbed the overhead throttles and eased into full power.

Gathering speed, the PBY shot down the field trailing a white cloud of coral dust and wobbled into the air. Like dogs on a Sunday afternoon drive, the men in the aft blister compartment stuck their noses in the wind cooling off in the breeze as bits of paper and dust whisked among them.

They smoked cigarettes in the PBY, chatted incessantly and swore at each other on the intercom, officers and enlisted alike. Merriweather and Hitchcock likewise blabbed at each other nonstop with Cogswell giving permission for Hitchcock to sit up in the tower and take it all in. Otherwise, Cogswell was easy with them. But there were times when he was professional. For example, they knew to shut up when they were setting up for a landing.

Ingram's first view of the *Dunagan* was one he would rather have forgotten. She looked pathetic, laying over to starboard perhaps ten degrees, about six hundred yards between the beach and a reef further out. But a barge was tied up to her port side and it looked as if there was a working party down there offloading ammunition. A tug, the USS *Ponca* (ATF 156) was anchored about a thousand yards seaward. Another barge was anchored farther out, this one a fuel barge, carrying all but ten percent of the *Dunagan's* allotment of naval standard fuel oil (NSFO).

Cogswell turned the wheel over to Johnson and let him do the landing.

Johnson eased her down and *Blind Date* kissed a very smooth Pacific

Ocean with hardly any bumping and bouncing. They turned and taxied back toward the *Dunagan*.

Down from the tower, Hitchcock joined Ingram at a window.

Shaking his head, Ingram said, "Looks pathetic." He continued, "Look Gilroy, I've been thinking about something."

"Is this where I learn you've wised up and decided not to take the job?"

Ingram snorted. "No, far better than that. That's one of our ships. She's in trouble. Somebody has to take hold and straighten things out."

"And you're not going to do it."

"No Hitchcock. I am going to do it. The time is right for me. It needs being done and there's nobody else around to do it. So, I'm stuck in the barrel.

"Well, when you put it that way..."

Ingram jabbed Hitchcock with a forefinger. "And I need a chief master at arms."

"Aww, bullshit. You are—" Hitchcock's eyes widened. "Holy shit. You're not thinking of me?"

"None better."

"You hardly know me."

"I've seen enough."

"But I got stuff to do. I gotta fix Lolli."

Ingram grinned. "For the next couple of weeks, you're gonna be sitting on your ass drinking beer and doing nothing while you wait for that engine to show up."

"But—" protested Hitchcock.

"You don't think that's productive time while our boys are being shot at, do you Gunny?"

Hitchcock sputtered.

Ingram's voice softened, "Aw, come on, Gunny. It'll only be for a week or two. And here's your chance to kick some ass and show these guys what Americans are made of."

"But—"

"Americans, Gunny. Real Americans. Not some candy-ass kid sitting around sniveling to his mother about what a raw deal he has."

"Two weeks?"

"Two weeks. Maybe three tops while the Navigation Department sends us a new CMAA."

"Free room and board?"

"That's the spirit."

"Just two weeks. Then I walk."

"Deal." Ingram stuck out a hand. They shook.

———————

Gus Johnson was driving as *Blind Date* flew around *Dunagan* in slow circles.

"Piece of shit," Hitchcock pitched his head down toward the ship. "What's with the working party?"

A group of men were gathered up near mount 52, just under the bridge on the foredeck.

"Lightening ship. Dumping ammo."

"At that rate, gonna take 'em all year."

"Umm." Hitchcock was right about that. There was just one working party. And that was just at the deck hatch near mount 52.

The water was calm with very little wind under a blistering sun. In fact he could see men splashing around under the bridge. Swim call.

Johnson set up for a landing and eased *Blind Date* onto a patch of oily smooth water and taxied to within 100 yards. Cogswell told the Duke to cut the engines, then looked up to Ingram, the question unspoken. *Nobody coming to get their skipper?*

Ingram checked under the bow. A twenty-six-foot motor whale boat idled among the swimmers. Ingram shrugged. "Looks like they have more important things to do." He rubbed his chin, pilot and copilot staring at him. "You sure they got the message?"

Cogswell turned in his seat and called back to the radio compartment, "Mickey."

"Sir?" Mickey Henderson an aviation radioman third class piped up.

"You sure the *Dunagan* rogered for that message?"

"They were loud and clear, sir. No glitches."

Cogswell looked back to Ingram, his brow knit.

"Okay, can you get me over there?"

"Curb service, skipper." A man hustled aft to get a life raft ready.

Ingram rubbed his chin for a moment. He looked over to Hitchcock. "Gilroy."

"Yes, sir?"

"You ready?"

Hitchcock gave him a long look. "Anytime skipper."

Ingram turned and offered a hand to Cogswell and Johnson. "A nice job, fellas. Thanks very much."

Cogswell popped a stick of gum in his mouth. "You bet, skipper," he said. "*Blind Date* Inter-island Airlines appreciates your patronage. Please come back soon."

10

The two gunners boarded the raft and sat and waited.

Ingram turned to Hitchcock, "Your turn, Gilroy."

Hitchcock eyed Ingram, "Navy regs, huh?"

Ingram patted him on the back "Navy tradition, really. Senior officers last."

His lip curled to a thin smile. "Got it. Last one in is a rotten egg." He said it loud enough so everyone in the compartment heard it and laughed, even Ingram.

Hitchcock scrambled through the hatch, jumped in the raft, and sat near the bow,

Inside, Cogswell offered a hand, "Looks like you got some work to do."

Ingram said, "Thanks." He took Cogswell's hand. "Please be careful with Hitchcock's gear. Some of that stuff is very, very personal."

"I'll pack it for him, skipper. Anything except the latest Jap newspaper will be overlooked."

"Excellent." Ingram shook and said, "Thanks, Homer. Take care of your boys. They're a good bunch."

"You bet."

With the raft bouncing up and down, Ingram crawled out and dropped on the rubber flooring. He sat at the aft end, arranged himself and waited, looking like an underfed Captain Bligh.

He shaded his eyes looking over to the *Dunagan*. With the starboard list, sunlight glinted off her exposed port side. He could hear more than see the working party off-loading ammunition onto the barge moored to the starboard side under mount 52. Even at this distance, there were guttural shouts and occasional screams.

A tug was anchored 200 yards further to starboard of the *Dunagan*. A portable steel ladder had been dropped over the port side at the quarterdeck.

Cogswell untied the painter and tossed it onto the raft. "You two deliver Commander Ingram to that ship yonder and then hustle back. We gotta get airborne, chop, chop."

"Yes, sir," they responded.

Ingram pointed to the folding steel ladder hanging over the destroyer's side. "You guys see that?"

"Yes, sir."

"That's where we're going."

"Yes, sir." They dug in with powerful strokes and covered the distance quickly. The raft softly bumped the ship's port side. One of the gunners grabbed Ingram's bag and hoisted it to a man waiting up on the main deck.

Grabbing the ladder, Ingram called over to the gunners, "Thank you. See you in a couple of hours."

"Yes, sir."

Ingram grabbed one of the ladder rungs, jammed in his foot and scrambled to the main deck.

He rose to his feet to see a second-class boiler tender staring at him. Ingram saluted the flag at the fantail then the man before him. "Permission to board the ship, sir?"

After what must have been a strenuous internal debate, the man returned the salute. "Uh, welcome aboard, sir."

The man wore a light blue chambray shirt caked with grease. All the buttons were undone save one, holding everything in. The sleeves were rolled all the way up. He was unshaven, he wore unlaced black shoes, his shirt was not tucked in and worse, he wore no cover.

"Where's the exec?" asked Ingram.

With a prolonged glance at Ingram's collar tabs, the boiler tender straightened up. "In his rack, sir. Had a rough night. Who may I say is calling, sir."

"I am Lieutenant Commander Alton C. Ingram, your new commanding officer. At least I will be after I read my orders on the fantail in about five minutes. Now please summon your executive officer."

The boiler tenders face went from red to white. "Uh, we have no watch messenger, sir, nor a QM."

Ingram futzed in his B-4 bag and pulled out some papers. They rattled, all flimsies. He drew off a copy and handed it over. "Those are my orders. Log them in."

"Logbook is on the bridge, sir."

Ingram drew to within inches of the man's face. He waited. No alcohol. At least he couldn't smell anything, except terrible body odor. "What's your name,

sailor?"

"Uhhhh, Roberts, sir."

"Well Roberts, I have news for you. You are now going down to rouse the exec. Tell him he is to be here, chop, chop. Then you will go straight to the bridge, bring back the logbook and log me in. Immediately after that, you will find a proper watch quartermaster and messenger."

"But—" Roberts looked around wild-eyed.

"In the meantime, I will stand your watch for you. For the moment, you are relieved. Now get going," Ingram barked.

"Y-Y-Yessir." Stammered Roberts.

"Go! On the double!"

"Yes, sir!" The man ran off, unlaced shoes and all.

An officer walked past wearing just a bathing suit and garrison cap. An officer. A single silver bar. A lieutenant j.g. "You there!"

"Huh?" The officer turned, surprised to see the man shouting at him and especially the man's rank. "Errr-sir?" He looked from side to side.

"Yes, you. Come here, please."

The man turned and walked over. He was five-eleven, sandy blond hair and fair complected with a pencil thin moustache. But thin. He looked as if he'd been on a starvation diet for six months.

He took in Ingram's collar tabs, and in an instant, his expression changed from irritation to servility. He saluted, "Yes, sir?"

Ingram returned the salute. "What's your name?"

"Eckert, George R., sir."

They looked out as the demanding roar of twin R-1830 engines captured their attention. *Blind Date* was all white spray and water vapor heading out to sea as she lunged into her take-off run.

"Billet?"

"Communications officer, sir. And if you don't mind, sir. What is your business here?"

"I'm your commanding officer."

"Holy cow."

"You're the communication officer and you don't read your messages?"

"Just got up, sir. Working all night and conked off for four hours." "We sent you a heads-up from the dumbo advising you of my

arrival."

"You did?"

"And your radioman acknowledged receipt. Looks like your radio gang was asleep like you."

The man's shoulders slumped. "I'm sorry, sir, It was me who was asleep. They probably tried to wake me. But I'm an assh—real jerk when it comes to waking me up. My fault."

A man rushed up, out of breath. Lieutenant's bars were precariously stuck on his collar. He brushed sleep from a bright red face. He was well over six foot two and muscles bulged on beefy arms and his likewise muscled chest. His nose, bent to the left, had been broken several times. He'd jammed a garrison cap over a dark brown butch cut.

A boxer. At least at one time.

He stuck his face in between Ingram and Eckert. A deep baritone voice rumbled with sarcasm, "Anything I can do to help?"

Ingram asked, "And you are..."

"And who the hell are you? And what are you doing on my ship?" His breath was bad. Not alcohol. But there was a stench. Just then, he took in Ingram's collar insignia. His expression didn't change a bit.

Ingram peeled off a copy of his orders and jammed them in the man's top

pocket.

"I'm Alton C. Ingram, Lieutenant Commander, United States Navy, your commanding officer. That's a copy of my orders that I wish to read to the crew in the next five minutes. Accordingly, you will get your men and those men," he nodded toward the swimmers, "out of the water and formed up on the fantail where I will read these orders. Upon which time I intend to take immediate command of," he looked the man up and down, "your ship. After that, you may be up for some brig time if you don't recall your Naval protocol. And that includes your manners, mister. Now what is your name?"

"I saw no notice."

"We sent you a message, as recently as from the dumbo. Your radio gang acknowledged receipt."

"I didn't see it."

"Nor did your communications officer." Ingram looked to Eckert, then back to the lieutenant. "I asked for your name."

"Childers, sir. Tyler Childers."

A loose circle had formed. At the center was Ingram. Towering over him was

Childers who towered over George Eckert, the communications officer. Even

Roberts, the fat boiler tender, stood among them, deck logbook in hand.

Ingram continued, "Now we're getting somewhere. And you are the executive officer?"

"That's right."

Ingram stared at him. Thirty seconds passed.

"Ahhhh....that's right, sir."

Ingram nodded and waved the back of his hand to Childers. "Very well,

Mr. Childers. Now, while Mr. Eckert here relieves me as officer of the deck, you will assemble the crew on the fantail. I expect to read my orders in five minutes. After that, I want an officer's call in the wardroom. All officers and senior chiefs. Is that clear?"

"Yes."

"Yes, what?"

Childers actually braced himself. "Yes, sir!" Then he walked swiftly away.

11

---

9 August 1943
USS *Dunagan* (DD 504)
Aground: 14° 41'3.84"S, 166° 34'6.24E
Espiritu Santo, New Hebrides

The word for an officer's call circulated quickly and they fell right in, lined up in two ranks on the port side by seniority, Childers standing before them. Ingram and Hitchcock stood off to the side as they gathered. Many were in bathing suits still dripping from their swim call. A minor miracle was that boiler tender second class Frederick Roberts was freshly shaven and dressed in clean dungarees with decent shoes. Ingram learned later that Hitchcock had 'spoken' with him.

Calling them to attention, Childers yelled loudly, "You've all heard our new skipper is aboard." He nodded in Ingram's direction. "He'll be speaking in a moment. He is Lieutenant Commander Todd Ingram, having recently spent time with Brent Moosbrugger in the Battle of Vela Gulf where we whacked the Japs three to zero. Presently, he's going to read his orders and then help us get this ship off the rocks."

Childers thrust out a hand, "Commander Ingram, welcome aboard."

Ingram stepped up and said, "Stand at ease, please gentlemen. There's not much time. We have to get this ship off the reef now. I'd like to know," he pulled a notebook from his pocket and checked a list. "Lieutenant Huber?"

"Sir?" The man was right in front of Ingram. Dressed in khaki shorts and shirt, he was about five foot ten and near to two hundred pounds. A real fire plug. With all that, his head looked too large for his body, especially with a liberal dose of five o'clock shadow. A typical looking gunner.

"How's the ammo offload?"

"We've offloaded about seventy percent, captain. At this rate we should finish tomorrow morning at zero eight hundred."

"We have to hurry it up, Mr. Huber."

Huber spread his hands. "Don't know how, skipper. We're going as fast as we can and still observe safety regulations."

"We may have to deep six safety regulations."

"But captain, we—"

"We will hold that in abeyance for now," interrupted Ingram. "But in the meantime, I'd like to add some more men."

"Where are they coming from, uh, Captain?" Huber's voice was a bit sarcastic.

"This answer is obvious. From the men in the water. Cancel the swim call and put them to work."

"They've been working their tails off," said Huber. "They're dead tired."

Ingram said, "Well Mr. Huber. What would you rather have? Dead tired sailors on a ship once again underway with a breeze in your face, or dead sailors on a ship on the bottom?"

Huber shook his head.

"Do it, Mr. Huber." Silence. Not a sound on the quarterdeck. Ingram said softly, "Mr. Huber?"

Huber nodded slowly. "Yes, sir. I'll get it done."

"Very well," said Ingram. "As soon as I've read my orders."

"Yes, sir." Huber looked up to the sky.

Ingram's eyes swept the two ranks of officers and chiefs. Then he gestured to the Marine standing beside him. "I'd like you to meet Gunnery Sergeant Gilroy Hitchcock who is our new master at arms until BuNav sends a regular. You can see by the wings on his chest that Gil is a flying sergeant which could come in handy for us. At the least, he has a TBF nearby that is going through an engine change. So, once that is done, he'll be returning to his regular duty. In the meantime, he's agreed to make himself useful and help us out. Thank you for being with us, Sergeant."

Hitchcock took a half step forward and waved. There was no response. He stepped back.

Ingram continued, "Okay, I will be meeting with department heads right after the reading of orders to discuss issues."

Ingram took a deep breath. "One more thing, gentlemen. It's obvious this offload is not going quickly enough. Even as we cancel swim call, we're doing one more thing."

All eyes returned to Ingram, now intense.

Ingram said loudly, "Junior officers, all ensigns, and lieutenants junior grade will join the working party. They will pass ammunition until the job is done."

There was a buzz from the officers. A look of anger flashed over Childers' face. On the other hand, Hitchcock flashed a quick thumbs up to Ingram.

Childers' face was red as spring cherry. "But captain. We can't have officers workin.'"

"Why not, Mr. Childers?"

He sputtered, "Because...because they're officers."

"What's wrong with that?"

Childers walked over to Ingram. "They're officers. They don't do manual labor."

"They're red-blooded American boys. We need them. This is an emergency. They can pass ammo. They will handle ammunition. Is that understood, Mr. Childers?"

Childers stepped close to Ingram.

"No, it's not, and furthermore—"

Gunnery sergeant Gilroy Hitchcock moved between Ingram and Childers, his arms folded. He was six inches taller and looked down to Childers.

Childers growled, "Where did this ape come from?" He doubled his fists. "Call him off."

Ingram spoke softly into Childers' ear. "That, my soon to be relieved executive officer, is your new chief master at arms. Weren't you listening when I introduced Gunnery Sergeant Gilroy Hitchcock, United States Marine Corp? His top responsibility aboard this ship is to maintain good order and discipline, of which, so far, I see very little from you. Now if you don't step back, I'm going to order Gunnery Sergeant Hitchcock to beat the shit out of you and then throw your dead ass into the brig. Do you understand what I just said Mister Childers?"

Childers' face grew redder. His lips were pressed, and five seconds passed. He sighed. His fists undoubled. He stepped back a pace. "Yes, sir, sorry sir. But that's such an extreme move. It's never been done before."

"It sure as hell has been done before, Mister. And you're looking at one who has done it. Yes. Me. A ring knocker to boot. In 1942, when the Japs were trying to sink our ship. I was passing ammo, like everyone else."

"Uhhh...don't mind me asking, where was that, sir?"

"Corregidor."

"Corregidor? You were on Corregidor?"

"That's affirmative."

Childers stepped back two more paces.

Ingram said, "Don't you realize we're a sitting duck? Someone is going to come along and blow us to kingdom come if we don't get moving."

"Yes, sir."

"We'll take this up later. But for now, let's assemble so I can read my orders. Now. Dismiss the officers."

"Yes, sir."

Childers did a correct about face and bellowed, "Dismissed. Everyone to the fantail where the captain will read his orders."

Tightly packed, they stood facing forward, all three hundred and fourteen of them, leaving twenty-two two-man skeleton watches in the foward fire room, the forward engine room, combat information center, bridge, radio central, and quarterdeck.

They brought up a cane-back chair for a pedestal. Childers stepped up, braced by two enginemen, and called: "Ship's crew. Stand easy. Lieutenant Commander Alton C. Ingram will now read his orders." He stepped down.

The chair was shaky with the ship at a ten-degree list. Nevertheless, Ingram wiggled up making the chair slide to starboard. In the end, Hitchcock and Huber stood fast and braced him. Finally, at a semblance of upright, Ingram called, "Closer, you men. Don't be afraid to pack it in. This won't take long."

He pulled a flimsy message from his pocket and began reading.

Lieutenant Tyler Childers wanted to make sure he read what it said. He pulled out his flimsy copy and followed along as Ingram barked it out:

BT
CLASSIFICATION: SECRET AS PER ORDER 17210843/N01321
FROM: CHIEF OF BUREAU OF NAVIGATION
TO: ALTON C. INGRAM, LIEUTENANT COMMANDER, UNITED STATES NAVY
SUBJ: BUNAV ORDERS: 17210843/N01321
INFO A. BUNAV; N443P
B. CINCPACFLT
C. COMDESPAC
D. COMPACWEST: N4
E. COMDESRON 6
1. WHEN DIRECTED BY REPORTING SENIOR, DETACH IMMEDIATELY FROM TRANSIT ORDER 021080443
2. PROCEED TO PORT IN WHICH USS *DUNAGAN* (DD 504) MAY BE.
3. UPON ARRIVAL REPORT COMMANDING OFFICER AS HIS RELIEF. REPORT IMMEDIATE SUPERIOR IN COMMAND, IF PRESENT, OTHERWISE BY MESSAGE.
BT

12

---

9 August 1943
USS *Dunagan* (DD 504)
Aground: 14° 41'3.84"S, 166° 34'6.24E
Espiritu Santo, New Hebrides

After reading the orders, they broke for chow, sandwiches mostly, and a thin, watery tomato soup.

That was when Ingram heard Huber mutter about not being efficient on the guns. That they'd not worked the loading machine for a couple of months. Right away Ingram drew Huber aside and ordered practice on the five-inch loading machine near the quarter deck. Each mount crew was to take a fifteen-minute break from offloading and work the loading machine.

Twenty rounds each. Then withdraw and let the next gun crew work it. Five-gun crews in all for mounts 51, 52, 53, 54, and 55 on the fantail.

With the heat, some of the kids passed out. Childers suggested an awning overhang. The bosun's mates rigged a canvas awning and twenty minutes later, each gun crew was able to toss off twenty dummy rounds without too much trouble.

Ingram and Hitchcock stood off to one side watching mount 53's gun crew exercise the machine. The crews growled and cursed and sweated as dummy rounds clanked onto the tray and into the breech.

Ingram and Hitchcock exchanged glances. *Slow*, they thought. But after the

second cycle of five rounds, their rhythm was better. They cut thirty seconds off their time. And the rhythm was smoother, the cursing less as the rounds flashed in and out. Even better in the third round.

After the noon meal, Ingram called a department head meeting in the wardroom to summarize the ship's status:

He started by pointing to the opposite end of the table. "Okay, gentlemen, first things first. I'd like to start by introducing our temporary, but gladly welcomed, Gunnery Sergeant Gilroy Hitchcock of the United States Marine Corps."

The officers rendered thin smiles. Hitchcock obliged them by smiling and waving.

Ingram continued, "Sergeant Hitchcock is a mud Marine with service in China, the Philippines, and more recently Guadalcanal. Just before the war's outbreak, Hitchcock decided he wanted to fly and spent fourteen months at Pensacola learning to fly. He is now a flying sergeant and earned those wings you see above his breast pocket. They have him on hazardous duty, the most recent of which was in a clapped out TBF with contaminated fuel. On our way here, that airplane, correction, our airplane was within a sixteenth of an inch of ditching in the blue Pacific. But he performed some miracles that kept that rattle-trap airborne long enough to make an emergency air strip just down the coast at Olpoi." Ingram pointed, "This man knows how to take care of himself and knows how to think on his feet. So please feel free to work with Sergeant Gilroy Hitchcock on any issues you may have.

"With DESRON 23's full approval, I have given Sergeant Hitchcock complete authority as Chief Master at Arms of this ship until BuNav sends a new replacement. Now, are there any questions?"

It was quiet so Ingram continued with, "And welcome aboard, gunny."

Hitchcock spread his hands and smiled.

He received nods in return.

"That said, gentlemen, I'd like to begin with the ship's status. Let's begin with...ahhhhh," he pulled a section of paper from his top pocket, "with engineering. What's the status of the plant, please, Mr. Shorter?"

A thin, wiry, sandy-haired Lieutenant Clinton T. Shorter sat slumped in the chair to his left. He smoked Lucky Strikes, one after another, and his eyes were half closed, like he hadn't slept much, which he hadn't. He wore sleeveless khakis and shorts with stains dating, it seemed, back to World War I. Why was it, Ingram wondered to himself, that engineers took great pride in their oil-stained clothing? They refused to throw them away. Each blotch, many faded with washing and with time, were like decorations, all standing round to claim some disaster that was quickly overcome, the ship still delivering full power.

Shorter spoke with a mid-western accent through a chipped front incisor. It looked good, Shorter was like the battered runt playing flag football with the big boys—*do or die*.

Shorter went through the litany of lighting yet another Lucky. He exhaled. His face nearly disappeared. At length, he summarized, "After fire-room, boilers three and four on the line, captain. Also up are the after-engine room, forward engine room. Split plant. Generators one and two on the line, no problems." The sky cleared. He flicked an ash and stared at Ingram.

"That's it?"

"Yessir."

Ingram smiled, "Well then, is the ship ready for sea?"

The question startled Shorter. He jumped. "Well, I didn't mean that, sir."

"Mr. Shorter. If that's not the case, please tell me what you meant."

Childers, on Ingram's right, said, "What we have here captain is a—"

Ingram waved him down. "I have it, Mr. Childers." He turned back to Shorter. "Mr. Shorter, you are the chief engineer aboard this vessel, is that not correct?"

Shorter glanced at Childers. "Yes, sir. Sorry sir. Yes, you are correct. There is more. The ship is aground. But I had nothing to do with that."

"I didn't say you did, Mr. Shorter. Now please proceed," said Ingram.

"Yessir. We are—"

Childers said, "Perhaps we can—"

Ingram silenced him with a stare.

"Go on, Mr. Shorter," said Ingram.

Shorter's voice was up an octave. "We are perched on some sort of rock or coral structure that has covered the main induction for boilers one and two. But that's okay. We can still make fresh water with what we have in the aft fire room. There seems to be no damage there, sir. Just the main induction is plugged. Oh, yeah, the sonar dome and transducer are goners and that's it."

"I figured that. Fuel oil?"

"We offloaded most of it, captain. We're down to about twenty percent." He pointed over his shoulder. "Now parked on oil barge 2868 over yonder." He waved.

"Ship's structure?"

"We put a diver over. We look okay, other than being on this damned rock."

"Very well, Mr. Shorter. Thank you."

"Yes, sir." He lit another Lucky Strike.

Ingram sipped coffee. It was excellent. He noticed Hitchcock emptied his own cup and tapped his belly with the top of his fist. He belched softly and winked.

13

9 August 1943
Wardroom - USS *Dunagan* (DD 504)
Aground: 14° 41'3.84"S, 166° 34'6.24E
Espiritu Santo, New Hebrides

"Time to hear from operations," Ingram said. He looked down at his scrawled list; Jonathon J. Grout was written in as the Operations officer. He sat to Ingram's left.

Grout started right away. "Embarrassed to say we're safe and secure, captain. All stations are manned, circuits up and being guarded, equipment fully operational. Surface search radar on the line with no contacts the past twenty-four hours. Because of the list to starboard, the air search radar is secure. Don't want to strain the bearing."

"Crew?" Grout answered his own question with, "all safe and healthy." He sat back.

"That's it?" Ingram asked.

"Yes, sir." Grout was a tall sandy-haired man. He also wore a pencil thin moustache, and in any other setting would be an attractive man. But his working khakis were wrinkled and he slouched. His short hair was mussed.

Worst of all, he didn't look at you when he spoke or was spoken to. His eyes were always directed to the deck.

I hate that, "Mr. Grout." Ingram waved his hands before his face.

"Huh? Yes sir?"

"Here I am, Jon."

He sat up straight. "Yes, sir."

"Good. Now, I want you to energize that air search radar."

Grout squirmed in his chair. "But sir, the bearings."

Ingram smiled. "But Jon, the Japs."

"Sir?"

Ingram sighed, "Visualize, if you will, Mr. Grout, a Japanese twin-engine Betty flying right toward us carrying torpedoes. Wouldn't you like to have a little advance notice?"

"Uh, yes, sir."

"Bearings or no bearing?"

"I get your point, sir. We'll light it off."

"Very good. And just a relative scan. Let's say a one hundred eighty degree sweep every two minutes. Will that make it easier on your bearings, Mr. Grout?"

"Y...Yes, sir. Every two minutes. Yes, sir. Thank you, sir."

Ingram smiled and looked them in the eye. "That is all for now. But later—" he snapped his fingers and then pointed. "Mr. Grout, one more thing."

Grout faced Ingram, "Yes, captain?"

"You have a man, George Eckert, working for you?"

"Yes, sir. Our communications officer. Lieutenant jay gee."

"Who doesn't like to be awakened to stand a watch?"

"Well, sir, that's true. We had to take him off the watch bill. He gets quite violent. Sorry, sir."

"Well, put him back on the watch bill."

"Sir?"

"You heard me. Put him back on the watch bill. I don't care if he screams in his sleep and foams at the mouth. If you can show me something in his medical folder that says he should be taken off the watch bill, then I'll consider it. Otherwise, he does his job, just like everybody else."

"He's not going to like this, captain."

Ingram froze in his chair. There was a deadly silence in the wardroom for thirty seconds. Finally Ingram said in a stone-cold voice, "Mr. Grout. I advise you. This ship is a United States Navy man of war, not something to suit one individual's tastes and preferences. Do you understand that?"

"Yes, sir."

He pointed to Hitchcock seated at the far end of the table. "You see that man sitting there?"

"Y...yes, sir."

"He is Gunnery Sergeant Gilroy Hitchcock of the United States Marine Corp. Now before all these men, I am ordering Gunnery Sergeant Hitchcock, who as you know, is now the chief master of arms, to accompany the messenger who wakes Mr. Eckert. If Mr. Eckert resists or makes a scene, the gunnery sergeant will dump a one-gallon bucket of cold water over Mr. Eckert's head. If he further resists, the gunnery sergeant will...ah...help convince Mr. Eckert that proudly standing a watch is every officer's duty. If that has no effect, then our Chief Master at Arms will throw Mr. Eckert into the brig. No questions asked. Mr. Eckert will then be charged with dereliction of duty and turned over to the nearest Marine brig to await trial. And all penalties will apply. Is that clear, Mr. Grout?"

"Yes, sir."

"Why does your Mr. Eckert get a free pass to sleep while others are forced to take his load?"

"No reason, captain."

"All right. Now go and energize your air search radar and then have a little séance with Mr. Eckert. You have permission to take him out of the ammunition passing line to convey this latest piece of news to him."

"Yes, sir." Grout nearly shouted like a recruit in boot camp.

"Okay, gentlemen. Let's get at it. Secure."

Chairs scraped as they stood. Childers called across the table to Grout, "It's okay. Maybe with your radar, we can see who's been firing those flares."

"Yeah, maybe so," replied Grout.

Ingram froze in his place. "What? Say again, please."

Childers waved his arms nonchalantly. "Somebody been shootin' flares at us last couple of nights."

"What kind of flares?"

"Well, you know, the ones that light you up and float silently down."

"Illumination flares? You mean illumination flares?"

Childers stood straight up. After taking a deep breath, he said, "Well, yes, sir. Like illumination flares. But nobody is shootin' at us. So I figured that—"

"Did you report this?"

"Well, no sir. They're just flares. We figured somebody was practicing out there."

Ingram slowly shook his head.

Childers asked, "You think it was a Jap, sir? Couldn't be a Rufe. We heard no engine noise. Besides, too far for a Rufe—out of range. Anyway, there was no engine sound. So it wasn't a Betty either. We definitely would have heard that. So?"

"Was it entered in the logbook?"

Childers looked to Grout who nodded 'yes.'

Ingram said, "Sound general quarters, immediately." He turned to Grout. "And get that damned radar going, now."

14

9 August 1943
USS *Dunagan* (DD 504)
Aground: 14° 41'3.84"S, 166° 34'6.24E
Espiritu Santo, New Hebrides

"GQ, sir?" Childers asked. "They're passing ammunition."

"That's what I said, Mr. Childers," said Ingram.

"But—"

Over the 1 MC the command went out. "Now general quarters, general quarters. All hands man your battle stations."

"I will be on the bridge, Mr. Childers, and you will be in CIC?"

"Yes, sir."

Ingram dashed into the passageway and jumped inside his in-port stateroom finding his B-4 bag atop the bunk. Quickly, he unzipped it, grabbed a stop watch and clicked it on as he continued his trip up two ladders to the bridge.

He dashed outside to the starboard bridgewing and leaned against the bulwark, watching...and watching...

Evident was the sound of mayhem drifting up to him: men growling, yelling, shoving.

"Run forward on the port side! Run aft on the starboard side! Look out! Make a

hole...Get a move on!"

A man stepped up to him wearing headphones and mic. A helmet was hooked

onto his belt. He was a yeoman first class in dungarees and very skinny, no more than 140 pounds nor taller than five feet eight. It was hard to see his eyes as he wore aviator glasses and had cauliflower ears. He wore his hair in a butch and kept it scrupulously trimmed. Yet, he stood assuredly with his finger on the mic button, ready to transmit the captain's orders. Proudly tattooed on his right biceps was a U.S. shield with *United States Navy* and just below that was *Mother*.

Looks okay, worth a try. "You belong to me?"

He spoke. Ingram was surprised to find his voice a smooth baritone. "Afternoon

captain. I am Norman Lutz, your talker."

"Glad to meet you, Lutz. What's going on?"

"All manned and ready, captain, except...except," he spoke into his mike,

"Bridge, aye." He turned to Ingram, " That was gunnery manned and ready, we still have Main Control...Wait one...Bridge aye," He looked back to Ingram. "That was...yes, main control and...and...Bridge aye. That was CIC, sir. All stations manned and ready, captain."

Ingram clicked the stopwatch. 4:23. "Ugh!"

"Sir?"

He flashed the stopwatch. "We have work to do, Lutz."

"Yes, sir."

Just then, an officer walked through the hatch. He approached and saluted, "Afternoon, captain." He wore headphones and battle helmet.

"And you are—"

"Your GQ OOD. Clinton Shorter, Lieutenant, USN, Engineering Officer. I hope

you'll be pleased, sir."

"So far, so good, Mr. Shorter." Ingram waved him over. "Except," he raised the

stopwatch. "Four minutes and twenty-three seconds. Unsat."

"Yessir."

"We have to bang it down to three minutes and thirty seconds. And then maybe

three minutes. And we don't have much time."

They stepped to the bulwark and, leaning on their elbows, peered over the side. "Not to sound sarcastic, captain, but we ain't going anywhere as far as I can tell."

Ingram sighed, "You have a point and that means we could just sit here until the

ship rots, or some Jap finds us, or the Navy sends out a monster fleet of tugboats, to drag us off. During which time we wait and catch up on our sleep, maybe roast marshmallows on the fantail after sunset."

Shorter shrugged and gave a smirk.

"Well, I ain't doing that, Mister," Ingram growled. "I'm not sitting on my butt while

this ship is in danger. Nor is anyone else. We'll be getting this ship off the reef one way or the other. Do you understand me?"

They locked eyes.

Jeeeez. "Er...yes, sir."

Ingram cast a hand toward the water. Together, they viewed the crystal-clear

water and the bottom, about thirty feet down. It was light sand with a few rocks scattered about. Ingram asked. "What do you think, Mr. Shorter?"

Shorter clasped his hands. "Water is very clear, sir."

"I can see that."

"But the bottom is ragged. Unpredictable."

"What do you mean?

Shorter paused and then said, "We put a diver over yesterday."

"Who?"

"Ensign Becker. Our DCA[1]. Belongs to me. He's a qualified diver."

"Good move. Did he find anything?"

Shorter shrugged, "Maybe a nick in the starboard propeller blade and yet a little

one. But I still worry about shaft alignment there."

"I don't blame you. Anything else?"

"Not really, captain. Outside of scrapes and scratches, it looks okay. But the bottom? It's weird. I can't tell what's going on there."

"Meaning?"

Shorter pointed, "See that dark slash over there?"

Ingram leaned out. "Yes."

"That could be the lip of a chasm, meaning, that if it gives way, we could slip into it and be afloat, but also be land bound. No place to go."

Ingram rubbed his chin. "Then we blast our way out."

"How do we do that?"

Ingram pointed to the tug anchored out. "Rig a delayed fuse on a depth charge.

Push it off the *Tillamook's* fantail and run like hell."

"Don't know if they would approve that chit, Captain."

"Who?"

"DESRON 23. Our home."

Just then, Lieutenant Huber called down from atop the pilot house. "Gunners

mates report all ammo offloaded, captain."

Ingram shaded his eyes and looked up. "Very well, Mr. Huber. Does that mean

everything is off the ship?"

"Affirmative, captain."

"Okay, here's what I'd like to do. Do you have any VT frag in your inventory?"

"No, sir. Not yet. On order but not here yet."

'Okay. Let's take back aboard twenty rounds of able-able-commonfor

each mount to be stowed in their upper handling rooms. Once that is done, secure the ammunition party, pull off the barge and anchor it a thousand yards away. But keep the *Tillamook* close by. We may need it. Got that?"

"Will do, captain. Give us twenty minutes, and I believe we can button it up."

"Very well." Ingram looked up. The air search antenna was rotating slowly back and forth. He doubted if anything would show up but it was good to give the boys in CIC something to do. And the surface search antenna was swinging in circles, doing its job.

Shorter wandered into the pilot house.

Speaking of something to do, Ingram stepped to the open bridge and the surface search radar repeater. He checked to find the surface search radar energized, pushed his face down to the rubber hood that kept daylight from washing out images on the radar screen. The cursor swept slowly around. Espiritu Santo's landmass clearly 'painted' to starboard. To port was all black; all ocean for forty miles out, the extent the radar could see ocean-based objects.

He made to turn away, but then...something.

A little tiny blip about...he ran the cursor: bearing 281°, range: 8,200 yards. He watched. The cursor painted it once, twice...then not on the third time nor after that. Harmlessly, it kept sweeping with no little blip.

What the hell?

He grabbed a phone from its bracket and punched CIC.

"Combat, Allred speaking, sir."

"Allred, this is the captain. You have a contact about 8,200 yards bearing 281°?"

"Yes, sir, intermittent. We're watching it."

"Why haven't you designated it?" Ingram looked up. Hitchcock stood before him giving a mock salute, a smirk on his face. Ingram returned it with a cursory tip of his fingers to his forehead.

Allred replied, "Such a weak contact, captain. Most likely a reef being washed over."

"Is it underway?"

"Not as far as we can tell."

"Very well. Keep a watch on it. It's a strong echo at times, more than a reef, I'd say. Designate it, please."

"Yes, sir, captain. We can call this skunk Charlie. Right now DIW[2]."

"Thank you, Mr. Allred. Now, put the exec on, please."

"Er, ah...not here, captain."

"Not at his GQ station? Then where is he?" barked Ingram.

Allred said, "Stateroom, I believe, captain. Paperwork."

"Thank you, Allred. Hold a moment, please." Ingram held the phone away and looked at Hitchcock. "I don't believe this. Childers not at his GQ station."

Hitchcock looked about the open bridge. Except for Lutz, there was nobody close by. "That's why I'm making this little visit. To inform you about this. But you just found out the hard way."

Ingram looked again at the radar repeater.

Bleep! There it was again, this time much brighter. "Take a look, Gilroy. Tell me what you think."

Hitchcock pulled a grimace then pressed his face to the hood. He muttered, "Just a stupid jarhead. What the hell do you expect from..." He concentrated, stepped closer, then looked again.

At length he raised his head and moved away. "I ain't nothin' but a stupid jarhead, who..."

"Come on, Gilroy. What the hell do you see?"

"Intermittent contact, sir."

"I know that, damnit."

"Strong echo. Metallic, I'd say."

"Now you're talkin'," said Ingram. "Combat has designated it skunk Charlie."

Hitchcock shrugged and moved away. "Wonderful."

Ingram checked the range again. Still 8,200 yards.

He called into the phone. "Okay, I have it Allred. Thank you."

"Yes, sir." Allred rang off.

Ingram punched the *XO Stateroom* station.

"Childers here."

"Tyler. What are you doing there?" demanded Ingram.

"Captain Gillian wants his reports, sir." M. J. Gillian was the commodore of Destroyer Squadron 23.

"And what about the Japs? What do you suppose they want?"

"Sir? His people get quite...ahhh...pesky...when it comes to this. They want a complete hull report. We should—"

"Mr. Childers. I order you to your GQ station. Is it necessary that I send Mr. Hitchcock down there to drag you up there?"

"Captain, I would like nothing better than to see Mr. Hitchcock at my door."

"You're out of line, Mr. Childers. Get back to your GQ station at once."

"Yes, sir."

"We have an intermittent surface radar contact. It could be a Japanese submarine."

"Indeed?"

"For the last time, get up there."

"Yes, sir. On my way."

Ingram jammed the handset in its bracket and muttered, "What the hell am I going to do with that guy?"

15

9 August 1943
USS *Dunagan* (DD 504)
Aground: 14° 41'3.84"S, 166° 34'6.24E
Espiritu Santo, New Hebrides

Ingram checked the sun. Nearly three in the afternoon. And hotter then blazes, he reckoned, inside the ship. They'd been at GQ more than an hour. And no change with skunk Charlie, still stationary at eight thousand yards.

He walked into the pilot house, yanked the sound powered phone from its bracket and punched CIC.

"Childers."

"Ahh, good, Tyler. Sorry to take you away from your paperwork. Welcome back to CIC." He waited. No response. So he said, "Any reply from VP 54?" VP 54 was a PBY squadron based in Espiritu Santo.

"No sir. Not yet."

"How about DESRON 23?"

"Negative."

"COMSERVESOPAC?"

"They're sending a couple of tugs up from Noumea. Message just came in."

"Very well, thank you." Ingram hung up.

Ingram turned to Lutz. "Tell all stations to stand down to condition three, except for main control, CIC, and the bridge."

"Yessir." Lutz keyed his mic and began spewing orders.

Ingram walked to the port side of the pilot house. He grabbed the handset and punched up the gunnery officer's line. "Huber, this is the captain."

"Yessir."

"We have a radar contact: 8,200 yards bearing 281°. Think you can get a visual? Maybe see what it looks like?"

"Not a bad idea, captain. We'll give it a shot." Huber keyed his mic and within seconds, the main battery director whirred around to the bearing. Ingram gave a thought to the optical range finder. It was a giant telescope with lenses mounted on either end of a fourteen-foot tube for stereoscopic range finding. Developed in the mid-thirties the image was stabilized from ship's movement in a seaway and very accurate. Not as accurate in range as the radar but far better than visual estimates.

Huber called down, "Mr. Buckner reports Damico sees an indistinguishable slab-sided object, dark gray in color, and, get this, from time to time, he sees a very slender mast-like object sticking up."

On tiptoes, Ingram motioned Huber down on his haunches. He spoke sotto voce. "Your range finder operator. He's okay?" He knew operating a range finder was as much an art as it was a science.

"He's a second-class FT, sir."

"That's nice. Now, how is he at operating that range finder?"

Huber's face spread to a wide grin. "No worries about Lorenzo Damico, captain. With a naked eye, he can spot a rabbit turd at four hundred yards."

Ingram said, "Glad to hear that. We need more like him. Carry on."

"Now with a naked girl, he can—"

"Very well, Mr. Huber. Thank you."

"Yes, sir."

The open bridge phone buzzed. Ingram stepped back and yanked it from its bracket. "Ingram."

"Childers, captain."

"Go ahead."

"VP 54 Noumea advises a dumbo is enroute for assistance."

"Assistance. Is that it?"

"Yes, sir. That's it."

"ETA?"

"I'd say about an hour, sir."

"Very well. Thank you."

Childers hung up.

Ingram silently shook his head. *What am I going to do with this guy*?

"Sir?" asked Lutz.

"It's all right, Lutz. Just thinking. I get a little dangerous when that happens."

Lutz took a deep breath.

"What can I do for you, Lutz?"

"No, sir. It's the other way around. How would you like a nice tall glass of ice water?"

The corners of Ingram's mouth raised a bit, "Only if you'll join me, Lutz. Make it two."

Ingram heard it all the way down to the bridge. "Sheeeeyat!!!"

The invective had echoed from the main battery director just above them. He looked up to Huber who keyed his mic.

Huber finished and looked down at Ingram. "That was Buckner. They just blew the magnetron."

Dammit. Of all times. The Mark 37 fire control system was notorious for faulty or substandard magnetrons, a major component in fire control radars. The whole system depended on operating magnetrons. Otherwise: nothing.

"ETR?"

"Yes, sir, we have spares on hand. Leon's pretty good with that. I'd say ten minutes tops."

"Switch to optical."

"Done that, Captain."

"Who's on it?"

"Damico, Captain."

"The guy with the rabbit turds?"

"No sh—er, yes, sir. That's Lorenzo Damico, all right."

"I'd like to speak with him."

"Yes, sir."

Ingram twisted the barrel switch nearby. He landed on the main battery director circuit after three tries.

Voices came up. "And you should have seen the boobs on this one. She lifted up her—"

"Silence," roared Ingram. There was silence. Then Ingram said, "This is the captain. Which one is Damico?"

"Here, sir."

"Here, what? How do you announce yourself?"

"Range finder 51, sir."

"Very well, range finder 51, did Mr. Huber designate a target for you?"

"Yes, sir."

"Did you acquire it?"

"Yes, sir."

"Very good, Damico. Now, I'd like you to tell me what you saw."

"See, sir."

"What?" demanded Ingram.

"I'm still watching it. Right now. While we're talking."

"Go ahead, please."

Damico took a large lungful of air, then said, "Eight thousand yards, four miles. Makes it tough. Half a flyspeck, maybe." He paused.

Ingram waited.

"A lot of haze out that far, the target wiggles, almost disappears, and then clears up momentarily."

"And so...?"

Damico went sotto voce and said, "Mr. Buckner thinks I'm crazy. Told me to shut up. But I think...I think..."

"Go on."

"A submarine. It's a submarine. Nearly bow on. But he ain't movin', captain. Like he's fixed. Bow stickin' up in the air. Maybe aground, like us."

"That's it?"

Damico exhaled loudly. "That's my best guess, sir. And now, it sounds like them guys on the radar have it pretty well wrapped up. They'll be after me to shut up in a moment."

"Radar or no radar, Damico, you keep doing what you're doing. Report any changes to Mr. Huber immediately."

"Yessir," Damico fairly shouted.

A tap on his shoulder. It was Lutz. "Yes?"

"Director 51 reports fire control radar working one hundred percent, captain."

"Very well."

Lutz' hand was out. Ingram looked down. A frosted glass of ice water. "Thank you." He meant it and took three large swallows. "Wow. Thank you."

Lutz had his own glass, already half-drained. He held it up, "And thank you, sir." He tipped it and drank more.

Ingram stepped into shadows onto the open bridge and checked his watch: 1537. It ran through his head: *I've been aboard this beast a little over six hours and nothing's fixed. In fact It's getting worse. I still have no idea how this ship ended up on this reef. Worse, I can't tell the commodore that we can survive this mess even as we sit here, high and dry. And now, I may have a Jap submarine out there with me in his sights.*

It hit him. Time to shoot back. "Mr. Huber," he called.

"Sir."

"I intend to take that target, skunk Charlie, under fire."

"You concur with Damico, Captain?"

"Indeed I do. Please designate mounts 51, 53, and 55 as the firing mounts. Just two rounds each, in order. Director control."

"Are we sure about this captain?"

Ingram smiled for the first time. "Let's put it this way, Mr. Huber. It's not one of ours. We know that, right?"

"Yes, sir."

"It appears to be an enemy submarine according to a trained and resourceful operator."

"I'll buy that, Captain."

"Well then, I'd rather give it to him than sit around and give him time to figure out how to give it to us."

"Ummm, makes sense to me, Captain."

"Then make it so. Let me know when you're ready."

"Sixty seconds, Captain."

"Make it fifty-nine."

Huber snorted and left the circuit.

"Bridge combat." It was Childers on the 21 MC.

"Go ahead."

"Dumbo on his way in. About a minute out. Due south. It's that crazy Cogswell on *Blind Date.*"

Ingram grinned. "Tell him 'Welcome aboard.' Now, did you hear my conversation with Huber?"

"Yeah, makes sense to me."

"Very well. Then please relay our intentions to *Blind Date.* Ask him to exercise caution as we open fire. By the way, did he relay his ordnance load?"

"Eight 250-pound bombs. Lots of fifty calibers."

"That sounds nice." Ingram checked his watch. "We're about ready here. We'll begin with Mount 51."

"Aye, captain."

16

9 August 1943
USS *Dunagan* (DD 504)
Aground: 14° 41'3.84"S, 166° 34'6.24E
Espiritu Santo, New Hebrides

It seemed to happen all at once. First, Ingram, his palms pressing his ears to his head, felt and heard the strident 'crack' of *Dunagan's* mount 51, the forwardmost five-inch gun mount on the ship. 'Strident crack' really is an understatement. The round erupts with an ear-splitting 'WHAM.'

The five-inch naval rifle cranks out a fifty-four-pound projectile at the rate of 2,600 feet per second; the blast often called louder than that of a battleship's sixteen inch cannon with the same muzzle velocity.

And next, for the people topside, was the growl of *Blind Date's* R-1830-58 engines as she blasted right over the top, saluting with a wing-wiggle, and heading directly for the Japanese submarine. "Glad he's on our side," grinned Lutz. The PBY looked deadly as it dwindled from view, eight 250-pound bombs hanging beneath her wide, parasol wing.

Ingram yanked the R/T handset from its bracket. Holding it for a moment, he asked Lutz, "What's our call sign?"

"Haystack, sir," replied Lutz.

With a nod, Ingram pressed the transmit button and said, "Poor Alimony, this is Haystack, over."

With static, the reply came back, "Hey, Mr. Ingram, it's Gus Johnson. Homer's a little busy right now. Can I put you on hold?"

Ingram said, "Not necessary, just wanted to—"

WHAM! It was mount 51's second round.

"Welcome you aboard. Haystack out."

But the Japanese weren't caught napping. As Ingram had feared, the submarine had decided to send a round from her four-inch deck gun, the two projectiles passing each other in flight. He looked up to Huber. "See anything?"

Just then, the Japanese four-inch round splashed about 400 yards short and 200 yards to port. Ingram mused, *crappy shooting.* No need to take evasive action yet. Ingram shook his head. *How can you take evasive action when you're high and dry on a coral reef?*

Huber called down. "Not bad. I think we're 150 short and 200 to the left."

Ingram called, "Apply the spot. All mounts open fire and have fun."

"Yes, sir," called Huber.

Just then, the R/T went off. "Haystack, this is Poor Alimony. Be advised, two torpedoes fired from the Nip. Headed your way ."

Ingram felt as if he'd been speared by a four-foot icicle. With a great deal of effort, he grabbed the R/T and keyed it. He could hardly find his voice. "Uhm, Poor Alimony, Haystack. Understand two torpedoes."

"Wait one, Haystack..."

Ingram looked out to the PBY, a dot out to sea. He was in a shallow dive. Then he leveled out.

WHAM, WHAM. Mounts 53 and 55 cranked out their rounds.

Just then, the PBY pulled up sharply and climbed. Visible, were a series of splashes, explosions...yes...bombs...walking their way across the water.

The reports of their explosions dimly echoed across the water.

Suddenly, a flash. Debris twirled into the air. Smoke, a lot. A bit of flame glowed, then disappeared. But smoke tumbled up into the sky four or five hundred feet, Ingram guessed. He keyed his mike. "Poor Alimony. Did you do what I think you did?"

Static. They looked to the overhead-mounted speaker. Finally. Cogswell's voice was hoarse. "Yeah, Tojo and his buddies just said goodbye. The thing is obliterated."

"Wow. Congratulations."

"Not without a cost, Todd. They put up flak, plenty of it. Gus was hit pretty bad. Head wound. Not sure if he'll make it. Shrapnel right above his eye. Cockpit is a mess."

"I'm sorry."

"Worse, that Jap had pretty good aim. Just caught up to his two torpedoes. Close to the surface. Running right toward you. About halfway there. Batten down, Todd."

"Right, thanks Homer. Haystack, out."

Ingram jumped in the pilot house and keyed the 1 MC. "All hands. This is the captain speaking. The PBY just destroyed the Japanese submarine. But not before he fired two torpedoes at us. These are Jap fifty knot torpedoes and they should be here within the next two minutes. Secure all loose gear. Close all water-tight hatches. Hang on and pray. We'll get through this. That is all."

He stepped back and said to Harvey Truesdale, the boatswain mate of the watch. "Sound the collision alarm." And then to the men in the pilot house he said, "These things have one hell of a wallop. Grab on to something solid."

He told Lutz to relay that to all stations on his circuit. Then he grabbed his sound-powered hand-set and jabbed CIC.

"Combat, Childers,"

"Okay, Tyler, it's Ingram. You up on the torpedoes?"

"Yeah, we copied your gab with *Poor Alimony*. Then I got them on a mark. A little over a minute and a half to go."

Just then, *Poor Alimony* roared overhead, waggling its wings. Ingram, Lutz, the lookouts and the 40-millimeter gun crews waved back.

"That sounds about right. Hang on to something solid."

"You can bet we're doing that. Those things have crappy warheads?"

"Uh, I wish. They carry each a little over a thousand pounds of torpex."

"Aw, shit."

"Yes."

"Speaking of shit. You shitting your pants?"

Ingram forced a laugh, "Hell, yes. Like a racehorse."

"Me too, enough to fertilize the White House rose garden."

Ingram said, "Gotta go, Tyler. Good luck." He bracketed the phone and stepped on to the port bridgewing. Lutz followed, his mouth gaping open.

Ingram pounded the bridge bulwark. "Grab on, son. These things will rattle your brains."

"Yes, sir."

Propping his elbows on the bulwark, Ingram raised his binoculars and stared out to sea, looking for torpedo wakes. Just then, one jumped the surface, a glistening silvery fish, Porpoising through a wave, it actually jumped through and plopped back in the water.

About 500 yards out but running erratic. Bad depth correction. Good news.

But it was headed right for them. Amidships. *Bad news, Very bad, Forward fireroom. We're screwed. Really screwed.*

He checked his watch. Then he spotted the other wake. This one about 600 yards out. But it looked as if it would miss aft by about one to two hundred yards. One torpedo would be bad enough. Possible survivable. The other one will miss but not by much. A near miss.

The second torpedo passed the first torpedo which was still jumping out of the water.

But it was holding steady on its course. In fact, it had pulled a bit left now. No longer for the forward fire room. This bastard is going to hit right beneath the bridge. The thought flashed; this has to be the shortest time in command anyone has ever had in this man's Navy.

Ingram looked over to Lutz. The yeoman's hands were grabbing tightly to the bridge bulwark, his head was bowed beneath his arms; a rivulet of sweat ran down his cheek.

Ingram reached over and slapped him on the back. "You're doing fine, son."

"Captain, I'm scared, shitless," he wailed.

Ingram grabbed the bulwark and said, "You and me both, sailor."

Surprise registered on Lutz's face. His mouth dropped open. He went to speak.

Ingram's last thoughts were of Helen.

That's when the torpedo hit.

17
---

9 August 1943
USS *Dunagan* (DD 504)
Aground: 14° 41'3.84"S, 166° 34'6.24E
Espiritu Santo, New Hebrides

Lightning bolts danced before his eyes. Ingram remembered flying backwards, his back slamming against the pilothouse bulkhead. Then he was on the deck, looking up at a once cloudless sky. Junk. Rocks. Debris cascaded over him. Water. It seemed like tons of it showered on him all mixed with bottom sand, vegetation. Detritus. Unrecognizable. And then the ringing in his ears. Sound seemed to have taken a holiday. There was activity all around but he couldn't hear.

Five seconds passed; he wiped at bleary eyes.

A second explosion. As loud and as tearing and as devastating as the first.

More rocks, more water, more detritus splattered on the deck. There was a sting. A fist-sized rock had landed on Ingram's right shoulder. Not coral. A rock. Heavy. Ingram looked to see his shirt ripped and a bloody cut on top of his shoulder. The culprit lay on the deck beside him.

His ears rang. He still couldn't hear a damned thing.

Lutz lay next to him, his nose bleeding. Three other crewmen were scattered on the deck, one or two propped on their elbows. Blinking their eyes, wiping water and sand off their faces.

Something else.

Jeeeez. Ingram rolled to his hands and knees and looked about. It seemed as if the water would never stop. It still came down and down, soaking all on the open bridge.

Men cursed. One or two shouted at the unhearing sky.

Ingram rose to his feet. Still dizzy, he braced himself against the bulkhead.

Something else.

"Holy shit, Mr. Ingram."

Surprised, Ingram could hear. "What?

"Do ya feel that?" Lutz gasped as he stood next to Ingram running the back of his hand across his nose.

Feel what? Then *What the hell is that*? They were rocking. Side to side.

Afloat!

"Good God! We're afloat," Ingram gasped.

He steadied himself against the pilothouse bulkhead. Grabbing the hatch coaming, he leaned inside and spotted the boatswain mate of the watch. "You! What's your name?"

The man's white hat was jammed askew. He was skinny and his dark brown hair stuck out underneath his white hat. Blinking, he tried to get his bearings. "Uhhhh,"

His teeth were stained from too much smoking. He pressed his hands to his temples. "Truesdale, captain."

Truesdale, damnit. That's right. "We're afloat. Got it?"

"Uhhhh. No shit?"

Ingram stepped through the hatch and grabbed Truesdale's shoulders. "Yes. No shit. Wake up. There's lots to do." He nodded to the helmsman and lee helmsman. They hung on to their helm or the engine room telegraph. "Take these two guys and go down and drop the port anchor."

Ingram shook his head, "No wait. Delay that." He turned to Lutz, "Call the forward repair party—what do you call them?"

Lutz's jaw worked as he searched for words.

Ingram said, "You okay, son?"

Lutz held up a hand, "Can hardly hear you, captain, those explosions were so loud. But okay, I got it. Repair one, sir."

Same thing. Ingram realized his ears were still ringing. He wondered if his nose was bleeding, too, and ran his hand beneath. Nothing.

"Right, call repair one and tell them to drop the port anchor. Hold it at short stay

but make sure it's holding."

Lutz wiped at his nose with a handkerchief. "Yes, sir." Lutz pressed his mic key and began talking.

Truesdale held up a handset. "XO for you, sir,"

Ingram shot back, "Tell him to wait one."

He stepped to the 1 MC and flipped the 'all stations' switch. His voice echoed throughout the ship as he said, "This is the captain speaking. Well, providence has dealt us an interesting hand. That Jap did us a favor. His two torpedoes, instead of blowing us to smithereens, did something to blow up the coral reef we rested on and set us afloat. So strike one up for the good guys. I intend to remain anchored here for a short time and check the ship for structural security. I also want to send out a diver to see if it's safe for us to back clear. Hopefully, we'll be able to do that. Once clear, we will be taking our fuel oil back and our ammo. Okay, for now, I'd like us to stand easy, especially those of you topside, check for any damage and then get ready to reprovision.That is all."

Ingram stepped back, letting out a lungful of air. *I should be dead. Instead, we're alive and afloat. Amazing. Survivor's guilt. Get on with it, you idiot.*

"Mister Shorter," he bellowed.

Shorter, the GQ OOD, stepped before him, his garrison cap jammed askew. He looked at Ingram, the corners of his mouth raising.

"What the..." Ingram began

Lutz reached up and correctly positioned Ingram's cap on his head. The three looked at one another.

Shorter bellowed with an enormous laugh. Finally, he wheezed with, "You...you look like Elmer Fudd."

"And you. You're out of uniform, sailor," cackled Ingram as he reached up to adjust Shorter's cap.

Shorter dipped his head in a slight bow. "How can I help you, captain?"

"We need your diver to go over the side and see if we have a clear path to back out of here."

"Give us twenty minutes, sir."

"Very well."

Lutz nudged him.

"What?"

Lutz said, "The exec holding on the phone, sir." He handed it over.

"Ingram," he growled.

"Are you all right up there?"

"Yeah, that was a hell of a blast. Put us off the air for about thirty seconds, I'd say. You okay?"

"Frankenstein fell out of his chair. Hit his head. Big bump. Bleeding. We bandaged it. So, he's okay now. Equipment seems to be working okay."

"Who's Frankenstein?"

"Excuse me, sir. Wallenstein, radarman second class. One of our best."

"Was he out?"

"Yeah, actually about five minutes."

"Have the doc check him."

"He seems okay."

"How do you know?"

"He's walking and talking and telling dirty jokes."

"Have the doc look him over. See if he has a concussion."

"He's our top radar whiz on the watch. We need him."

Ingram stood up straight. "I have a question for you, Mr. Childers."

"Sir?"

"What medical school did you attend?"

There was silence on the line.

Ingram said, "I take that as the Chop and Scream school of medicine in Punxsutawney, Pennsylvania."

"Well, not exactly. I—"

"Get him checked now, damnit. While we have this little interval. Starting with ammo passing, we're going to need everybody. And I leave this up to your judgement, to consider putting him on light duty for a couple of days."

"Ahh, yes, sir. Just wondering, what medical school did you attend, captain?"

For some reason, Ingram grinned. He would rather have this sort of back-and-forth crap than a sullen non-committal exec. He needed every inch of Childers. "It's the I-am-your-boss school of medicine."

"I got it captain. Frankenstein goes to sick bay, immediately."

"Thank you XO."

"Yes, sir."

"Incidentally, how's the air search radar working now?"

Ingram heard static, then nothing. "Hello, Tyler?"

"Ahh, wait one, please. We're checking."

Ingram could have laughed aloud if the situation were not so serious. Then the thought struck him, time to get a SITREP (situation report) out to DESRON 23 and to ComCincPac. And then, once free of the inland waters of Espiritu Santo, the *Dunagan* would most likely be ordered north to Pearl Harbor for a new sonar dome at the least; possibly some propellor shaft alignment depending how the ship performed on her way up. Accordingly, there would be a lot of preparation for all that.

Childers came back. "We don't have enough quarters to get the thing running."

"What?"

"Sorry sir. Just a little post-traumatic euphoria. It's working fine. As far as I can tell, all of our gear is working fine."

"Very well. And I'll expect some of your guys in there to pass ammo as well."

"Yes, but..."

"But what, Mr. Childers?"

"Yes, but...okay...yes, sir...we'll contribute three or four guys to the cause."

"Make it four."

"Aye, aye, captain."

PART II

<hr>

Code of a Naval Officer
John Paul Jones

"It is, by no means, enough that an officer of the Navy should be a capable mariner. He must be that, of course, but also a great deal more. He should be, as well, a gentleman of liberal education, refined manner, punctilious courtesy, and the nicest sense of personal honor. He should not only be able to express himself clearly and with force in his own language both with tongue and pen, but he should be versed in French and Spanish.

He should be the soul of tact, patience, justice, firmness, and charity. No meritorious act of a subordinate should escape his attention or be left to pass without its reward, if even the reward be only one word of approval. Conversely, he should not be blind to a single fault in any subordinate, though at the same time he should be quick and unfailing to distinguish error from malice, thoughtlessness from incompetency, and well-meant shortcoming from heedless or stupid blunder. As he should be universal and impartial in his rewards and approval of merit, so should he be judicial and unbending in his punishment or reproof of misconduct."

18

19 August 1943
USS *Wahoo* ((SS 238)
Etorofu Strait, Kuril Islands

Wahoo was a *Gato* class submarine of 1,525 tons, 311 feet in length, and carried a crew of 85 officers and enlisted volunteers. Laid down at the Mare Island Naval Shipyard on 28 June 1941, she was commissioned on 15 May 1942 and began her first war patrol on 23 August 1942. The *Gato* (and later *Balao*) fleet submarines were specifically built for the Pacific war. They had a range of 11,000 miles and were powered by four Fairbanks Morse diesel-electric engines that provided a speed of twenty-one knots on the surface and up to nine knots submerged, depending on the battery status.

Recently, at Mare Island, she had been overhauled extensively. She'd received brand new battery cells fore and aft, her engines were overhauled and now were better than new. Her bridge and her cowl were cut down to where, it was hoped, her nighttime silhouette looked like one of those innumerable trawlers darting about the Japanese home islands.

Born in Kentucky and raised in Florida, *Wahoo's* skipper, the charismatic Commander Dudley W. Morton, became her commanding officer after her second war patrol. After that, she had sunk sixteen Japanese ships for a total of 87,000 tons during an intense period of just five months.

Early on, at the U.S. Naval Academy, Morton's thick southern accent gave rise to a nickname of "Mushmouth." Later, it was shortened to "Mush" as he progressed onto active duty in the Navy. But as Morton grew in stature and rank, "Mush" was set aside as a personal salutation. By the time he became a lieutenant commander and ultimately commander on board *Wahoo*, Morton was addressed as either Dudley (in the wardroom) or Captain in the presence of others. But ashore, and especially as his reputation grew, Morton didn't mind as senior officers (even Vice Admiral Charles Lockwood, Commander submarines—Pacific) called him *Mush*. It was catchy. *Mush Morton*. The news media loved it.

During *Wahoo's* overhaul, Morton found himself in Hollywood at Warner Brothers Studio in Burbank where they were filming *Destination Tokyo*. It was a rousing war movie starring Cary Grant and John Garfield about a U.S. submarine entering Tokyo Bay and scouting Japanese defenses in advance of the Doolittle Raid of 18 April 1942. A lot was made of this as Morton and his wife, Harriet, met Cary Grant who played the lead submarine captain in the movie.

Submariner and famous actor meeting one another, an unbeatable pair.

There were smiles all around as Morton, the authentic submarine captain, stepped on the set cracking jokes and pushing war bonds, but saying nothing about the dismal failures of the Mark 14 torpedoes coming from the Naval Torpedo Factory.

And in this war patrol, *Wahoo's* sixth, nothing had gone right. With Morton's highly experienced attack team, they had fired ten torpedoes throughout nine attacks at six ships in or around the Sea of Japan. None had exploded against their targets. Some had porpoised revealing their position to the enemy. Others exploded prematurely or had struck their targets without exploding. Some torpedoes had wandered off never to be heard or seen again. A few Mark 14s made hair-raising circular runs right back to the submarine which launched them.

Time and time again, all of the torpedoes had been pulled and closely examined. Suspicion centered on the 96-pound Mark 6 exploder along with the depth mechanism. But nothing really significant was discovered during these inspections.

It was frustrating. *Wahoo's* crew had exposed themselves while hauling these

3,040-pound torpedoes over five thousand miles.

For what? Just duds. Nothing else.

After the tenth torpedo, also a dud, Morton sent a message to Admiral Lockwood requesting permission to return to Pearl Harbor in order to learn more about why their Mark 14 torpedoes were not exploding.

In essence, they were not advancing the war effort in favor of the United States.

Morton knew other submarines were having the same problem. And the collective howl must have been loud enough, for Lockwood granted permission for Morton's immediate return. And that included specific orders to bring back the ten remaining torpedoes to, hopefully, find out once and for all what in the hell was going on.

19

29 August 1943
USS *Dunagan* (DD 504)
Approaches to Pearl Harbor
Territory of Hawaii

The sun greeted them about the same time the mountain tops of Oahu peeked over the horizon. It was going to be another slice of tropical splendor; a Sunday to cap off 3,600 miles of steaming. But, as an anti-submarine measure, they laid down a sinuous course, which meant they had to zigzag, adding five days to the trip. So the *Dunagan* steamed the distance at ten knots, the whole voyage taking twenty boring days.

Landa had given Ingram his choice on whether or not to zig-zag. Ingram decided it was his job to deliver a fairly new *Fletcher* class destroyer and her crew minus a sonar dome rather than a ship ripped by Japanese torpedoes. So they zig-zagged at ten knots in full knowledge that Japanese submarines swarmed around the Hawaiian Islands looking for a quick, juicy target. Accordingly, ships, large and small, including submarines and destroyers, were escorted from as far as fifty miles out.

Dunagan was vulnerable. Once refloated, thanks to the Imperial Japanese Navy, divers in Vanuatu swarmed about the destroyer for close inspection while sections of a new massive floating drydock lay close at hand, her crew rapidly putting the 927-foot monster together.

Good news and bad news. Aside from the sonar dome being scraped cleanly off, there were no major holes in the hull. The bad news was that the port propellor was missing a blade and that the shaft was out of alignment. It was a yard job for sure, the closest one being in Pearl Harbor, Hawaii. To get there, ten knots was all that would be available on the starboard shaft, much of their headway impeded because they had to drag the port shaft with its propellor locked in place,

The sun's first light found them in the outer fringes of the harbor entrance mine field. The sea was a rich, oily calm as they stood at special sea and anchor detail to meet the escort who would guide them through. She was the USS *Litchfield* (DD 336), an old four-stack destroyer which had popped up on radar a half hour ago. She took shape in the morning mist as, for some inexplicable reason, she was twenty-four miles off Oahu instead of the usual fifty. Possibly, it had something to do with another ship which had shown up at the twenty-five-mile circle. Flashing lights stabbed the early morning as the three blinked and blabbed recognition signals.

They stepped carefully for they were on the edge of the minefield guarding the entrance to Pearl Harbor. Each knew they would have to be extra vigilant. But the *Litchfield* would lead them through. It was her job. All the others had to do was sit back, hug her transom, and hope for the best.

Litchfield flashed formation instructions ordering *Dunagan* to fall astern of the *Litchfield* by one thousand yards. The other ship was to go in the middle between the two destroyers.

So they hung back and waited. Ingram, Tyler Childers, Gilroy Hitchcock, and Clinton Shorter stood at the port bridgewing, peering aft. Soon they felt the other ship, rather than seeing or hearing it. It began with a low rumble, turning to a collective thunder hawking at the new day.

Diesels. Four of them unmuffled, ripped at the dawn as the all black submarine caught up and eased past, her bow wave gurgling. Closer up, she was matted with grey blotches where the black paint had flaked off. Her crew, in undress whites mingled about on deck, breaking out mooring lines, getting ready to enter port.

Ingram felt good about that. After much debate with Childers and a few naysayers, he had the *Dunagan's* crew also turned out in undress whites.

The submarine drew abeam with the men on her bridge waving.

Sailors aboard *Dunagan* waved back with Ingram noting her bow number painted in white: 238.

"Geeeez," said Childers. "Now, those guys have been out there mixing it up with Tojo."

"That's for sure." Ingram turned to Johnson, quartermaster of the watch, and asked, "You have an ID on that ship?"

Fifteen seconds passed as Johnson flipped pages. Finally, he whistled.

"What?" demanded Ingram.

Johnson cleared his throat. "She's the USS *Wahoo*, captain."

Automatically, Ingram called to his talker, "All stations on deck, form up to port. Prepare to render honors."

Johnson continued, "He's a commander, senior to us."

Ingram nodded and said quietly to Harvey Truesdale, the red-headed bosun
mate of the watch, "In more ways than one, boats. It's your show."
"Yessir."

Childers chortled, "Render honors at sea? And going into a minefield? Are you—"

"For these guys, yes I am," said Ingram quietly.

Quietly, almost reverently, Johnson said, "Yes, it's commander Mush—"

"Dudley W. Morton," finished Ingram.

Wahoo seemed to understand, for their cadre of thirty to forty men quickly lined up on the starboard rail, actually an imaginary rail. There were no safety rails on submarines.

Ingram called to the bosun mate of the watch. Truesdale, It's all yours."

Truesdale answered with, "Yes, sir."

Immediately he got on the 1 MC. His voice, loud and resonant, echoed across. "On deck. Attention to port."

In the glow of the dawn, the crews on both ships snapped to attention.

Truesdale keyed in the 1 MC and called, "Hand salute."

Officers on deck of the *Dunagan* saluted for their men who stood at attention in ranks.

As they held perfect salutes on *Dunagan's* bridge, Childers muttered, "Lucky bastards, stayin' at the Royal Hawaiian."

Ingram gave an eye roll.

Hitchcock countered with, "Maybe you should join the sub-service, Tyler?"

"You ever been on one of those sewer-pipes, Jarhead?"

"Yup. It's like crawlin' in a Jap binjo ditch."

"I suppose you have," shot back Childers.

Hitchcock said quietly, "Ever heard of Guadalcanal?"

Childers countered, "Yes, and I—"

"Knock it off, you two," said Ingram.

In the silence, *Wahoo's* bow wave gurgled a bit louder as she moved in to take her place. From the *Wahoo's* conning tower, someone called, "Hand salute." Then, "Ready...two."

"Two," called Truesdale. Then, "Stand easy."

They waved. Ingram shouted, "Welcome home."

An officer silhouetted in the conning tower shouted back, "Thank you."

By then, *Wahoo* was well ahead and almost in place, a mini-cloud of diesel fumes trailing back and settling on the decks of the *Dunagan.*

With that, Ingram felt a great relief to shift off the sinuous course clock and follow *Litchfield's* white stern light just ahead and let someone else do the thinking, especially in this minefield.

They set a course of 358°T, speed ten, and headed for the harbor entrance, twenty-

two miles distant.

The wind didn't oblige them and it remained calm and humid the entire way. Their speed seemed like a funeral march as the three ships entered the massive Pearl Harbor basin.

Once inside, the *Wahoo* headed for the submarine base while the *Dunagan* headed for the ten-ten dock across from Battleship Row.

One sniff told Ingram that things hadn't changed much. It was easy to lose your temper as you gazed on the graves and temporary graves of ships sunk at Pearl Harbor. And the odor was still overwhelming, more than what he could remember from last being here. Fuel oil, the dead intravenous medium from dead ships, was everywhere, stuck to the sides of the live ships, fresh from the states. And stuck to the shoreline as if a greasy giant had once bathed here.

But the dead ships on Battleship Row, of course, was the worst. *California*, *West Virginia*, *Tennessee*, and *Maryland* had all been raised, temporarily patched and sent back to the mainland for complete repairs.

But the worst and most devastating were the hulks of the battleships *Arizona* and *Oklahoma*. A 500 kg bomb from 5,000 feet had penetrated *Arizona's* forward powder magazine, the whole conflagration basically obliterated the forward end of the once powerful ship. *Oklahoma* was just as worse off. At least five Japanese type 93 torpedoes found her hull, all watertight doors laid open for inspection on a bright Sunday morning. She was capsized nearly upside down and her fuel oil spewed up then as it still does every day covering the entire area with a necrotic stench.

This is what Ingram wanted his men to see, to sense what had happened here just over two short years ago. To momentarily be with these lost sailors, at least in spirit, comfort them to whatever extent possible, and avenge them to the utmost.

20

---

31 August 1943
Room 201-B
CinPac Headquarters
Pearl Harbor, Territory of Hawaii

Helen hadn't slept well the night before. Today was the day they wanted her to
testify.
Testify?
Where in blazes did that word come from? This had the makings of a legal hearing. Lieutenant Lamar had said nothing about that.
They were in the new three-story rectangular CinCPac headquarters on Makalapa heights with its magnificent view of Pearl Harbor. But room 201-B on the second deck had all the trappings of a court room. A call board outside the room announced:

NAVAL TORPEDO FACTORY
TOP SECRET PROCEEDINGS
AUTHORIZED PERSONNEL ONLY

A Marine guard stood outside the door checking IDs against a page on his clipboard.

Inside, defense table and chairs were on the left side. Plaintive to the right. In the center was a platform for officiating individuals or groups. And now, senior officers entered the room and sat at a long, green felt-covered table in front: two commanders and a captain. Immediately, they bent toward one another and deliberated among themselves.

Lamar had not been able to attend the meeting and had designated this morning, a subordinate, Lieutenant (j.g.) Daniel J. Palomino, a fine-looking Italian kid, to be Helen's contact for the next day or so for the duration. He seemed a decent sort. With close-cropped hay-colored hair, about five foot eleven, he seemed in good shape. He had shiny white teeth which he displayed with a wide grin. Except he chewed gum. It detracted. He clacked it a lot and even blew bubbles.

After small talk and a few quick questions, Helen learned Palomino had just graduated from law school at UC Berkeley. After that, he went through ninety-day wonder school and had just been newly assigned to Admiral Nimitz' staff.

She leaned over and asked, "Lieutenant Palomino?"

He threw a dazzling glance at her. "It's Dan, captain."

She offered a quick smile. "Thank you, Dan. My question is, why are you here? What are you supposed to be doing?"

Palomino looked down and then whispered, "Making sure they respect your rights, captain."

"What about my rights? Aren't I protected? What is this?"

Palomino said, "We wondered about that, too. And then we learned they had sent Robert O'Connor out."

"Who's he?

"The guy in the middle, the commander. He just got in last night."

"What about him?" She glanced at the commander. His uniform too tight, he'd already loosened his tie. In spite of an ill-fitting uniform, he was thin with dark, swept-back hair and a tiny moustache. But his eyes, Helen couldn't see his eyes. Couldn't even find them.

"He just put on a uniform a couple of months ago. He's not a Navy man. He's a prosecutor, through and through. Top prosecutor of the City of Philadelphia staff. They call him the hangman of Philadelphia. O'Connor could get you in jail for spitting on the sidewalk in front of Independence Hall even though you were in Iowa at the time."

Another man stepped to their table. He smiled with a muted, "Good morning." He was a Lieutenant Commander who appeared rather athletic. Helen couldn't help noticing that he looked drawn in a way, peaked, maybe without sleep.

"May I join you?" he asked. "I am also one amongst the pilloried."

"Please." Palomino waved to a chair. "Misery loves company."

"For sure." The lieutenant commander yanked out a chair, sat, and whipped out a copy of the *Honolulu Advertiser* and, rattling pages, began reading. He had two solid rows of ribbons, some with stars, meaning he'd been in battle. And above the ribbons was a gold piece, a piece that Navy men held dearly. Not wings, but the fish, the...dolphins. The man was a submariner.

She looked over to the group of senior officers. They were nodding, having just reached some sort of agreement.

The captain stood and rapped his knuckles on the desk. "Good morning gentlemen and Captain Ingram. It's time to get started." He gestured to himself. "At the head table we have me, presiding, James Blackshear. On my right is commander Robert V. O'Connor, of the Naval Torpedo Factory and to my left is commander Russell Hartley, a medical doctor from the Bureau of Medicine. We are assembled today via an order from the Bureau of Ordnance. Our purpose is to review and hopefully settle some issues relative to Mark 14, 15, and 18 torpedoes in general and the most recent patrol of the USS *Wahoo*." He looked about the room. "Is Commander Morton present?"

Palomino cleared his throat and rose to speak

The man with the *Honolulu Advertiser* sat up, waved him down and rose instead. He said, "Here, sir. Uh, he's otherwise involved, sir. I am Lieutenant Commander Verne l. Skjonsby, executive officer of the USS *Wahoo*."

The captain's eyes narrowed. "Where is Morton?"

Palomino went to stand but Skjonsby grabbed his elbow, brought him down, and then whispered something to him.

At length, Palomino went, "Uh huh, okay."

Skjonsby cleared his throat and said crisply, "In a meeting, sir."

The captain took a sidelong glance at Robert O'Connor. "What meeting could take precedence over this? After all, we're attempting to determine the problems, if any, with the Mark 14, 15, and 18 torpedoes."

Skjonsby shot his left sleeve and checked his watch. "Sir, Captain Morton is in a meeting with Admiral Nimitz, Vice Admiral Lockwood, several submarine skippers and technicians."

Silence swept the room. It was as if conversation had never existed amongst them. He added, "Yes, sir, he's spread kind of thin right now." He flicked imaginary pieces of dust off his sleeve.

In a clipped voice, O'Connor asked, "Are you tired, Commander?"

"Sir?"

"You look kind of tired."

"Well, that's SOP. Been up all night getting us home."

"Well, you're here."

"You bet. And you should have seen that minefield chart. Scare the crap out of you."

O'Connor waved and looked around the room. "And you have a navigator to do that for you."

"Yes, sir, we sure do."

"Okay, then. What is it that kept you up all night?"

Skjonsby jabbed a thumb at his cheek. "Me. I'm the damned navigator."

"Huh?"

Snickers ranged around the room.

"Gotta say one look at that minefield chart has you cleaning your shorts for the next forty years."

Laughter broke out. Even Captain Blackshear.

Skjonsby picked it up, "But we were lucky. The four stacker *Litchfield* led us through. We stayed glued to his transom. Interval was supposed to be five hundred yards, but I'll bet we had it down to a hundred, maybe less. I gotta tell you, nobody wants to screw with mines at four in the morning. We stuck to that guide like glue. And there was another can with us, the *Dunagan*. I could tell he was scared, too. He was riding right on top of us like we were riding on top of the *Litchfield*. He even—"

Helen screeched, "*Dunagan. Did you say the Dunagan?*

Skjonsby looked her up and down. "Yes, ma'am. The *Dunagan*."

She clasped her hands, "My God. That's my husband's ship. He's the skipper."

Skjonsby gave a lopsided grin. "I'll be damned. Todd Ingram?"

"Yes, that's him."

"Yes, we all made it through that minefield. Ingram especially. Had only one screw to work with. The starboard one. Hell of a ship handler. Never seen anything like it. He actually—"

Helen felt a surge of joy. Todd! And he's here in Pearl Harbor. What luck. It was hard to keep still, she felt like a ten-year-old on her birthday.

Blackshear rapped his knuckles. "Welcome to the reunification with your husband, Captain Ingram."

"Yes. May I be excused?"

"Not at the moment, Mrs. Ingram. You have key testimony we'd like to review."

"Well, can I do it now?"

"Soon, Mrs. Ingram. First, if you don't mind, I'd like to get back to Commander Skjonsby."

Helen rolled her eyes and bunched her hands. Palomino reached over and patted her shoulder.

O'Connor shot a question at Skjonsby. "And now, commander, could you please give us a brief summary of your most recent patrol and the problems you incurred?"

Skjonsby sat straight again, brushing away at flecks that seemed to float forever. "Yes, sir. It goes like this. We were on *Wahoo's* sixth war patrol."

"Where were you?"

"Sea of Japan via the La Perouse Strait.

"What then?"

"It was a bollix. A total damned bollix from one end to the other."

"I see. Can you please be more specific?"

"Yes, I can give you an idea, Commander O'Connor. We had a loadout of twenty-four Mark 14 torpedoes."

O'Connor pulled a sheaf of papers from a briefcase, separated one and ran a forefinger down. "Yes, the Mark 14s."

"That's what I just said."

"Go on."

"Do you know what a Mark 14 torpedo weighs, commander?"

"Suppose you tell me."

"I was hoping you had it on file there." Skjonsby pointed to the pile of paper accumulating beneath his arm.

Blackshear interrupted, "Please commander, we're only trying to help."

"Yes, sir. Well, one of your Mark 14 torpedoes weighs 3080 pounds."

O'Connor blinked then said, "Please go on."

Skjonsby laced his fingers across his chest, "At some risk to the *Wahoo* and to our crew, we hauled ten of those dead pieces of crap, that's thirty thousand pounds, over forty-four hundred miles only to have them malfunction. All ten of them. Duds. ComSubPac summoned us back with the rest.

"Ah, so we can examine them?"

"I wonder, commander. They were offloaded at Midway as we refueled on our return trip."

"Who authorized that?"

"The Naval Torpedo Factory."

"Are you certain?"

"I have a copy of the message aboard ship."

Blackshear waved a hand, "Commander. I'm sorry to learn your patrol was...ahh...ineffective. Can you summarize it for me?"

Skjonsby gave a smile that was not a smile. It sort of froze the room. "Well, let me put it this way, captain. After four thousand miles of hide and seek, we got into the Sea of Japan and fired ten torpedoes at six ships from an average range of a thousand yards. Some impacted the targets. Others simply wandered off and porpoised, giving our position to the enemy. But the torpedoes that did strike were duds. They didn't explode. After ten attempts and ten failures, we contacted NPM. They ordered us home."

"NPM?"

"Commander submarines, Pacific, Admiral Lockwood."

O'Connor rubbed his chin, "In your professional opinion, did your commanding officer and firing team employ all the proper procedures?"

"Nothing but the best, Commander."

"Why then doesn't Commander Morton man the periscope? What is he afraid of?"

Skjonsby, his fingers still laced on his chest, twiddled his thumbs for a moment. "Your question is inappropriate, commander."

O'Connor stood. "I'll be the judge of that. Please answer the question."

"How many submarines have you sailed on, Mr. O'Connor?"

"That's not the point. I asked you a question. Please answer."

Skjonsby shot to his feet. "I just did. You said you would be the judge of that. My question to you is how you can judge if you haven't stood a deck watch on a ship, let alone a submarine."

"May I remind you that you can be charged with insubordination."

"And may I remind you that Commander Dudley W. Morton is the recent winner of the Navy Cross, the silver star, the distinguished service cross, the purple heart, and the combat action ribbon among others. His record is above reproach. You and not—"

"Quiet!" yelled Blackshear.

The two became silent but stared each other down.

"Sit, both of you," ordered Blackshear.

Slowly, they sat.

Blackshear said quietly, "This hearing is recessed until after lunch. He pointed, "You two meet with me over there.

21

31 August 1943
Room 201-B
CinPac Headquarters
Pearl Harbor, Territory of Hawaii

After lunch, Blackshear stood and tapped a spoon against a half-empty water glass. It rang true; they quieted and looked toward him.

Waving a hand at Helen he said, "We are honored today with the presence of Captain Helen Duran Ingram. U.S. Army Nurses Corps, currently stationed at Fort MacArthur in San Pedro, California."

Helen sat up straight. She tried to smile. She couldn't. *Todd is here. Somewhere.* She hadn't seen him in light years. Must ask Lamar.

"Captain Ingram?" It was that snake O'Connor. He stood before her, licking his lips. She visualized a pitch-black forked tongue,

"Yes...sir. Oh yes, sir. Sorry, I was distracted."

"I was just saying you were on Corregidor. Is that right?"

"Yes, that's true. I was there."

"And what was it like?"

There had been sleepless nights in San Pedro. And Helen had spent hours and hours suppressing what she had seen in that terrible place; what she did there. And now, this animal was going to make a public exhibition of her.

"Horrible."

"Oh, come now. Can you please define 'horrible?'"

Shhhhhhhhhhh...Helen, don't...

"Captain Ingram?"

She sat bolt upright. "Dead, dead, everywhere."

"Go on. Please."

She barked, "Headless corpses in the Bay, their hands tied behind their backs. Floating there for days. Men screaming as artillery shells ripped them up. That's when we got them. Hideous wounds. Amputations all the time. Then, we ran out of anesthetics. Those were the worst. Did you ever have to saw off a man's gangrenous arm on the streets of Philadelphia, Mr. O'Connor?"

"Of course not."

"Well, I did. In Corregidor's Malinta Tunnel."

"Well, I..."

"Do you know what that smells like?"

"Ma'am?"

"Gangrene?"

"Well, no."

"It's rancid. And while Jap artillery pounded at us from above, I was inside

sawing off people's arms and legs. And, Commander O'Connor, they screamed, three, four, five guys holding them down. I still hear their screams. Some died right then and there. Some simply—"

"Doctors, you had doctors, didn't you?"

"Not nearly enough," she said. "And somebody had to do it. So there was me and three others. All happily killing Americans and Filipinos."

"Well...I suppose that..."

Her eyes were unfocused as she said quietly, "There was a fellow, a Filipino Scout, full of energy. It was his right arm—no, his left. He blessed me and blessed me and blessed me as I worked. 'May God bless you,' he would say. And then we were done. That's when he died." She snapped her fingers. "Just like that. Gone. Manuel Bauzel, a happy corporal. Can you believe it?" She looked up to O'Connor. "Just like that."

There was an extended silence.

She continued, "And you know what, Commander O'Connor..."

He stood back. "No, ma'am, that's enough. I get the idea. You have lived through hell. And I'm sorry for that, Mrs. Ingram." He went to pat her on the forearm but Helen yanked away. She clenched her fists.

He poured her a glass of water. She drank half, breathing hard.

A minute passed. It was quiet. "Sorry," she said.

"No ma'am the apology belongs to me. I had forgotten the brutal stories I'd heard of Corregidor."

"It's...it's okay. We can continue."

He stood close to her. "Thank you, Captain Ingram. Tell me, how did you escape Corregidor?"

"By submarine." She brightened at the thought. Todd had been there. Had helped her aboard...and then...

"And then what, Captain?" He was close to her, his tongue flicking.

"They dropped us at a local island and went back for more people on Corregidor." She waved a hand at the diminishing space between them. "Please."

"Yes, I'm sorry. Please continue."

"They left us with a Filipino family. They were wonderful, but the Japs came and killed them. Killed them all. Raped one of their daughters then shot her. Killed them all."

"And?"

"Two ghouls."

"What sort of ghouls."

"Lieutenant Tuga, from the *Kempetai*."

"What's that?"

"An organization separate from the Japanese Army. They're modeled after the German SS except these people go a step further. They have unlimited control over everything. Even what's in your mind. They're referred to as the 'thought police.'"

"And what did they want with you?"

"They're looking for names, for people in the resistance, the organized resistance."

"And did they get anything out of you?"

She looked off into the distance.

"Captain?"

"I...told them nothing."

"I see."

"But the little bastards tortured me. Still, I told them nothing. I almost died. Dehydration."

"And you survived that."

"Well, yes, sir. Lieutenant Ingram and his raiding party broke it up. Shot a bunch of the Japs and whisked me away. During that time, they were able to rehydrate me and get me going. Just in time. We had just reached Mindanao and the lumber mill where we thought it would be safe. But Tuga and his Japs showed up there as well."

"And then Ingram and his people saved you."

"Yes, sir. They did that, blew up the lumber mill, and got underway for Australia in that thirty-six-foot boat. And they made it all the way to Darwin, Australia. A magnificent escape of over nineteen hundred miles."

"Ingram was determined to get his boys out. What happened to you?"

"There was so much commotion, I got separated from Todd at the Lumber Mill. He got away. I was lucky, too. I got scooped up by Pablo Amador and his resistance. Later, Todd came back for me and I got out."

"And you two later married."

"We sure did." She smiled and flashed the wedding ring on her fourth finger.

"Back to the Japs. What did they do?"

"To me?"

"Yes."

"I mean it. Nothing. At the time, I knew nothing. Since then, I had been brought into the resistance. And I was safe."

"Is that it?"

"Well, Mr. O'Connor. Yes, there is more." She gave him a look.

"Please."

"You understand I am bound by the Espionage Act of 1917."

"To which you signed a waiver this morning."

"To which I signed against my better judgement. But Admiral Nimitz... he is such a nice man. He asked me as a favor." She didn't add that Nimitz had given her an out. Paragraph 4 (B) of section 22 of the waiver provided that *Captain Ingram, at her own discretion, may decline to answer certain questions.* She realized that Nimitz was vigorously pursuing his own investigation. It made her think he didn't trust the Naval Torpedo Factory people at all. So as far as Admiral Nimitz and the ComSubPac people were concerned, this hearing was a waste of time. My God. *I'm a pawn.*

O'Connor stood straight. "So please tell us about when they captured you."

This person is such an odious snake. See how he slithers about the room.

"Captain Ingram?"

She had signed and he had counter signed.

"They put me with a Filipino family as a sign of normalcy. I blended right in. I'm dark complected. I look very Asian."

"Duran is Indonesian then?" asked O'Connor

She took a drink of water and shook her head. "No. Swiss. There is a Mount Duran there. But Duran is also part Czech. We find it in Latin countries as well."

"So you were taken in? Again?"

"Conscripted really. They go about gathering women for forced labor. They don't kill anyone. They just grab women to do the housekeeping on a berthing barge they had moored there."

"Go on."

"I had an out."

O'Connor raised his eyebrows.

"Earlier, Lieutenant Tuga and his accomplice had tortured me with cigarette burns about my body."

"Indeed. Must have been very painful."

"Yes, I screamed a lot."

"I'm sorry." For an instant, O'Connor looked almost human.

And then he asked, "Would you mind showing us?"

"What?"

"You mentioned there were cigarette burns about your body?"

"Yes, everywhere. Even in the arch of my foot, my armpit, between my toes. They know how to get your attention."

"And how did this appear to everyone?"

"It was a good cover. Made everyone think I had leprosy—that I came from a local leper colony. I was avoided. They pinned a sign to my forehead and made me wear it. '*Leper*'"

"And so the report says that's how you got the Japanese torpedo manual. By supposedly cleaning an officer's cabin?"

"Yes, that's right."

O'Connor pointed to a disheveled volume laying open on a table. "Does this look familiar?"

She squinted. *Good God.* "I think so. Looks the same. Well, I was cleaning the captain's stateroom. He was messy. Stuff laying all around. One morning, I was by myself in his room. He'd been called out. I grabbed the manual and shoved it under my dress. At the same time, the resistance started a ruckus. The army kicked us out. Truly let us go during a firefight. Later that day, the barge was blown up with an American torpedo, an experiment. So we believe the Japanese wrote the manual off as a loss because of the American torpedo."

"Extraordinary." O'Connor steepled his fingers. "And yet guess work. We don't know for sure."

"I saw the explosion from a half mile away. It was a hell of a blast."

"Yes, and yet we're not sure if the Japanese knew the torpedo manual was missing."

"I don't get your point."

"Authenticity, Captain Ingram. Absolute authenticity."

"It's the best we can do."

"Except for one more thing." O'Connor's tongue flicked again.

She stared at him.

"We would like to examine your...ah, cigarette wounds."

This is stupid. "Here." She held out her arm and rolled up a sleeve. "Take a look."

Connor circled around. "Well, we need just a little more, Captain. Would you please show us the wound on the bottom of your foot and then one in your armpit. Dr. Hartley is a burn specialist and can authenticate them on site for us. It will take no longer than half a minute. You can go to the back of the room in the corner there for privacy."

"No."

"Captain Ingram, this will only take seconds. No one else will see. And we need this data."

"I said no."

Captain Blackshear said quietly, "Captain Ingram, this will show up on your fitness report."

"What?" She was astounded.

O'Connor chimed in. "Just thirty seconds, Captain, and we'll be done. You can be excused to go do whatever you wish."

She stood and bit her lip. These people were not trying for a peep show. But the whole idea was absurd. "Can you keep this confidential?"

Blackshear said, "Captain Ingram. May I remind you the entire report is classified as Top Secret."

She pointed to a corner near the back door. "Over there. And just Dr. Hartley. Nobody else."

Blackshear looked at Hartley, his brow furrowed.

Hartley nodded. "Yes, that's all right." He held up a camera. "But I would like to take a couple of close-up shots."

"None of my face, you little turd," she replied.

Hartley's eyes narrowed. "Of course not." Then he said, "Shall we?" He waved toward the corner.

Helen walked over, unbuttoning her jacket and her blouse. She looked back. "Face front, you perverts," she shouted.

Almost as if snapping to the command of a drill sergeant, they whipped around and faced toward the front of the room.

Her jacket and blouse were off. Her left arm was in the air, exposing a terrible burn wound in her armpit.

Hartley held up his camera and clicked off a picture. "Okay, just one more."

WHAM! The courtroom door whipped open and blasted against the stops. A man, a Navy Lieutenant Commander, walked in yelling, "What the hell are you doing you bottom-crawling bastard?"

He swung at Hartley. Another man, a Marine, rushed up and held him from behind. He was joined by another Marine from down the hall.

The punch missed.

"Todd!" shrieked Helen.

Todd Ingram and two Marines tumbled through the door, all fighting one another.

Hartley, the camera nearly knocked out of his hands, rescued the piece and ran for the front of the room.

"Uhhhh!" Ingram struggled against the two Marines but he fell to the floor with them on top of the swirling mass.

"Todd," screamed Helen.

22

---

31 August 1943
Room 323
CinPac Headquarters
Pearl Harbor, Territory of Hawaii

The room was small. It was a cubby hole and Ingram found the phone in a desk drawer.

It was ringing.

No place to sit. He parked on top of the desk and picked up the receiver. "Hello?"

"Ingraaaaaaam. You stupid son of a bitch." It had to be Landa. Even filtered over 2,600 miles of underwater cable to the mainland, no matter what else, he recognized Jerry Landa's voice.

"Good to hear from you, too, Jerry."

"Don't bullshit me." Landa's voice was clear and loud. "What the hell are you pulling out there?

Angry. Landa sounded very angry. "Are you pissed about something, Jerry?" Ingram looked down to his bandaged knuckles. Those Marines had subdued him with nightsticks but he had gotten in a couple of lucky blows: one of them to a loud-mouthed ex-prosecutor posing as a commander, and another commander, a doctor of some sort.

But Ingram had wrestled his way to Helen and she to him. They'd embraced and that was when that magniloquent lawyer yelled at him. One blow from the jarhead and he went down. But he found room to land a punch on the peace-keeping doctor, all smiles and bowing and making excuses for taking sleezy photos of Helen.

And then the Marines went to work on him. He woke up ten minutes later in the bed of a pickup truck, his face and head bloody, hands and feet in manacles, on the way to the brig. The trip took three minutes. At the brig, they dumped him in a cart and wheeled him to a cell that was open on all four sides. Nothing could be hidden. Completely subdued, they removed all the manacles and then all of his clothes.

Everything.

He was on a steel bunk when they told him to stand. When he did, they blasted him with a hose of cold water and told him to soap up. After that they blasted him again, rinsing him off. Then, they turned off the hose and had him sit. A heavy towel was thrown in. And then his underwear, all warm and dry. Minutes later, all of his clothes were returned: worsted khaki uniform, shoes, socks, belt, tie, garrison cap, all perfectly clean and pressed. Under the supervision of a Marine sentry, a pharmacist mate came in and dressed his cuts and bruises. Amazingly, all his teeth were still in place.

He stood in uniform feeling stupid. Then a balding fat sergeant walked up, unlocked the cell door, and told him to go to room 323 and answer the phone. The sergeant swung the cell door open and walked away.

Ingram needed no further encouragement. Dashing out the main door, he found a hallway with rooms. He found room 323.

Very dismal. He walked in, shut the door, and heard ringing right away. Opening the drawer, he picked up the receiver.

"Hello?"

Landa was yelling, sometimes screaming. That meant everything was okay. If he was serious about something, he never yelled, just a menacing soft monotone.

It went on for a while until Ingram shouted, "Do I get a chance to speak, damnit?"

The line went silent. Then, "It better be good."

"It's simple. I admit I went off the deep end, but shit, you should have seen what these guys were doing."

"I haven't got all day, ensign."

Ingram didn't miss the 'ensign' part but launched into it anyway, "I was up in Lamar's office, talking about a new gig. Then he told me Helen was here in the building and would I like to see her? 'Hell, yes,' I said and he sent me packing down to Room 201-B. It was a courtroom. So I looked through the little window to make sure I had the right place and here was Helen, backed in a corner right next to me, her jacket and blouse were off, and—"

"But her bra was on."

"Yes, it was on. But here was this idiot, a medic of some kind, with a camera pressed up to her taking pictures." He took a deep breath. "She looked so damned pathetic, like I hadn't seen since the Corregidor days. On the edge of terror and misery. I have to tell you I wanted to kill that guy. The Marine guard was right there with me and tried to grab me. But I shoved him aside, got through the door and started to beat the living shit out of that doctor.

"It was all insane. Another Marine showed up. They drew nightsticks and put my lights out. Then they took off my clothes, shoved me in a cell, then showered me, put me in a clean set of clothing, dressed my wounds and here I am sniveling to you."

It was quiet. Static ran along the line. Landa said, "I spoke with Helen. She's fine. She's up at the Admiral's house."

"He must be really pissed."

"We'll get to that. She tells me you cold-cocked that Philadelphia prosecutor."

"No kidding?"

"Yes. No kidding. On the other hand, the admiral told me—"

Ingram groaned. "You spoke to him?"

"Yes, I had to. Somebody had to clean up your shit."

"Jeez, I'm sorry, Jerry. I didn't mean—"

"We found a way out."

"Huh?"

"Lamar didn't realize those idiots would be yanking Helen through a knot hole. He thought he was sending you down for a session of sweet reunion and marital bliss. And the admiral apologized to her for their bizarre tactics. That was uncalled for.

"You, the outraged husband, showed up at the perfect time. Nimitz deauthorized the meeting and cancelled further proceedings."

"What way out did he find?"

"This is not a secure line, Todd. It's technical. They'll, most likely, tell you over there."

"Okay. So can I come home now, daddy?"

"Not yet. You and Helen are being kept incommunicado at an undisclosed location on Oahu's East End for a week."

"Holy cow. You mean—?"

"Yes, a snake pit. Just you and Helen. All expenses paid."

"Wow. Thanks, Jerry."

"Don't thank me. Thank the admiral. If it were up to me, I'd have you chipping paint on the *Dunagan's* forty-millimeter gun tubs. Beyond that, we need you aboard for a couple of weeks for a little gig up in the Solomons."

"Are you volunteering me for another shit detail? If so, count me out. I've had enough of that."

"No, no. To begin, we need your evaluation of Tyler Childers. We're thinking of bumping him up to CO. What do you think so far?"

"Childers? He's his own man. Pro-Navy. Loves his men. Loves his ship. Used to love his wife, but then she sent him a dear john letter."

"So, that's over?"

"She tried to clean him out. He got some of it stopped. But now, she's moved to Reno for a quickie divorce."

"What do you think?"

"Still trying to decide. Some parts I like. Some I don't. I'll let you know."

"Okay. You don't mind staying aboard a few more weeks?"

"You just said a couple of weeks."

"That's what I meant to say. Just a couple of weeks, well, maybe three."

"Jerry, must I have this in writing?"

He went to a falsetto, "Oh, Todd, I may need your written apology for your performance in the courtroom to include in your fitness report."

He's got me. "Okay, okay. What can you tell me about the gig?"

"Unsecure line, Todd. But thanks for agreeing to participate. Lamar will fill you in. How's your ship doing?"

"Just went into drydock. New sonar dome and transducer were there, waiting."

"Good."

"And they're installing two new hedgehog racks."

"Wow. We're finally getting them in the Pacific."

"Should be out in three to four days."

"Excellent."

"I want a bottom job."

"What the hell for?"

"She's been living in the South seas. Have you forgotten that they cook in those waters? There's cancer all over the bottom. I want it done."

"Jeez, Ingram. Sand blast and paint. Another couple of days. You're beginning to sound like a commanding officer."

"You're beginning to sound like a bean counter. Never thought I'd see the day."

"Okay, okay. I'll take care of it."

23

---

31 August 1943
Liberty House Department Store
1432 Fort Street
Honolulu, Hawaii, Territory of Hawaii

Lamar had them in a little one bedroom bungalow a half block from the beach. It was on the same property as a sprawling beachfront residence owned by Sandy Walker, a close friend of Admiral Nimitz. To the Ingrams, it was paradise. And Lamar made sure it stayed that way. He kept the pantry shelves generously stocked, including the refrigerator.

On nights with an on-shore breeze, Helen and Todd would lay back and listen to the surf crack and roll while staring up to the sky and its billions of mysterious pinpoints of light.

And always, when he looked at her, Helen's eyes would reel him in. He would be finished. He was hers for whatever she wanted. Her eyes and her ebony ponytail that constantly swished silently from side to side—he always wondered if she consciously did this just to keep him on edge.

They could talk about anything, anything, from the state of the coal mines in West Virginia, to hoot-less hoot owls, to the latest uprising in the Belgian Congo. Just the sound of her voice nailed him to a wall. He was cooked and he knew it. A sucker and yet she didn't push it. Somehow, it was her effect only on him, and he to her. Both knew it. Both kept it to a level where it was just between themselves, not obvious to others and, yet, sometimes explosive when off by themselves. They'd broken a creaky wooden bed frame that way.

They'd moved in two days ago. That was equal to two light years in time and lost opportunity aboard the *Dunagan*. So it was time to go see what was happening. Using the Jeep provided by Lamar, he'd driven her into Honolulu and dropped her at the Liberty House for a morning of shopping and an early afternoon in the beauty parlor. He'd parked, pecked her on the cheek and watched her disappear inside, then he found a payphone and dialed the base. After transferring three times, he got through to Lamar.

"Cinpac."

He was tempted to call him "Hal," as those closest to him did. The man had done so much. "Good morning, Lieutenant. It's Todd Ingram, returning your call."

A chair squeaked; Lamar was leaning back. "Commander Ingram. Why are you wasting time blabbing at me? You are supposed to be on the beach digging for sand crabs."

Ingram gave an obligatory short laugh. "Actually, I did that yesterday. Clam digging. Caught six of them. Big ones. We made a clam chowder. Best I've ever had."

"Now you're talking."

"You called, Lieutenant," Ingram reminded.

"That's right. I did, You have a man in your wardroom, Sergeant Gilroy Hitchcock?"

Ingram stiffened a bit. "Yes, I do." He almost asked, *what's he done now?*

"He's put in papers. He wants out of the Marine Corps."

"Holy cow. Gilroy Hitchcock?"

"I think there's only one. He's your Master at Arms, is he not?"

"That's right. But how did it get to you?"

"This fellow is no dummy. He's got over thirty years in the Corps. He's over fifty-five, fifty-seven, I believe, so we can release him with our blessing.

And it looks like he gave it all to me to process since you were frolicking on the beach."

"Well, I'm in town to check up on the ship. I'll see him and find out what's going on. But thanks for the heads up."

"I'll not tell Zero Zero what you just said."

"Why not?"

"He would be displeased. He wants you and Mrs. Ingram on the beach sifting sand and barbecuing Hawaiian style pork ribs."

"Oh."

"Besides that, there's one other thing."

"Yes?"

"Sergeant Hitchcock is not aboard the *Dunagan*."

"What?"

"You'll find him at the US Naval Hospital and Health Clinic on the base here."

Hitchcock was in room 242 B sharing with three other Marines. One, a tanker, was lashed up in traction. Another was a burn victim who seemed to be coming out of the worst stages of a plane crash. The third was a victim of a stomach wound who slept a lot.

And then there was Hitchcock who lay on his bed, feet spread, fingers laced behind

his head.

Ingram walked in. "Hey goldbrick."

Hitchcock's mouth drew to a large grin. "Jeeeez, Todd. What the hell you doin' here?"

They shook. "Out looking over our ship. Those yard birds don't screw around. Sonar

and a new dome are installed and functioning as far as we can tell. Have to put to sea to calibrate it, but so far, so good. The port shaft is aligned. New screw to be hung tomorrow. They even did a new bottom job. So, she's about ready to go."

"Sounds good."

"And that's not all. They're giving us two hedgehog mounts."

Hitchcock spat out, "Hedgehog what?"

"Ahead thrown weapon. A-T-W, Most of our destroyers in the Atlantic have

hedgehogs. Supposed to be five times more effective than depth charges."

"No shit?" Hitchcock gave a slight belch.

It drifted to Ingram. Beer. The sonofabitch was drinking beer.

Hitchcock caught his look. "Todd, look. There's this nurse here who—"

"No need to make excuses to me. But to tell the truth, if your retirement hadn't already been approved, I'd have your dead ass up on charges."

Hitchcock drew a plaintive face. "Aw Todd, you wouldn't do that to me would you?"

"Well..."

Hitchcock reached under his covers and began fumbling. "You want one?"

Ingram shot out a hand. "Jeeeez. Gunny. Take it easy. Save that for later when the lights are out." He paused and looked from side to side. "Errrrr... what do you do with the empties?"

With a half grin, Hitchcock jabbed a thumb at an open window behind him. It was an eight to ten foot over-the-head shot.

Ingram whistled. "You ever miss?"

Hitchcock winked.

"You are one lucky bastard."

"I wish. Just have to get my temperature down so I can get the hell out of here."

"Quit drinkin' beer then."

"It makes me happy.""

Ingram looked around, "What's not so happy?"

Hitchcock shrugged. "Malaria. Comes back and bites me in the ass once in a while. I go into these shaking spells that scare the crap out of people. They say I look like Frankenstein on a binge. They lock me up for a couple of days. Throw atabrine at me and I'm all well again."

"That's nice, Gilroy. So when can we see you again?"

"Well..."

"Yes?" Ingram dragged a chair over and sat.

Hitchcock unlaced his fingers and began to twiddle his thumbs. "I should tell you..."

Ingram settled back and stared.

"Aw, don't do that, Todd."

Ingram said nothing.

"Aw right. Aw right. Here it is. I put in my papers."

"So I've heard."

Hitchcock started and sat up for a moment. "Who told you?"

"Does it matter?" asked Ingram.

He relaxed and exhaled. "No, I suppose not. Here..." He reached to the nightstand and produced a sheaf of papers. He handed them over.

Ingram leafed through it. One batch was a set of government documents. The word RETIREMENT prominent. At the bottom of the pile was a letter. He tried reading it, then said, "This is in French?" He handed it all back.

He smiled, "It's from Lolli. Her mother wrote it. Beautiful handwriting, huh?"

"Wonderful. What's it say? "

Hitchcock rose and propped on an elbow. The letter was three pages long. "I can hardly read the stuff myself. But I got this. Oh, did I ever."

Ingram was beginning to catch on. "You mean, she's preg—"

"Hot damn right. Ingram, you crazy son-of-a-bitch. I'm going to be a dad!" He thrust both fists in the air. "Uhhhh-Rah!"

Ingram stood and reached for Hathcock's hand. They shook. He said, "You're the crazy son-of-a-bitch. Congratulations. Yes, of course we'll approve your retirement."

"Thanks, boss." said Hitchcock.

"When do you want to pull the trigger?"

"Whenever it's convenient for Tojo. Don't want to set him and his precious schedule back a notch."

"Perish the thought. Tell you what. How about making it contingent on me finding a new CMMA?"

"Eh." Hitchcock tipped a hand from side to side. "I could lose on that one. Who the hell would want to serve with you?"

"You have a point, but then, what if I task you with finding your replacement?"

"Another Marine?"

"Makes no difference to me."

"Okay. They're supposed to release me tomorrow morning. Then I can jump right on it."

Ingram put a finger to his lips. "I need someone who can stand up to... to..."

"Tyler?"

"Yes. Tyler."

Hitchcock lay back and said. "You know, Todd. Tyler ain't such a bad guy."

"Oh?"

"I got to know him a little better since we been in drydock. Did you know, he's a teetotaler?"

"Now that surprises me. How did—"

"Chiefs told me. Tyler Childers has saved more of our guys from water-front brawls than I can count. Beats the shit out of anything in his path getting it done."

Ingram rubbed his jaw. "Amazing. No I didn't know that."

"He's all haze gray and underway. Rough edges but still, pro-Navy."

"I'll be damned."

Across the room, the man with the stomach wound muttered, "Hey, can you guys hold it down, I'm tryin' to sleep?"

Hitchcock lowered his voice, "So tell me about hedgehogs."

24

Hitchcock's head was propped up on an elbow, his professional interest getting the better of him.

Ingram explained, "A hedgehog is like a mortar. It's shot from a mount off the forward part of the ship, usually the oh-one level. They're putting ours in place of the forty-millimeter mounts there, port and starboard. The rounds launch with an impulse charge like a mortar. Each mount has twenty-four rounds that go off in ripple fire, about six to eight seconds to empty a mount. The hedgehogs fly forward about 250 yards and land in a one-hundred-foot perfect circle. Each round weighs about sixty-five pounds, thirty-five pounds of which is torpex."

"Torpex? Hot damn."

"That's right. One mount fires the little suckers in ripple fire. Unlike a depth charge, the thing won't go off unless it hits the target. It does, that torpex is enough to blow a major hole in the submarine. Then it's curtains for the submariners."

Hitchcock clicked his teeth and pulled up a blanket. "I'll say. That torpex is mean shit." He began to shake a bit, his speech slurred.

Fortunately, a red-headed nurse with a large overbite was walking past. Ingram signaled her and she stepped over and felt his forehead. "Hmmmm."

Her nametag announced, **AGNES WALKER, RN.** She produced a ther-mometer and

took Hitchcock's temperature. After two minutes, she pronounced Hitchcock on the edge of a malaria seizure,

She kicked Ingram out of the room, saying he could come back in an hour when his newest round of atabrine took effect.

She added, "The USO is handing out coffee and doughnuts." She pointed, "Right around the corner."

So, with an hour to kill, Ingram meandered over and found the USO window. A line was long, about twenty people, all service men. He gave his name to a volunteer. Another, at the head of the line, was calling names. Despite this, he felt relaxed, unchallenged, at ease with things for a change as men, from dress uniform to bandaged on crutches, learned against a wall waiting for their names to be called.

"...Cooper, Ross, USS *Talbot*."

"Yo." A shiny new ensign walked toward the window.

"Cortea, Calvin. USS *Essex*."

"Here." The Sailor walked over and collected his coffee and doughnut.

"Arana, Steven, USS *Dunagan*"

"Yo."

It hit Ingram like a lightning bolt. Arana? Arana? *He's supposed to be Stateside, isn't he?* Jeeeez...off the *Dunagan*.

"Ingram, Alton, USS *Howell*." Ingram waved a hand and walked forward, passing Arana, shoulder to shoulder. In a hospital bathrobe and head bandage, Arana's eyes were wide open when they passed. He carried two coffees and four doughnuts and gave Ingram a once over as they passed. Ingram pretended not to notice and moved quickly to the window, grabbed his coffee, and waved off the doughnut. He was thankful he had, from habit, given the name of his old ship, the *Howell*, now a twisted wreck off Mondo Island in the Central Solomons.

Quickly, Ingram walked around the corner. He stopped and looked back. There, he saw Arana's bandaged head bobbing down the hall that ran the length of the building. Soon, he disappeared into the crowd.

Ingram found the floor nurses' station. Seated at a desk nearby was a woman with grey, pulled-back hair and quick, intelligent eyes. One instinctively knew one didn't fool with this lady. She looked up from a logbook. "Yes?" She had a professionally sweet voice. Her Bakelite name tag read, **LT. DARLENE N. INGALLS. RN**

Ingram mellowed. "You have a chief bosuns mate Steven Arana here on the floor?"

Ingalls' eyes narrowed. "Who's calling, please?"

Ingram took a breath. *I'm not too good at this.* "Lieutenant Commander Alton C. Ingram."

"Of?"

Ingram nodded. "Of what, Ma'am?"

"Sir, your duty station, please." She waved a pencil over a pad.

Here we go, Todd. Deep, dark brown smelly stuff. "CinCPac staff."

She snorted. "Oh, come on, Commander. Everybody seems to be working for Admiral Nimitz these days."

"You can check with CinCPac Fleet Flag Lieutenant Arthur Lamar on extension 3521." *Ingram, you really are a bullshitter.* But the number was authentic. He'd just dialed it this morning.

She picked up the phone and started to dial. But then her eyes landed on Ingram's blouse.

And on his Navy Cross. "My, oh my, you've been busy." Her voice turned sweet.

"Yes, ma'am."

She found a page under the logbook. "They're in room 262 B."

"They?"

"Well, yes. Chief Arana and Commander Ron Keating. They're in together...Say, are you all right, commander?"

Keating? What the hell is going on? "Yes...of course." Keating and Arana. It made some sort of bizarre sense. Although he did feel stunned for a moment. He pointed down the hall. "262 B, right?"

"Yes, go that way. Almost all the way to the fire escape. Right hand side."

"Thank you, ma'am'" He started walking.

Nurse Ingalls's voice shifted to full siren of the Rhine River, "You are most welcome, commander."

Her voice trailed away as Ingram headed to 262B. He dodged several lunch carts serving rooms along the way reminding him that the noon hour was upon him and that his stomach was growling along with untold others in this hallway.

Two minutes later, he was there: 262B. And a lunch cart was being pushed in as another attendant, both young Hawaiian males, held open the door. Ingram walked in close behind. The room was barely large enough for two beds, a hanging closet and a small washroom with toilet and basin. With Ingram in the room, it made five men jostling back and forth, with trays and water glasses clanking and people grunting. Finally the attendants backed away and closed the door. Ingram stood at the foot of Keating's bed as both he and Chief Arana unwrapped sandwiches and futzed with milk cartons and straws.

Arana examined his sandwich. "Same old cheesy shit. Even the bread is stale." He took a large bite and sat back, noticing Ingram for the first time. His eyes grew wide. He muttered something around the food in his mouth.

Casually, Keating took him in. He was an extraordinarily handsome man. A year ahead of Ingram at the Naval Academy, he was extremely popular with the local women. Indeed, he had no trouble getting dates and no trouble getting dates for his classmates. But right now, he looked as if he'd been in a train wreck. His jaw was wired, and various bandages were stuck to his face and neck. Both eyes were black and blue, his left arm was in a sling, and he made a raspy noise when breathing.

"Lemme take care of this, Skipper." Arana moved his tray aside and made to get out of bed.

Ingram shot out a palm. "Stay there, Arana. And shut up. Or I'll get a couple of Jarheads in here to make life a lot less comfortable for you, like in a closet."

Ingram shifted his focus to Keating. "You look pretty good, Ron. Maybe hit a couple of speed bumps since I last saw you." Ingram hadn't seen Keating since his graduation seven years previously. But he knew the man had gone surface Navy. Started out on the battleship *Tennessee*, if memory served him right. His hair was still blonde-streaked, his California-bred olive skin, a mellow forever-tanned look. And his teeth, a white, dazzling—wait, an upper bicuspid was missing. But the rest of Keating was placed on a well-proportioned body of six-two and a hundred and seventy-five pounds.

"You're not so bad yourself," rasped Keating. "Filled out some. You were a skinny kid. And look at the salad on your chest."

"They make me wear it."

"Well, it needs wearing. Too many chickenshits running around. They need leadership."

"It doesn't come easily."

"Not supposed to. You were at Corregidor, I hear."

Surprised, Ingram nodded and kept silent.

Keating waved to a chair. "Sit please, Todd." He leaned back in his bed. "How can I help you?"

"That's very nice of you."

"So now, you're the commanding officer of the *Dunagan*?"

"That's right."

"I may not be able to speak to you."

This guy is brazen. But he always was. Conned his way out of everything at the Naval Academy. Learned from his Dad, Chairman and Chief Executive Officer of United Oil and Natural Gas. Carmen Keating's fingers were in pies world-wide.

Ingram said, "Let's try, anyway, Suppose you tell me what happened, Ron."

Keating pressed his lips and then drummed his fingers. "I didn't know."

"Know what?"

"That she was the exec's wife."

Ingram gave a look that said, '*Oh, come on.*'

"I mean it, Todd. You think I'd go off and start banging my executive officer's wife? It wasn't like that."

Ingram kept silent.

"We met at the Coronado 'O' Club. She was alone. Beautiful. A really gorgeous woman. But sophisticated. Very smart. Her name was Renée. We

talked for a while. I'm a bachelor. She wasn't wearing a wedding ring. So...
we had a couple of drinks and things moved on from there."

"To your place," said Ingram. It was a statement. Keating's tastes were
upper crust. Off base, he had a waterfront apartment that was furnished to
the tastes of King Louis XIV. He wore finely tailored uniforms and drove an
aquamarine blue Duesenberg convertible. All served to represent a gigantic
bull's eye on Keating's chest.

"Yes. And she ahhhh...visited me several times."

Seeming relieved, Keating kept at it. "One time we were sitting at my
coffee table. No lights, just candles."

"And a little wine," Ingram added.

Keating confirmed with a nod. "And a little wine."

"So, this one night, we spoke of shoes—and ships—and sealing-wax—
of cabbages—and kings—[1]."

Ingram smiled at the poem drilled into them in their sophomore years.
Apparently, Keating remembered, too. He was no dummy.

"An ornate cigarette box was on my coffee table. An antique, made in
Italy. A beautiful piece. One of a kind." He laughed. "A present from Mom
and Dad on their latest trip to Europe. It was right there. I gave it to her. I
insisted. She thanked me profusely. It fit perfectly in this large purse she
carried. And she took it home and set it on her coffee table.

"Well, Tyler recognized it. This woman, Renée, was, unknown to me. I
had no idea she was my XO's wife. He'd been to my place socially a few
times, but without his wife. And he saw and admired the cigarette box like
so many people had. And then, the damn thing turns up at her place—at
Tyler's place. He spotted it the night before we got underway for SoWesPac.
We were headed to Tulagi to join up with DESRON 23.

So we got into Espiritu Santo for fuel. We also picked up mail and got
underway for the final leg. That's when Tyler opened an envelope and
discovered he had a "Dear John" letter from Renée, his wife. That's when
Tyler Childers went batshit on the bridge and started beating the crap out
of everything in sight, including me. And that's when we went aground at
Espiritu Santo."

25

31 August 1943
Room 262 B
US Naval Hospital and Health Clinic
Pearl Harbor, Territory of Hawaii

"And then the ship ran aground," Ingram said.

Keating clasped his hands, "Indeed she did. The noise was terrible."

"Must have been God awful."

"But the fighting continued. I was out cold by that time. And it took eight guys to eventually wrap up Tyler Childers and manacle him to his bunk. We left him that way for a full day. Then he quieted down and became the model exec." Keating took a deep breath. But it rattled and he had trouble. Finally, "Do you realize he's a four-oh Lieutenant? High marks in everything. Several times recommended for command."

"Yes, I saw his fitness reports."

"The guy is amazing. From one extreme to the other." Keating rubbed his hands together. "How did you get her off the reef? As I recollect, we were doing ten knots at the time. Thought she was high and dry."

"Your recollection is good." Ingram told Keating how they got off the reef.

"Those torpedoes are big and long and very, very nasty. You were lucky."

"I'll say. And then the PBY blew it to kingdom come. Not much of it left after we floated off."

"Is there anything I can do for you?"

Ingram thought at first the man was joking. He felt like laughing. Keating was in deep, deep trouble. But then Ingram steadied on Keating and saw that he was serious. "No, Ron. We're okay. We're about ready for sea. We take her out day after tomorrow and hot rod a bit after that, then out to SoWesPac. But they'll need a skipper. Overall, I'm working for Jerry Landa in DESRON 6, So, it's essential they find a guy, chop, chop."

Ingram held up a hand. "But it's curiosity more than anything else. Where do you go from here, Ron? What in store for Ron Keating?"

Keating had been sitting erect on his bed. Now, he exhaled and seemed to collapse internally. He raised his hands momentarily, palms up. "I...I... the Navy is done with me."

"But surely they can—"

"Too many people have been exposed to this. It...it wouldn't look good. They want the slate cleaned. Now. There's too much of this crap going on.

"It even got to Nimitz. He put the final kibosh on it." Keating shook his head slowly.

Ingram thought of the plight of Gilroy Hitchcock and what he'd just gone through. Keating continued, "Dad played his last ace...my last ace. He called Ernie King."

Ingram recalled Carman Keating, where the sale and provision of Navy Standard Fuel Oil (NSFO) was concerned, dealt at the highest levels in the Navy. And that included four-star admiral Ernest J. King, Chief of Naval Operations and the highest-ranking officer in the Navy.

Ingram sat forward. "And...?"

"For a clean slate, it was decided to take this beyond the naval judicial system. No trials, no hearing, no public exposure. Only that I be released from the Navy without prejudice and that Tyler Childers be allowed to keep his rank and career with all the accoutrements.

"A nationwide manhunt is now underway for Renée," he chuckled, "Or perhaps I should say nationwide woman-hunt is underway.

"But you said 'Reno.'"

"As of last week. But now, they can't find her there. Nor anywhere. They're thinking she left the country."

"Holy cow."

"They're embarrassed. They've called in the FBI. And the FBI called INTERPOL. They'll find her, all right. She's a lightweight. And I'm glad they're taking those steps. She tried to clean us out."

"Us?"

"Yes, me and Tyler. Financially. She tried to take us to the cleaners. Visited the right banks but gave the wrong answers. Now she's on the lam."

Keating lowered his voice to barely a whisper. "Come here," he rasped. He beckoned with his fingers.

Ingram stepped close and bent over.

Keatings breath was labored. He barely croaked. "Tyler has been unlucky in love. Two divorces. And he dates really sleazy women."

"Hmmmm."

"So, in desperation, he ups and marries this one. They do all right for a year or so. I never met her, but Tyler seems happy. Then I come along and meet this very, ahhhh very..."

"I got it," whispered Ingram.

"At the 'O' Club bar. And then one thing leads to another."

"Hmmmm."

"Then I discover I'm porking the exec's wife."

"At the same time, he gets a 'Dear John' letter. He puts two and two together and confronts me on the bridge.

"Well, we're both kind of pushing hard. I get angry too." Keating slowly shook his head. "Stupid. I called her a whore."

"Wow!" said Ingram.

"Which she is. Nevertheless, Tyler really got uncorked at that. That's when he started to beat the shit out of me."

"Jeeeez. What did—?"

The door opened and a young officer walked in, a lieutenant.

Ingram stepped away.

Keagan gave an eye roll. "Todd, say hello to Jacques Giguere."

Ingram extended an open hand. "How do you do?"

Giguere, a short, balding man, had massive shoulders and a generous overbite that made him look rather foolish. Ingram took in right away that the man wore the legal designators on his khaki sleeves. And his eyes. Tucked behind thick tortoiseshell glasses, were narrow eyes that were difficult to find.

Moreover, he didn't shake. Ignoring Ingram's hand he said, "I'll have to ask you to leave."

Ingram shifted his glance to Keating who said, "Jacques is my attorney."

"He's trying to kick me out," said Ingram.

Keating shrugged.

So that's the way it is. He turned to face Giguere. "Who are you working for?"

"Eleventh Naval District. And you are treading upon the lawful conduct of proceedings that—"

"You are in a war zone and are interrupting government business." With a forefinger, Ingram jabbed him in the chest. "I am the commanding officer of the USS *Dunagan* attempting to determine details for the smooth transition of the change of command of that ship. I have high priority since our ship gets underway for southwest Pac in the next few days and I need his input to determine our approach to operations in the near future."

"Such as?" Giguere demanded.

"Classified," barked Ingram. "Now you better get out of here before I call the shore patrol and have them throw your dead ass into the brig."

"You can't—"

"Out!" yelled Ingram, pointing at the door.

Giguere turned to Keating. "Mr. Keating. This is not—"

"Out!" rattled Keating, likewise pointing.

Giguere leveled a stare at the two of them. "You'll hear about this," he muttered. He straightened his shoulders and walked out the door.

It started with a chuckle from Arana, then Keating, then Ingram. All three laughed for a good thirty seconds.

---

26

1 September 1943
Beverly Hills Hotel
Beverly Hills, California

The limousine picked up Commander Dudley W. Morton and his wife, Harriet, promptly at ten o'clock in the morning. Taking Coldwater Canyon 'over the hill' (the Santa Monica Mountains), they pulled up to the main gate at Warner Brothers Studios in Burbank at ten thirty-five. The guard waved them on and they drove straight to sound stage 15.

A young man stepped from the shadows as the limo pulled up. He was dressed in coat and slacks but no tie. He opened the door as Morton stepped out.

He held out a hand, "Wilford Thomas, commander. Welcome to Warner Brothers Studios. It's my honor to be your escort for today. I'm an associate producer on the movie you'll see being filmed today."

Thomas had a strong grip, solid build, and an easy, youthful grin that caused Morton to wonder about his draft status. "Not at all," Morton said, "The honor is all ours. Thank you for inviting us."

"Here, allow me."

Morton stepped aside as Thomas, freckle-faced and red-headed, moved with the grace of a sixteen-year-old boy scout, helping his wife, Harriet, from the car. She stood to her full height, a broad smile stretching from ear to ear, enjoying the moment.

Turning to them, he asked, "You've heard of the film we're doing?"

Morton and Harriet exchanged glances. "Something about Tokyo," he said. "That's all Compton could tell us." Lieutenant Commander Phillip Compton was the technical advisor to the film. He'd called Morton four days ago with the invitation to watch the live filming, a submarine film with a cast of superstars including Cary Grant.

"Uh-oh." Thomas reached for a door and snapped it open for them. "He didn't brief you?"

"He was in a hurry. Gave us the essentials. We said 'yes,' and here we are. But no, not much else. And I understand he's not here today?"

"That's right. We had to send him off to a production meeting with Mr. Warner. So, I'm sorry if this sounds like a typical foul-up."

Morton clapped Thomas on the shoulder. "My boy, one gets used to it. Foul-ups are the story of World War II. You learn to live with them. It is said victory goes to the one who screws up the least."

Thomas stood there open-mouthed.

Morton continued, "One learns that as he goes along. And I'm sure you see it in your business as well. Yes?"

"Now that you mention it, yes. Plenty of screw ups."

"There, you see?"

"And yelling and screaming as well."

Morton gave one of his signature churlish grins. "Ah, but that's the secret."

They stepped through a dead space guarded by an interior door. Thomas opened that, asking, "Sir?"

Morton and Harriet stepped in, saying, "It is also said victory goes to the one who remains calm and screams the least."

Thomas steepled his fingers and nodded. "Yes, I like that."

He waved them through to the sound stage. He said, "So, welcome to our submarine movie titled *Destination Tokyo*."

"Wow." The Mortons gasped as they walked onto a large sound stage with an enormous water tank in the middle. The tank looked to be about

60 by 50 feet. Planted in the tank was the center section of what looked like a *Gato* class submarine with a conning tower and 20-millimeter cannon mounted on the afterdeck. Also mounted were periscope shears, radio antennae, and other authentic topside gear. The water tank was full and a dark green life raft was tied to a submarine's cleat and bounced in little wavelets beneath the conning tower. All the overhead stage lights were on, making everything glisten with the water as men scurried over the submarine's deck, hammering things into place, and shouting at one another.

Two men were seated on a portable dolly-mounted platform that reached out over the water nearly to the submarine. One man sat behind an enormous camera and held five fingers up in the air. The back of his deck chair read Bert Glennon. Sitting beside him was another man smoking a pipe. Also with five fingers in the air. He shouted, "Quiet!" His deck chair read Delmer Daves.

It was amazing. Instantly, all the hammering, casual chatter, electric machines and banging from behind the submarine stopped instantly.

Harriet squeezed her husband's arm. He looked at her and winked.

A man held a clapboard before the camera. "Take four," he said, then ducked back.

Glennon hunched over his camera, his face pressed to the view finder.

A man, a sailor in dark foul-weather gear, stood in the life raft and braced himself against the hull with one hand.

Harriet squeezed harder. '*Wow*,' her mouth formed.

Morton realized what she saw. *The sailor was the actor, John Garfield.*

Sailors on deck untied the bow line from a cleat and tossed it aboard. Garfield smiled, threw a mock salute to the conning tower, and then sat and paddled away.

"Cut," yelled the director. "That's good. Back to scene one twenty-two."

Morton tipped his hat back. "Amazing," he muttered.

"Shhh," said Thomas.

"Quiet," called the director.

The man with the clapboard held up his device and clicked it off.

The scene was an easy one of the sailors on the submarine untying the liferaft's bow-line, throwing it into the raft and John Garfield shoving the raft away and sitting to paddle back to shore.

The director peered down at a manuscript, found a page, and called loudly. "Okay, one-twenty-three is next. Fifteen minutes."

Thomas looked at them. "Well, what do you think?"

Morton said, "I am overwhelmed." He spread his hands. "Everything is so realistic. Where do I sign?"

Thomas chuckled, "Thank you. High praise coming from you." He turned to Harriet, "And you, ma'am?"

"Oh, he's more handsome in person than on the screen."

"Are you sure about that ma'am?" They turned. The voice behind them was that of John Garfield wearing a broad grin.

Her hand went to her mouth, "Oh, my."

They laughed as Garfield gave Harriet a great hug. Then Garfield and Morton

shook hands.

Right behind Garfield, puffing on a pipe, was Delmer Daves, director and one of three screenwriters of *Destination Tokyo*.

Cary Grant, star of the film, stood off to the side. Grant was dressed for his role as Lieutenant Commander Cassidy, skipper of the USS *Copperfin*, wearing undress khakis with no blouse. His thumb hooked a foul weather jacket over his shoulder. With his broad smile and universal good looks, he certainly rivaled Lieutenant Commander Dudley W. Morton as far as appearance goes.

The two shook warmly.

Grant rubbed his chin and asked, "Excuse me commander, but do they really call you Mush?"

Morton slammed on his thickest Kentucky accent, "Sumpin' I picked up at the Naval Academy. Can't seem to shake it."

"Oh, I don't know about all that. People still give me heat about my British accent. And here I thought it was all gone."

Harriet popped up with, "Oh, you keep it, Mr. Grant. The ladies love it."

Grant wrapped an arm around her. "I think I'll fire my agent and hire you as his replacement." He tossed at Morton, "Nice, Mush. She's a keeper."

Delmer Daves checked his watch. "Back to work, boys and girls." He turned to Morton. "I hope you'll join us at lunch today. It's being catered by Bruce Wong."

The Mortons looked perplexed. He asked, "Of course. Sounds nice. Er... Bruce Wong? Is he a big deal?"

Daves replied, "Best Chinese food in town. Has a great restaurant down-town. Really good. People go nuts. You'll see what I mean."

Harriet said, "Chinese. We love Chinese."

Morton nodded, "Amen to that." He turned to Daves, "Please count us in. Thank you."

Grant said, "It gets interesting. We needed an oriental to play a Japanese radio direction finder operator. Wong fits the role perfectly. No dialogue. He just sits there and twists the loop antenna. Plus, he's been in the restaurant business for a long time. We all go there. He's good at what he does, food or film."

"Amazing," said Morton. "I can't wait."

Daves said. "I would be glad to put you into the scene as an extra but time is short and you're not quite dressed appropriately."

Morton laughed, "Oh, no. That's all right. I get plenty of experience at this when I'm out there. Fun to watch it from the sidelines for a change."

Daves said, "Okay, let's go then." He called loudly, "Take your places: scene one-two-three."

Morton asked Daves before he walked away, "What's this scene about, anyway?"

Daves rubbed his chin. "Sure. Last year's Doolittle air raid on Tokyo, right?"

"Yes."

"What we're doing here is our submarine, the *Copperfin*, has crept into Tokyo Bay. They landed a shore party in a remote spot. That's Garfield as the character named Wolf, along with two other guys."

"Okay."

"The shore party collects weather data while the *Copperfin* collects data on ship and aircraft movements in Tokyo Harbor. It's supposed to be in little books Cary hands over to Garfield."

"I see."

"So, what we're filming now is Wolf paddling out to get the *Copperfin* data. You'll see that in the scene we're about to do. Then Wolf takes it ashore where they've set up a powerful broadcast station. It's all collated and broadcasted to the USS *Hornet*. Now, the B-25 pilots have up-to-date dope for the raid on Tokyo and the other cities of Japan." Daves puffed his pipe and smiled.

"Aha," said Morton. He knew that the aircraft carrier USS *Hornet* was indeed the ship that carried Doolittle B-25s to bomb Tokyo and other cities. What Delmer Daves didn't know was that the *Hornet,* after participating in the Battle of Midway, on 4 June 1942, was sunk at the Battle of Santa Crus Island (Solomons) on 26 October 1942.

Daves continued, "So, what we see here is the data going to the shore party to be broadcast to the *Hornet*."

Morton clasped his hands, "Neat. Can't wait to see it."

Grant, standing close, furrowed his brow as he began donning his foul-weather jacket. "I just hope we can pull it off." He yanked at the jacket. A button snagged on his belt. He groused, "Damn."

Morton turned, unhooked the button, and yanked it up for him.

Grant turned and said, "Leave it to the U.S. Navy to bail us out."

Morton chuckled, "We're here to serve, Captain Cassidy."

They laughed.

Daves said, "You'll get screen credit."

Grant said, "Indeed, as Chief Unhooker." He squared his shoulders, looking marvelous. "But thank you, sir." Cary Grant saluted.

Morton returned it. "My pleasure, sir. The least I can do."

Delmer Daves whistled. "Very impressive. Two of the very best on my set. Amazing." He turned to Morton. "Thank you for being here."

"You're welcome. But the thanks go to you." He looked around. "I'd say you have a winner, here."

"Well, your opinion matters a lot. So, if you see anything, please sound off."

"Yes sir," said Morton.

Daves smiled, "Okay. Back to my office." Thomas and the Mortons stepped back about ten feet as Daves again climbed onto his rig and sat beside Bert Glennon. Others moved away and remained quiet.

"Lights," shouted Daves. The Mortons watched as magic was performed with the overhead bank of flood lights going off, while smaller more powerful lights took over for the scene and character lighting. The effect was phenomenal.

Daves shouted: "Quiet," then, "Roll 'em."

It is a night scene with Wolf climbing from the raft onto the *Copperfin'*s deck and walking to the conning tower. He looks up to skipper Lieutenant commander Cassidy in the conning tower, now in his foul weather jacket.

WOLF: (Walking up to the conning tower.)

Ready and waiting, sir.

CASSIDY: Enjoying your shore leave Wolf?

WOLF: Yes, sir.

CASSIDY: Here's the Tokyo and Yokohama dope.

(hands down a packet of journals)

We'll surface again at 0330. Good luck.

WOLF: Yes sir.

(dashes for the life raft)

"Cut!" shouted Daves. He leaned over and began talking to Glennon. The flood lights went up, making Morton wish he'd brought sunglasses.

Daves conferred with Bert Glennon at length. Then he slapped his forehead and summoned Thomas.

Thomas came back saying, "They're wrapping up for this morning. I'm going to take you over to postproduction and let you see some footage. Then it's lunch."

"Yum," said Harriet.

"This afternoon, they're doing a battle scene. A depth charging. Do you mind staying for that?"

"Sure," said Morton. "I always wondered what those were like."

Thomas cocked his head in a weird way.

Harriet fell asleep right away. Morton lay back on his pillow, his hands splayed behind his head. These fellows did a good job today. Of course, he could say little about the authenticity. There were so many things wrong but with what little information they had, Delmer Daves, Jack Warner, and their people had done a decent and compelling job. Good for the folks at home and even good for the boys in the Navy to watch, pure entertainment with not too much obvious claptrap.

But his mind wandered to why he was here in the first place. Heads were rolling, mostly in the Navy Department in Washington DC. The Mark 14 submarine torpedoes were complete failures. The evidence was overwhelming. Hit and detonation rates were horrendous. Submariners needlessly endangered their lives in attempts to line up perfect shots, only to see or hear them fail, dismally.

It had become cumulative over the past decade, due to the long-term effects of the depression, but also due to poor design, poor production and finger-pointing and inter-agency squabbling. That much was obvious to Morton. And nobody wanted to take responsibility. To take over and sort it all out.

What was the problem, they asked innocently from under their desks?

Four little ones were the universal answers from the submariners who risked their lives against the enemy:

The Mark 14 torpedo ran ten feet too deep.

The Mark 14 torpedoes' magnetic exploder detonated prematurely.

The contact exploders malfunctioned and didn't detonate.

The Mark 14 torpedo tended to make a circular run, endangering the firing ship.

That's why he was in the States this week to meet with a design staff in San Diego, look for answers, hammer it out, and then more meetings in Pearl Harbor. After that, climb back into *Wahoo* and go back to sea, this time, hopefully, with a batch of torpedoes that worked. And right back to the Sea of Japan with its plethora of fat, juicy, targets.

Dudley Walker Morton ran it through his mind again and again. Another two hours passed before he went to sleep.

PART III

At Danger's Ebb
When vigilance sleeps,
Beware my friend,
Thine enemy creeps.
—John J. Gobbell

27

10 September 1943
Henry Walker Beach House
East Oahu, Hawaii
Territory of Hawaii

Lamar sent a pool car, a haze-gray Navy Plymouth four-door sedan with black numerals on the door panels. A step up compared to the open-air Jeep they'd been using the past ten days. But the Plymouth made him miss the cut-off shorts and barefoot style of living to which they'd become accustomed.

Ingram tossed his B-4 bag and Helen's luggage in the trunk. And they were off.

A young lieutenant (j.g.) with straight black hair and bushy moustache rode in the front passenger seat. His name tag read **RAPP**. He said to the Navy driver, "ten-ten dock, Nelson."

"Yes sir," was the reply.

Ingram and Rapp wore working khakis, a comfortable form of dress with just a worsted short sleeve shirt and open collar and garrison cap. For her travel today, Helen was in the Army's summer service uniform, also with garrison cap.

In the back seat Helen grabbed her husband's hand and held it.
Tightly.

She turned to the rear window to squint at the Walker's little beach house outlined by the rising sun. She said, "I could stay there forever."

Ingram squeezed back and said, trying to sound nonchalant, "Not with that plumbing system." The toilet had stopped up two or three times, a grumbling Ingram having to thump the toilet plunger in the wee hours.

Rapp grinned at Nelson, who made an effort to keep a straight face.

Rapp called over his shoulder, "Sorry about that. It keeps happening."

Ingram said, "I had to walk out back and bury it in a palm grove."

Rapp said, "Oh no."

Helen laughed and smacked her husband across the shirt front.

Ingram said, "Sorry lieutenant. Bad joke."

"Yeah, I kind of wondered about that."

They sat close together as Nelson tromped the Plymouth's accelerator. The anemic six-cylinder sedan rattled and bounced down Highway H1 through Honolulu and directly toward the Naval Station.

Helen's eyes were closed tightly and her foot jabbed an imaginary brake on the floor. He wrapped an arm around her thinking, *It's going to be a while before you do this again.* Sleep dragged at him. Helen too, he was sure. They hadn't slept well last night. They kept reaching for each other.

Like now.

"Maybe," she whispered in his ear.

He looked down at her, his eyebrows raised. "No foolin?"

She whispered back, "Never can tell, you were so...so..."

He laughed aloud, "So it's Hitchcock and me?"

She jabbed him with a thumbnail to the ribs.

Ingram made squealing noises.

Nelson's eyes snapped to his rear-view mirror.

Rapp started to look around but then centered his eyes on the road. "Careful," he muttered.

Nelson's foot left the accelerator. The Plymouth lost speed, with the car behind, a 1936 Ford convertible, honking furiously.

Ingram said aloud and with bluster, "Ten-ten Dock if you please, Nelson."

Rapp's hands shot out to brace himself on the dashboard. "Nelson, goddamnit."

Nelson punched it. The Plymouth jumped ahead just as they reached the Naval Station Main Gate.

And then Nelson was forced to brake hard. The Plymouth screeched to a stop right before the Marine sentry, tires smoking.

Childers was the model executive officer. He had the *Dunagan's* officers lined up in three tight ranks at the companionway. The ship was moored starboard side to, with lines all singled up.

Ingram stepped aboard first, throwing the proper salutes, then helped his wife aboard. Rapp and Nelson followed with luggage.

"Hand salute," called Childers.

Ingram returned it to the officers, then said, "At ease, please, gentlemen."

There was no doubt Helen had their attention. The officers, young and old, plus the nearby enlisted who happened to be in the area, gave Helen the once-over followed by many more once-overs. She rewarded them with a dazzling smile as she saluted the flag on the fantail and then the OOD, Lieutenant (j.g.) George Eckert.

Childers walked up, tipped a two fingered salute to Helen and then addressed Ingram, "Welcome back, captain. Ship is ready for sea, all lines singled up. A launch is moored to port ready to take Captain Ingram to the Ford Island Amphib Base."

Just then Rapp stepped up, "Mrs. Ingram's luggage is aboard the launch, sir. Your bag is on its way to your stateroom."

Ingram thrust out a hand, "Thanks for everything, Rapp. The house was fantastic. And you'll make sure to..." Ingram had given Rapp a fifth of Johnnie Walker Black scotch to hand over to the Walkers.

"All taken care of, captain. They'll have it by sundown."

"Perfect. Thank you."

Rapp flashed his watch. "And if you don't mind my saying sir, that Coronado is scheduled to take off within the hour..."

"Then let's get it going," said Ingram, with the realization that they had dawdled this morning, not wanting to leave. He continued, "That ride was better than the bumper cars at the Long Beach Pike."

They shook again.

Rapp grinned. "Thank you, sir. Nelson's a good man. I'll let him down easy." He turned to Helen. "Do you play cribbage, ma'am?"

Todd and Helen caught each other's eye with the slightest of smiles. "Well, er...Yes." She spread her hands. "Who doesn't?"

Nelson shrugged with, "It will be good if you do, ma'am. There are

two captains aboard that flight who are cribbage junkies. They cleaned me out a couple of months ago. But it was fun. Breaks the monotony of a ten-hour flight. Maybe they'll invite you."

Again, Helen looked at Todd. He recognized her *well, bring it on...* expression. She smiled back. "Well, I suppose I can give it a try."

"That's the spirit," said Rapp. "Well, goodbye, you two, and safe journey." With a nod, Rapp turned and left the ship, saluting as he went.

Ingram turned to Childers, "Okay, Tyler. This is all very nice." Ingram took a deep breath. A lot depended on what Childers said next. "Are we really ready for sea?"

"In all respects, captain."

Ingram knew he had to buy into it. Ready or not, he had to show confidence. "Very well. Please lay to the bridge, I'll see Mrs. Ingram off and be up shortly. And if you're ready, remove the brow[1]."

Childers gave a quick salute then said. "Thank you, captain." He called to the officers in ranks. "Secure. Lay to the special sea and anchor detail."

Ingram took Helen's arm. "Okay, babe." Together, they walked across the quarterdeck to the port side. Waiting was a forty-foot blue and white admiral's barge. Her crew of five were in dress whites standing at their stations, the barge's engines softly rumbling.There were four bronze stars clustered on the bow. "Holy cow," said Ingram. "You got pull around here."

"Is this his?" she asked.

"This barge belongs to the one and only Chester W. Nimitz, Admiral, USN, who also happens to be the Commander in Chief of the Pacific Fleet. For now, it's your boat. You shout, the admiral bends over backwards to get it done."

"Please thank him for me."

"He's kind of tough to get an appointment with."

"Then talk to Lamar."

"That I can do."

"My, oh, my." She stepped to the quarterdeck ladder. And then looked up to him. Her eyes were misty.

He grabbed her and held tightly.

Softly, she said, "I don't want to go..."

He kissed her. "Back soon.Then we'll all be together at Olsen's."

"Won't be soon enough...You'll write every day?"

"Best I can."

"Sometimes you don't and I get worried."

"Well, consider it my job to keep you from getting worried. I'll do my best." He hugged her again.

"I know you will."

A whistle from down below. The launch. A Navy captain stood near the quartermaster pointing at his watch. For emphasis the quartermaster revved the engines.

"Gotta go," she tapped him on the nose. "Love you."

"Love you back." He let go.

Saluting the OOD and flag, she was down the ladder and stepping aboard the barge. The navy captain made a great show of taking Helen's hand and helping her aboard. Then he looked up to Ingram and grinned.

Ingram stood to attention and saluted.

The Navy captain drew to attention and started to return the salute.

That's when the barge's quartermaster hit the throttles. All the way. The Navy captain lost his balance and pitched aft. But quickly, he grabbed a handrail and stood straight up. He looked back up to Ingram, grinning again.

Ingram grinned back and they waved to one another.

From inside the hatchway, Helen joined them, the three smiling and waving as the admiral's barge rose up on the step and headed across the channel to the amphibious base at Ford Island.

28

Jerry Landa took the 'O' Club steps two at a time, walked into the dark foyer and threw his suitcase in a corner. He reveled in the soothing rattan furniture wishing he could plant himself here. *What the hell? Let's do it.* He sat. And he wanted that beer. That iced, cool Pabst Blue Ribbon beer, the bottle covered with delightful little rivulets, all waiting to be tilted toward the ceiling, giving comfort to Landa now suffering from the aftermath of a nine-hour flight aboard a C-54 from Long Beach. He'd sat outboard, over the wing and could hardly hear with those engines blasting away. He had a head cold and talk was impossible with those engines, not that he could talk anyway. He checked his watch: nearly four o'clock. Yet his stomach was still on California time. His belly told him it was really seven o'clock and time for dinner. Where the hell was it? He could smell dinner odors drifting from the double doors across the room. Men laughed and chortled from behind those doors. His hunger wouldn't let up. And where the hell was Rocko

Myszynski, his boss? The rather strident message at the airport nearly ordered Landa to show up here as soon as he landed, four o'clock if practical.

Landa clicked his teeth. Dazzling, shiny white as usual, but they felt a little sandy, like it was time to go over them with a generous slug of pepsodent. Something to complement that Southern California tan he'd acquired, especially with golf twice a week at the Virginia Country Club. He really should get to the Pepsodent. However, it was in his bag against the opposite wall. After that, maybe sneak in a cold Pabst Blue Ribbon while he waited for—

A hand clamped him on the shoulder. "Jerry, welcome to paradise you old son-of-a-gun." He turned. Standing before Landa was Captain Theodor R. Myszynski, Commodore of Destroyer Squadron 12 and his immediate superior. They were in Hawaii for three days for a predeployment conference. However, Landa's squadron, now in the final stages of forming in Long Beach, was not quite available for operations.

He shook with Myszynski whose head tilted toward the empty table beside Landa, "What's this? No liquid libation for the great Jerry Landa?"

"Just got here, Rocko. You too?"

Myszynski said. "About ten hours ago. Had a little time to surf at Waiki-ki." He patted his belly. "Except this damn thing got in the way. Everybody laughed their asses off." He waved toward the bar. "Shall we?"

"I thought you'd never ask." Landa rubbed his chin as they emerged into the bar, about half-full. "Waikiki, tough duty."

They passed under the sign, now famous to Pacific forces:

"All those who enter covered here,

shall buy the bar a round of cheer."

Landa patted the top of his head just to make sure. He'd tossed his combination cap along with six million others at the front desk.

"Ah, that place spellbinds me. Even now. Would you believe it? They got barbed wire and sentries marching up and down the beach looking for Japs to shoot. But even with that, they still let us sneak out and surf the waves. With all the junk in the water the waves are still perfect. But dodging the barbed wire is a real challenge."

They sat, ordered Pabst Blue Ribbons, and Landa made a big show of wanting to pay. But Myszynski had his wallet out and yanked out a pair of two-dollar bills.

Landa said, "Next round."

They raised their glasses and quaffed half with the attendant "ahhhs" and belches.

Landa caught Myszynski' s eye.

Myszynski signaled for two more Pabst Blue Ribbons, drained his glass and nodded. He looked from side to side. At least ten feet separated them from anyone else. Even so, he kept his voice low. "Ever hear of Operation Blissful?"

Landa shook his head.

"Good, nor has anybody else. We're trying to keep it that way."

"Gotcha."

Myszynski ran a hand over his brow. "Halsey's getting ready to invade Bougainville." Bougainville was a major island in the Solomon Island group. "He and MacArthur have this strategy called 'hit 'em where they ain't.'"

"Which means?"

"Attack the enemy not in their strongholds like Rabaul, but take nearby lightly defended objectives. Bypass the big juicy targets, blockade them, bomb the hell out of them, and then starve them out."

"Okay," said Landa.

"So now, Halsey wants Bougainville. So do the rest of the Joint Chiefs of Staff as far as I know."

"So does MacArthur."

"For a different reason," said Myszynski, "With MacArthur it's political. But apparently back home, they've taken surveys. They've learned nobody gives a shit about the Pacific. What they want is Europe and the Mediterranean if need be. Then after that, maybe Japs in the Pacific."

"That's sad."

"Indeed it is. So when it comes time to pass out the resources, Europe gets first dibs."

"Why am I not surprised?"

"Which leads me to today's subject."

Landa studied his boss. Myszynski' s tone was quick, precise, to the point. He wasn't wasting time. Myszynski continued. "I need a destroyer. A loan if you will."

Landa gave one of his best, disarming grins. "Love to help you, Rocko, but I'm all sold out. All my ships are in training. Everyone committed. Beating their brains out so we can join up. Won't be anywhere near ready for another three weeks, maybe a month." Landa sat back and sipped. With his thirst quenched, he was past the guzzling stage. He snacked on popcorn and ordered two more beers.

"Are you sure, Jerry?

"Absolutely."

"I need just one ship. Seven days. Ten tops."

"All used up. Sorry."

"I promised Vandergrift." The soft-spoken General Alexander Vandergrift, USMC, headed up the fabled First Marine Division on Guadalcanal.

"Rocko, I'm sorry."

There was a stony silence. Landa realized Rocko could have ordered Landa to give him one destroyer but had not. They stared at the floor.

"It's not easy," said Myszynski.

"No," agreed Landa. Then he asked, "What's not easy?"

"We lost the *Willets* two days ago." The *Willets* was a destroyer in DESRON 14. "Huh?"

"Refueling at sea. She got pooped by a rogue wave and was shoved right into the tanker. Two men killed. Twenty injured. Hell of a mess. They figure three months in the shipyard."

"Jeeeez."

"And now, I can't keep my promise for Operation Blissful."

Here it comes. Landa knew when he was being had. And, skillfully. Myszynski was not pulling rank. He waited, saying nothing.

But Myszynski wasn't about to yield to a stand-off, "I had promised two destroyers for 'Operation Blissful,' the *Conway* and the *Willits*. And now, the *Willits* is out. And Vandergrift still wants two ships, not just one."

"Why me?"

"Not you. Todd Ingram."

"Jeez, Rocko, that's a hot potato. He's all wrung out."

"Just for a week, maybe ten days. All he must do is sit back and unload five-inch on the Japs."

"I hadn't told him, but I was going to have him relieved as soon as he got to Noumea. He needs a rest."

"You got somebody in mind?"

"Jack Taylor," said Landa.

Myszynski pulled a face.

"Jerry? Jerry? Your highness?"

"Uh..."

"What's wrong?"

Myszynski said, "Taylor is too young, a lieutenant commander?"

"Yes. Actually, he'll soon be in the zone for commander."

"He looks like an ensign."

"Ranked sixth at his class in the Academy. Smarter than hell."

Myszynski shook his head, "He may be smart, but his voice sounds like he's been goosed with a pogo stick. No evident command presence."

Landa looked away. Taylor really was smart. And his marks were good, too. But people had to get used to him, he had to admit. "We...he's all I got, Rocko."

Myszynski rubbed his jaw. A full minute passed. Finally, he spoke. "Tell you what, Jerry. Let's take Jack Taylor in as prospective CO. Then when the time is up for Blissful and if Taylor cuts the mustard, we'll cut Ingram loose and he can go play."

"Not much playing," muttered Landa. "Ingram is supposed to be off to new construction in a month or so."

Myszynski pulled a cigar from his top pocket, bit the end off and spit it out. With panache he lit it and then said. "Okay Jerry. Jack Taylor prospective CO? Then you can send Ingram wherever you want." He blew smoke and then stuck out his hand.

Why is he doing it this way? He could just order me? Landa asked, "What is Blissful, anyway?"

"Halsey wants Bougainville. He and Vandergrift figure a good way to get it is to stage a fake diversionary raid on Choiseul Island next door. Make the Japs think that's the objective. Then when they're lookin' the other way, that's when we blast into Cape Torokina and secure Bougainville." He blew smoke.

Landa said. "Do I have a choice?"

"Not really. But I admire you standing up for your troops."

Landa took his hand. "Okay, Rocko, you got me."

They shook.

Rocko said, "Jerry, thanks. Tell you what. I'll send the orders to Ingram and to Taylor. That way, I'll look like the bad guy. You'll be squeaky clean."

Landa's stomach rumbled.

"Okay, Jerry?"

"I think so," muttered Landa.

"What is it?" Myszynski looked at Landa in a strange way. "Jerry, when was the last time you had something to eat?"

"Rocko, I thought you'd never ask."

29

26 September 1943
USS *Dunagan* (DD 504)
Noumea Harbor, New Caledonia

Ingram sat back and propped his feet on the desk. The captain's in-port cabin on the main deck felt like the Pope Suite at San Francisco's St. Francis Hotel. Both port holes were up and clipped to the overhead. A soft breeze blew through, airing the place. He'd just taken a shower, ten marvelous minutes of relaxation after picking their way through Noumea's minefield and torpedo nets protecting the outer harbor. They'd been given a berth of honor, moored starboard side to the U.S.S. *Argonne* (AG 31). Originally a repair ship, the Argonne was primarily a command ship doing repair work on the side. As such, she was headquarters for Admiral William F. Halsey, Jr., and his staff.

While working his way alongside, Ingram had glanced up at the *Argonne*'s flag hoist to see absentee flags for both admiral Halsey and the *Argonne*'s commanding officer, Captain Walter Roberts. They were not aboard.

His eyes snapped to the top of his desk and the IN basket: It was piled high with requisitions, plans of the day, logbooks, personal memos. On top was a red and white striped folder. It was marked CLASSIFIED in large letters and was secured with red tape.

With a sigh, he reached up, brought it down, and undid it. A message flimsy flopped out.

BT
CLASSIFICATION: SECRET AS PER ORDER 26092843DD4321
FROM: CHIEF OF BUREAU OF NAVIGATION
TO: ALTON C. INGRAM, LIEUTENANT COMMANDER, UNITED
STATES NAVY
SUBJ: BUNAV ORDERS: 26092843DD4321
INFO A. BUNAV; DD23P
B CINCPACFLT
C COMDESPAC
D COMPACWEST: N4
E COMDESRON 6
F. CODESRON 12
1.YOU ARE DIRECTED BY REPORTING SENIOR, TO RESUME FULL
COMMAND OF USS DUNAGAN (DD 504).
2.LCDR JACK A. TALOR, USN, IS UNDER ORDERS TO REPORT
DUNEGAN AS PROSPECTIVE COMMANDING OFFICER.
3.LCDR TAYLOR TO RELIEVE YOU SOONEST WITH CONCURRENCE
AND APPROVAL OF COMMODORE DESRON 12 .
4. UPON RELIEF YOU ARE TO PROCEED TO PORT IN WHICH
COMDESRON 6 MAY BE.
5.REPORT IMMEDIATE SUPERIOR IN COMMAND, IF PRESENT,
OTHERWISE BY MESSAGE.
BY DIRECTION
T. ACOSTA
BT

A routing slip was attached. Childers had initialed it as executive officer, George Eckert as Communications officer, and Harry O'Toole as radio officer.

Now, the whole world knows.

There was a soft knock at the door. Ingram called out, "Come."

It was Childers. A man was behind him but Childers squeezed through and quickly closed the door behind. "Sorry to intrude, boss. Your relief is here." He grinned from ear to ear. From behind his back, he whipped out a manila folder and handed it over.

Ingram nodded toward the door. "Is that him out there?"

"Yes, sir." The grin persisted.

"What's so funny?"

"Nothing, sir."

Ingram held the stare for three seconds. He sighed, "Okay, show him in."

"Aye, aye, Captain." Childers reached for the door and opened it. "Please come in, commander."

A tall thin man edged into Ingram's in-port cabin. The shirt and trousers of his working khakis were pressed razor sharp. His shoes had a mirror-bright spit-shine and his brass shined even brighter, almost as if he just bought it off the shelf. His blond hair was meticulously combed, his garrison cap clutched in his left hand. Tall, at least six-two, thin, as if he'd been on a starvation diet. He had a pencil-thin moustache and was otherwise clean shaven with crystal clear aqua blue eyes. He took a step forward and said, "Lieutenant Commander Jack Taylor reporting, sir." It had squeaked out, almost like a Porky pig characterization. Ingram almost laughed.

And then it caught his eye. Taylor had stepped forward to Ingram seated at his desk and stood there nearly braced at attention. Ingram's eyes were level with...Jack Taylor's web belt and his shiny belt buckle. He made to rise and shake Taylor's hand. But then he took in the reason for Childer's grin.

Commander Jack Taylor's fly was unzipped. All the way down. Light blue underwear peeked through.

Ingram flopped back into his chair and covered his face with his hands. After five seconds, he looked over to Childers, the man doing his best to hold it all in.

Ingram took a deep breath and barked, "You're done here, Mr. Childers, You are excused."

"But captain, I—" He waved to a stack of papers.

Ingram snatched them, "I said, 'excused' Mr. Childers." Ingram reached across and opened the door. "And would you please ask the steward's mate to bring in two coffees?"

"Two coffees. Aye, aye, captain. I'll send them right in."

"Thank you, Mr. Childers." Ingram closed the door softly behind the exec. Then he rose and faced Jack Taylor. "Welcome aboard, Jack." He extended a hand.

Taylor, a bit bewildered, took Ingram's hand. His grip was firm. "Thank you, captain."

Ingram reached over to a door beside his desk and opened it. It was a small but functional washroom with washbasin, toilet and shower. A full-length mirror hung on the inside. "In here, please."

"What?"

"Get in here, now, Mr. Taylor. And then do an about face."

"Wha—what? I don't understand."

"You don't have to understand, Mr. Taylor. I'm giving you a direct order. Get in there. Now!" He nodded to the washroom.

"But this—"

"Now!"

Taylor's shoulders slumped. But he walked into the little washroom.

"Turn around, Mr. Taylor."

Taylor did a perfect about face.

"Very well." Ingram closed the door.

He tried counting to thirty but there was a soft knock at the door. *Childers with the coffee. Good.* Ingram reached over and opened it. Before him stood Gunnery Sergeant Gilroy Hitchcock, United States Marine Corps, holding up a coffee service with two steaming cups of coffee. "What the hell?" gasped Ingram.

"The XO said you would be surprised." He walked in, gingerly set the coffee on Ingram's desk and, smiling, looked from side to side, his face saying, *where the hell is he?*

"Hello, Gilroy. What brings you here?" asked Ingram.

"The Corps can't cut me loose right away. They claim I have another sixty days to serve." With the back of his hand he parted the curtain to Ingram's hanging locker.

"Done with the malaria?"

"Nurses were ugly as all get out. I had to bail out or go crazy." He whispered. "Where the hell is he?"

Ingram pointed to the other end of the narrow room, to the washroom. "Well, welcome back, Gilroy. We need you here. Now, for the time being stand back there and don't say a thing."

"Huh?"

"Go, Jarhead. And don't say a word."

"Yes, sir." Hitchcock took three steps, turned, and stood at parade rest, a recruiting poster Marine.

"Excellent." Ingram reached back and opened the washroom door. Jack Taylor was also at parade rest. Ingram looked down. Taylor's fly was zipped up. He looked totally composed. Standing to his full height, he was a model of a parade-ground naval officer. "All two blocked?" he asked.

"Captain, I'm sorry. I—"

Ingram waved a hand. "Forget it. But I have to tell you, the quarterdeck guys you checked in with are a bunch of motormouths. By now, it's all over the ship. You're going to have to live this down, somehow."

Ingram nodded to Hitchcock. "Another surprise. Say hello to Gunnery Sergeant Gilroy Hitchcock. Just reporting back after a bout with malaria as our chief master at arms."

They stood close to one another and shook. Taylor said, "Nice to meet you, Gunny."

Hitchcock said rather formally, "And to you, too, sir. Welcome aboard."

They heard voices outside in the passageway leading to the wardroom. One was louder than the others. It was the deep baritone of Clinton Shorter, the chief engineering officer. He barked, "No shit?"

Another voice muttered something.

Then laughter from several others.

Shorter came back with, "Howz that for brass balls?"

Ingram yanked open the door and looked forward finding Shorter at the entrance to the wardroom. He snapped out, "Mr. Shorter. Would you kindly make your comments elsewhere? Perhaps in the officer's restroom down below?"

Shorter's meek reply was, "Sorry, captain..." Ingram slammed the door before the man finished.

Ingram turned to face Taylor. "Jack, to tell you the truth, I am pooped. I hate minefields. They take a lot out of you. We had a French pilot and that made it worse. His English was terrible and he kept yelling helm orders in French, just to piss us off. But finally, we're through and I'm a walking zombie." He pointed to the bunk. "This room is yours including that bunk. It's very comfortable. As of now, I'm shifting to the captain's at-sea cabin. Do you know where that is?"

"Just behind the bridge."

"Very good, Mr. Taylor. In the meantime, I'd like to ask Sergeant Hitchcock to

accompany you on a tour of the ship. Go anywhere. As prospective commanding officer, the ship is yours. Take a couple of hours. I need the sleep. We can talk then and I'll introduce you to the officers in the wardroom. Okay?"

Taylor nodded vigorously. "Thank you, captain. Very nice of you."

Ingram pointed at the door, "Then go. What are you waiting for?"

30

28 September 1943
USS *Dunagan* (DD 504)
S 15° 15.8' E 162° 45.0'
Course 321°T, Speed 18 Knots
En route Tulagi, Solomon Islands

It was a fair night at sea. Easily, the *Dunagan* loped along like the greyhound that she was. The sun was gone. There was no moon, and, except for the cornucopia of stars overhead, the night was pitch black.

Todd Ingram set his coffee cup in the mug holder and leaned on the bridge port bulwark just aft of the pilot house. He was glad to be done with the day's paperwork. And now...

He took a deep breath.

Quiet.

Except for the occasional strident 'clank' of the loading machine back on the quarterdeck. Innately, Ingram felt the men were getting rusty, so he ordered drills on the five-inch loading machine to make sure the gunners on all five mounts kept their edge. The sailors cursed and grumbled, especially now. Loading machine practice cut into their movie time. But Ingram and Guy Huber kept them at it. And actually, Ingram preferred the drills at night. Low visibility, hard to see, closer to dirty, confused, combat conditions—a better simulation. No place to go but up. And plenty of the most beautifully crafted curses one could ever hear.

Eventually, loading practice was done. The men rushed below to the mess decks to light up their cigarettes and watch their movie filtered through blue smoke. That is if the projectionist threaded the finicky 16-millimeter Bell and Howell projector correctly. If he hadn't, there was hell to pay. The mess-deck roar gushing all the way up to officer's country.

Without the cursing and screeching, it was indeed quiet except for the soothing, soft squeal of air being pulled into the uptakes to feed the boilers down in the firerooms. Indeed, just standing here on this beautiful balmy evening, with no direct threat, cast a cloak of tranquility around him.

He checked his watch's luminous dial: 2034.

With smooth oily seas, mother nature was playing games with the *Dunagan* this night. Large pools of plankton would light up like gigantic blue-green floodlights.

Some pools of light were big, as many as thirty feet across. The glow cast an eerie light on sailors peering over the side, making them look like characters from a Hollywood horror film.

Phosphorescence, it was called. It was a radiant glow similar to fluorescence. But fluorescence doesn't remain in its illuminating mode absent the source that excited it. It goes off right away. But phosphorescence does remain on and continues to glow long after the original excitation. In this case, the excitation came from the *Dunagan's* engine vibration when she either ran through a pool of plankton or steamed close by.

It was new and awe-inspiring to the kids—especially those who grew up in middle America or on the farmlands, those who'd never been to sea before.

Looking aft to the main deck, Ingram saw them in bunches, all blue green, gathered at the ship's rail, pointing and going "wowie."

He checked his watch: 2102. He'd ordered a change to a sinuous course beginning at 2000 in the night orderbook. So far, nothing had happened. He turned to shout at the pilot house when a man in khakis stepped up.

Illuminated just then by a ten-foot pool of phosphorescence, it was easy to discern a lieutenant (j.g.) with a pencil thin moustache. He was George

Eckert, the ship's CIC officer assigned to the 2000 to 2400 officer of the deck watch.

His light, sandy hair blended with the strange light as he saluted and announced in a staccato fashion. "Eight o'clock, captain. Ship secure. We're steaming on course three-two-one, speed eighteen." He took a breath, "Uhhhh...let's see, oh, yeah, boilers two and four are on the line along with generator two. All systems up and running. No casualties. Request permission to commence steaming on sinuous course 23 Baker."

Ingram returned the salute, "Make it so, George. Is the air search radar lit up and running?"

"Working like a champ, captain."

"Very well. Please tell CIC to be especially vigilant on the air search. With about five hundred miles to go, we're closing enemy long range air activity from the Solomons. If we have any trouble tonight, we'll see it on the air search first."

"Yes, sir. Then I'll get to that sinuous course clock." He made to leave.

"Hold on."

"Sir?"

Ingram waved a hand at the ocean. "With all this damned phosphorescence, I'd like to reduce speed to fifteen knots, so we can reduce our signature a bit."

"Yes, sir. Fifteen knots?"

"That's right. And go ahead and plug in our sinuous course." Ingram nodded toward the pilot house.

"Yes, sir." Eckhart quick-stepped into the pilot house.

Thirty yards to port, an enormous pool of phosphorescence lit up the night, easily forty feet across.

Tyler Childers walked up just then. With the green blue he looked like Lon Chaney playing the Wolfman. All that was missing were the fangs. Ingram almost laughed wondering what others thought of himself with the glowing in the dark.

Jack Taylor was right behind, looking just as sinister.

Tipping two fingers to his forehead, Childers said, "Evening captain. Eight o'clock reports. All secure. All systems running normally. We're at condition three watch, the ship is darkened and the smoking lamp is out on the weather decks."

Jack Taylor stepped forward and added, "We put another man on the air search radar repeater in CIC just to make sure we don't have any extra company this evening."

"That's it?" asked Ingram.

Childers said, "Ahhh, they will be rolling a movie in the wardroom and mess decks in five minutes in case you care to attend."

Ingram thought that one over. He supposed it would be okay. But while at condition three, there would be fewer officers and men to see the movie. "What's the flick?"

"*To be, or not to be*: Jack Benny and Carol Lombard. Shall we hold it for you?"

He'd already seen it three times. Besides, Carol Lombard had been killed in a plane crash just last year. It made him sad to see her up on the screen. "No that's okay. I'll pass. But go ahead," said Ingram.

Childers' eyebrows were raised. There was something else. He looked at Taylor. "Okay, Jack. Go ahead and roll the movie. I'll be down presently."

Taylor said, "Okay, Tyler. Evening, captain." He saluted Ingram and headed down the ladder.

With both palms, Childers leaned on the bulwark, his head bowed. He waited.

Ingram remained silent.

"I know I'm not supposed to ask, but I'm dyin' to know. You saw Ron Keating in Pearl?"

"Yes, I did. At the hospital."

"And...?"

Ingram turned to look at Childers. "Yes, you shouldn't ask. It's beyond me. I only saw Ron Keating since I knew him as an upperclassman at the Naval Academy. But right now, he's pretty banged up."

"Shhiiiit..."

"Missing teeth. Broken ribs. He can't breathe properly. Busted arm."

"I...I..."

"You're lucky they got this new penicillin stuff. Antibiotics they call it. Stops infection. He'll pull through."

One could feel it. A drop in the relative wind. Eckert had ordered the speed reduction. Only three knots; it was still noticeable. The bow and quarter wake sounds were less. And less luminous.

Ingram continued, "And for his trouble, he's being kicked out of the Navy. Admiral Nimitz engineered it so there will be no legal proceedings. The Navy doesn't need this kind of publicity, especially with Keating's dad being who he is."

"What about his dad?" asked Childers.

Ingram told him and added, "Keating will be okay. He'll get a civilian job Stateside. No problem there. But he's out of the Navy for sure."

A weak flickering pool of light brushed across Childers' face. He looked fierce. "I didn't know what I was getting into."

Ingram thought about Hitchcock and all his problems. *No, you didn't*, he thought. He didn't speak.

"A complete gold digger. She set this up. Scavenged my bank accounts. Damn near cleaned me out. Then I discovered Keating was porking her. All of a sudden, I was out of money and out of a wife. Now, I got debts. I can't pay 'em. I get threatening letters. And then she has the balls to send me a 'Dear John' letter like she's shoving it in my face. She tells me she's in bed with my skipper so *how do you like that, Jack*?

"All this piled up on me and, like a fool, I let loose on Ron Keating."

"Well, you still have a job. You're lucky. The Navy will take care of you."

Childers shook his head.

"I said you have a job, dammit."

"Sure."

"Take care of your men."

"Sure," muttered Childers.

Ingram offered his hand, "And they'll take care of you."

Childers looked up slowly. "Maybe I should think about that."

They shook. "Good idea, Tyler. Meantime...what's the story on Hitchcock? We got a replacement yet?"

"So, what's the hurry about him?"

Ingram smiled. "He's gonna be a dad. And he's way above the age limit."

"Lucky bastard."

"Which we will all become someday."

31

---

2 October 1943
Camp Crocodile
Headquarters, First Marine Division
Henderson Field (CACTUS)
Guadalcanal, Solomon Islands

The front office hadn't changed. Except for a large new bank of PBX equipment against the south wall. And telephones. Plenty of them. To Ingram, it seemed as if each desk now had at least three telephones. Some were white. One phone, it was in the back, was red. A Marine major sat there, smoking a cigar.

There were more men to man all the phones. It seemed everyone in the center was on the phone. Most of them Marines, many speaking urgently, some shouting, waving their arms in the air, almost everyone smoking cigarettes. The occasional bellowed epithets were very blue.

Led by a quick-stepping Marine pfc in jungle fatigues, Todd Ingram, Tyler Childers, Gilroy Hitchcock and Jack Taylor single-filed through a large room divided by a crude, unfinished counter made with rough-cut 2x6s, where servicemen of all the branches, pushed and shoved at each other trying to get their orders processed. Commanders, corporals, ensigns and bird colonels, many red-faced, demanded attention from one of the Marine-clerks for help to get processed and out of this fetid place.

Luther Honeykutt, the sergeant who shoved Ingram aboard Gilroy Hitchcock's

TBF, was still there. But now, his eyes were droopy and bloodshot. He was beyond bored. Ingram waved to him as he walked by. Honeykutt saw Ingram and barely returned his wave while a chief bosun's mate screamed at him. But Honeykutt and Gilroy Hitchcock recognized one another.

Instantly.

Ingram laughed nearly aloud as the pair automatically gave each other the finger. Then they went on with their business.

Childers, close behind Ingram, bent over and waved to Honeykutt with, "Nothing like old home week."

Honeykutt looked Childers up and down. With another glance to Hitchcock, he gave Childers the finger and then went back to the screaming chief bosun's mate.

Childers laughed, "How to get promoted in one easy step,"

A pfc led them through the crowd, down a hallway, through double doors, and into a connecting Quonset. This hut was air-conditioned. The relief was magic. Instantly, Ingram felt human. Without the pervasive humidity, he could deal with the world, no matter what.

They were ushered into an outer office. The door plaque read:

ALEXANDER A. VANDERGRIFT, MAJOR GENERAL, USMC

A cool-looking Marine captain sat at a desk surrounded by two type-writers and three telephones, one of those red. Two of the three were ringing.

The pfc handed IDs to the captain, then stepped back. Despite the ringing phones, the captain shot to his feet and saluted Ingram and Childers. "Welcome aboard, gentlemen.The general is ready when you are." He picked up the red telephone and spoke softly, nodded then hung up and waved to another door labeled:

KNOCK THEN ENTER

Ingram gave a wan smile then walked up to the door and rapped sharply.

Someone shouted, "Okay."

Two men were at a drafting table, maps scattered about. One was obviously General Vandergrift: two silver stars adorned his collar. He was tall, six-two, weighed about 175, chiseled features, had salt and pepper hair, and wore jungle fatigues, clean-washed and crisp.

Beside him was a Marine lieutenant colonel. The man was five foot four inches. No more. He weighed about 140 pounds, looked gaunt and had a severe haircut. Like the general, he also wore clean and crisp jungle fatigues. A set of paratrooper's wings were mounted over his breast pocket.

Vandergrift gave a short wave and smile and said, "Welcome to Crocodile, such as it is, gentleman. Please stand easy. There's no formality here. Obviously, I am General Vandergrift and," he nodded to the Marine colonel, "this is Victor Krulak, we call him Brute."

They shook hands all around as Vandergrift continued. "We have a little soirée coming up where we would like your help. Please step over here, gentlemen." He waved to the drafting table as they moved over. "I'm going to let Brute do the talking here, gentlemen. At this point, I believe he knows more about this operation than I." Vandergrift smiled, bowed slightly, and took a half step back.

Krulak bent over the table, organized some charts and then looked up, catching their eye. "Overall, the strategic view is that of Admiral Halsey and that general," he snapped his fingers. "That army guy. What was his name again?"

Vandergrift feigned disgust, "Very funny, Brute. MacArthur. General Douglas MacArthur."

"Ahh, yes," said Krulak. "MacArthur."

They all joined with the obligatory laugh.

Krulak continued. "Admiral Halsey and General MacArthur want to wrap up this Solomon Island nonsense as soon as possible."

"Nonsense?" muttered Hitchcock.

Krulak give a short smile and pointed to Hitchcock, "Okay, how'd you get mixed up in this, Gilroy?"

So, it came out that Krulak and Hitchcock knew each other. Compared to the other military branches, the Corps is relatively small and after ten or so years, one will have served with the other two or three times.

"Just askin'," said Hitchcock.

There was an uncomfortable silence among the Navy contingent as the Marines sorted it out.

Krulak exhaled and spread his palms. "Guadalcanal and all of that has been tough on a lot of guys, especially General Vandergrift here and his bunch. You, too, Gilroy. I heard of some of your stuff and I'm proud of you."

Hitchcock said, "You too, Brute. Your work with the Higgins boats was a masterstroke."

Vandergrift chimed in, "That's for sure. Brute Krulak was very instrumental in the development of the Higgins boat, the LCVP landing craft, a very successful program. Now, they're being built by the thousands for use all over the Pacific."

Jack Taylor said, "Wow. I saw one of those back in Norfolk. Really a trick little boat. The Gunny is right. That bow ramp. Who would have ever thought of that?"

Krulak shook his head. "Wasn't me."

There was a pause. Krulak was coming back with something. "It was the Japs. Before this war, I was a China Marine and traveled a lot. I saw stuff. Some of it good, a lot of it bad, especially where the Japs were concerned with their invasion of China. On the good side, I saw them experimenting with watercraft. Pieces of shit most of the time. But this one new model made me sit up and take notice. It had a bow ramp that dropped. A whole platoon ran off that boat in ten seconds. No kiddin'. Swords flashing, guys screaming '*Banzai*.' Off the boat and up the beach in ten seconds."

He held up the fingers of both hands. "Ten seconds. That was it. I figured, why in the hell can't we come up with something like that? So, now we're at war with the little bastards and I've been thinking about this. So, when the time came, I talked to Andy Higgins, and that's what he came up with. The LCVP. They assigned me to the program and I got to test them. I beat the daylights out of them until they worked properly. Me and..." Krulak threw a thumb, "No nonsense Gilroy Hitchcock here. Biggest bullshitter in the Corps. But a damn good boat driver. Then the program was up. I sent him off to flight school in Pensacola and...you still flyin' Gunny?"

"Got me a little TBF, Brute. Fly the island trade. Scotch, cigarettes, cigars—"

"Girls?" asked Krulak.

Hitchcock looked from side to side and casually ran a hand over his mouth, "Well..."

Vandergrift barked, "Gentlemen, can we continue, please?"

Krulak bent over the chart. "So, as I was saying, the intent is to wrap up the Solomons campaign. We have guys scattered all over the Pacific and it's time to coordinate things. So they organized it into three groups. Admiral Nimitz will head up the effort to knock out the Japs across the Central Pacific. Admiral Halsey is now trying to finish the Solomon campaign, which for now means taking Bougainville, the largest enemy stronghold. General MacArthur is to secure New Guinea and drive north from there to secure the Philippines or Formosa, or maybe both, they haven't decided yet. Within eighteen months, we'll have them in a pincers from which there will be no escape." His hand slapped the back of a chart with a 'crack'.

Ingram felt compelled to ask, "And our job...you know...the good old U.S. Navy?"

Krulak leveled an eye at Ingram. "Taking Bougainville won't be easy. We're going to try it at Cape Torokina on the western side. But there's at least twenty to twenty-five thousand Japs there. We want to keep them off balance and confused. Sooo," He looked to Vandergrift who nodded.

"We're going to fake an attack on Choiseul first to make them think that's where we're hitting next. Here. Look at this map."

"Chart," Jack Taylor corrected with a thin smile.

Krulak looked up from his map and raised an eyebrow.

Ingram offered softly, "For the good of interservice cooperation, we will agree that the term map is appropriate."

Childers wiped a hand over his mouth, smothering a smile.

Keeping his eye on Taylor, Krulak said, "That's fine with me. Anyone else?"

There was another silence. Vandergrift tapped the face of his watch.

"Yessir," said Krulak.

Ingram nodded and said, "Makes sense. Halsey and his forces have successfully driven up the central Solomon chain." He ticked off on his fingers. We've taken Rendova, New Georgia, and Munda. And now, we're in the process of taking Vella LaVella. The arrow points north. Any reasonable planner would take into consideration that the next logical target is Bougainville." He fell silent, his hands clasped behind his back.

Vandergrift picked it up with, "You're on the right track, Todd. But with a feint to Choiseul, the Japanese would have to re-direct their forces to that area,"

Childers said, "Bait and switch. Nice."

Vandergrift nodded. Then he raised a hand, "Incidentally we have orders." The others fell silent as the general went through a stack of paper on his desk. "Came through about an hour ago. Ah!" He held up a manila folder. Then he looked at Hitchcock, "You're fired, gunny."

Hitchcock blinked, "Sir?"

"Your papers came through. You are being detached from the United States Marine Corp as of tomorrow morning."

"Huh?"

Krulak leaned toward Hitchcock, cupped his hand over his mouth and said, *sotto voce*, "He appreciates being addressed as 'sir,' Gunny."

It was the first time Ingram had seen Hitchcock flustered. He sputtered, "What? I mean, what, sir?"

Vandergrift continued nonchalantly, "Seriously, Gunny. It's our screw up, actually. This stuff has been out there," he waved toward the door, "for at least ten days.

"Ummmm," went Hitchcock.

"So, to continue, you are being retired with full pay as of tomorrow. And funny thing here says your preferred destination is Noumea. Now, that's a screw up I can get fixed for you."

Hitchcock said, "No sir. Noumea is correct."

Vandergrift's hands fell to his side, his face saying *what the hell*?

Hitchcock twirled his garrison cap in his hands. "My wife, or my wife to be, Lolli, she lives there. On a beach on New Caledonia. We're getting married. We...we...are going to..."

Ingram blasted out, "He's gonna be a dad." He stuck out his hand. "Congratulations, Gunny."

They swarmed around a grinning Hitchcock, slapping him on the back and shaking his hand.

Krulak added, "That's a relief. I was trying to figure out how to get rid of you. Now it's all taken care of. Anyway, congratulations, Gilroy." They shook again.

Vandergrift added, "Now I understand. For the past six days, we've had an extra TBF named *Lolli* here at Henderson field. Looks like a wreck, but with a new engine. Orders say that she is your transportation to fly to Noumea. Then after that, you return the aircraft to us in decent shape. Make sure you sweep out those beer cans."

"Wow! Thank you, sir."

With arms folded, Vandergrift leaned against his desk and muttered, "Okay, Brute. Finish it up."

"Ummm." Krulak shoved some charts around the table and muttered, "Where were we?"

Ingram said, "You were saying that you want us to support your landings?"

"Jeez, commander. You catch on quickly," said Krulak.

Ingram said, "Elementary, dear colonel. How can we help you?"

Krulak looked around the room. "Actually, there's supposed to be two of you."

Ingram said, "I beg your pardon."

Krulak said, "The *Conway*. She's supposed to accompany us also.'"

Ingram said, "*Conway*? Nate Prime's ship?"

"I think so." Vandergrift walked over to his desk muttering, "*Conway, Conway*. Hold on." He rummaged through a pile of messages. "Ah." He held it up. "I'm sorry, I'm late with this. *Conway* is still down in Sydney Australia finishing up yardwork. Getting underway tomorrow to join us. He tossed the flimsy aside,

Childers said dryly. "One final night of R and R."

Hitchcock said, "Correction, sir. In the Corps, we call it I and I."

"I and I? What's that, Gunny?" asked Jack Taylor.

Hitchcock came right back with, "Intoxication and intercourse."

Krulak slapped his forehead.

Vandergrift rolled his eyes and groaned.

32

USS *Dunagan* (DD 504)
Officer's call – Eight o'clock reports
5 October 1943
Choiseul Island, Solomon Islands

The crew was uneasy. For sure, the honeymoon was over. Something was up. But nobody knew. Except the captain. And so far, he hadn't said anything.

Ingram had ordered a hundred and fifty gunny sacks. During the two previous days, he had the crew filling them with sand from the beach. With that, he had the cumbersome sacks distributed about the ship, primarily in the battle spaces. Twelve bags were scattered about the bridge, five bags in each gun mount, another twenty for the 40 millimeter gun tubs. Ten bags were reserved for the torpedo mounts; more were distributed on the main deck near the 20 millimeter canons. Five went into CIC and ten each were distributed into the engineering spaces. Extras were stacked around the depth charges on the fantail.

In the tropics, the sun goes down suddenly as if some ghoul, just off stage, has thrown a gigantic switch. There's hardly any twilight. It's - BAM —lights out. *Where's my flashlight, damnit?*

Same thing in the morning. Like a raging volcano, the sun explodes above the horizon and one suddenly has the gift of full daylight. Tonight was no different. Sunset was at 1923. Lights out. Ships were not lighted in wartime. One had to trip and stumble his way about the decks, trusting the errant pad eye or coiled dock line to memory.

Tonight, the officer's call was held in the passageway just outside the wardroom. It extends fore and aft to the main deck where the mast was stepped. They were in a condition III watch which meant a limited number of men were at battle stations.

Childers called them to order and made a few announcements. Then, he had Clinton Shorter, the engineering officer, talk about conserving water. It was the age-old warning about the tropics and the ship's evaporators, that they were not keeping up well with the demand for fresh water for the boilers and that careful attention had to be paid to water use, lest water restrictions go into effect on board the ship. With that, showers would be greatly restricted along with washing of clothes and everyone going around smelling like goats.

Childers and Shorter stood side by side detailing the water restriction program when suddenly, Ingram appeared beside them.

Now, this was something. The captain never participated in officer's call. It was part of a rather imperial system aboard Navy ships. The captain often took his meals alone, he conducted surprise inspections in the crew's quarters but never participated in morning quarters or officer's call in the evening. It was better for the men to hear from their direct superiors than from someone removed by higher rank.

Punishment was something else. In the Navy, it was called Captain's mast or more formally, non-judicial punishment. In this role, the captain was in full authority. From his uniform and its badges of rank, to the participants in the mast, to the actual procedure itself. In daytime, "Mast" was usually held outside in an open space, on the foredeck, or maybe on the fantail. For muscle, a master-at-arms was present, maybe two. Also in attendance was the accused's division officer and perhaps a legal officer if the issue was complicated.

With all the evidence presented, the captain rendered judgement. The offender was ordered to uncover and stand at attention for judgement.

With others also standing at rigid attention and fully covered, there wasn't a *mast* that went by, that the offender didn't feel just a little bit naked when he yanked his dixie cup off his head and his hair blew with the wind.

The captain could be easy in his judgement or he could put the hammer down meaning the poor offender before him, twisting his hat in his hands, could be sentenced to miserable days and weeks in the Marine brig[1]. Usually, sailors returning from the brig had been stretched to their limit. Wide-eyed, they came back changed men, sometimes not.

At captain's mast, the offender stood at attention as charges were read. He was given an opportunity to plead his case. Then the captain rendered judgement: Tough, beefy masters at arms were posted on either of the offender's sides and he was ordered to remove his cap while the captain read his verdict. If judged guilty, a commanding officer could render a judgement that could effect a man's career for years. A common violation was *going over the hill*, (absent without leave) with offenders spending months in a Marine brig. Worst offenders were sentenced to Fort Leaven-worth Federal Military Prison in Fort Leavenworth, Kansas. Indeed, in the case of a court martial, a wartime penalty could include death for something serious such as murder or even falling asleep on watch.

In other words, the captain was sacrosanct. It was a strictly military system.

This evening, it was something else. They could tell as Ingram edged between Childers and Shorter, his hands clasped behind his back.

Parade rest.

Shorter became nervous in his delivery. He was talking about no fresh water washdowns on the weather decks and cutting back on the laundry service. But then, he looked at Ingram.

Ingram nodded with, "Good evening, Mr. Shorter."

Shorter glanced at Childers who shrugged. The officers themselves were on edge, their eyes directly on Ingram. Shorter looked about and then said, "You want to say something, captain?"

"Only if you are finished, Mr. Shorter," said Ingram.

"That I am, captain," said Shorter. He backed a half step into ranks at the bulkhead and stood quietly at parade rest.

Quiet reigned. Except for various sounds around the ship: a voice growling on the R/T next door in CIC, or a pump squealing below the deck in the forward fire room.

Ingram began, "First, I would like to introduce our new chief master at arms. Please say hello to Chief boatswain's mate, Lyman Griswold." A man stood in shadows behind Ingram. Ingram said, "Front and center, Chief."

The man stepped forward. He was no more than five feet six, but must have weighed in at 170 pounds. Rock solid, with a large nose bent to the right, he looked as if he could give Childers a run for his money. Everything about him exuded strength and stability. Remarkably, he waved and gave a large grin. All his teeth were there, shiny bright. "Good evening gentlemen."

Ingram offered, "Chief Griswold joins us from the USS *San Francisco*, which, as you know, put up a hell of a fight with the Japs, and is now on her way back to the States for complete overhaul. Originally, he's from Texas."

Griswold raised the back of his hand to Ingram and said, "I wuz born in Mississippi, but ah grew up in Texas, sir."

"So, we call you Tex?"

"If you wish, captain. But ahm hopin' there's nobody from Mississippi around."

It wasn't necessarily what he said. It was the way he said it. He punctuated it with a wink.

Ingram smiled. "Welcome aboard, Tex."

The officers relaxed.

Griswold nodded and stepped back.

Ingram continued, "Thank you chief. Now, you're wondering about the sandbags." He folded his hands. "Everyone is concerned with the sandbags. Well, I wanted to tell it to you directly because you will be explaining all this to the crew at our next muster tomorrow morning. And there's no easy way to tell you except to say it's for soaking up blood."

He paused as the youngsters in khaki's stood before him, their eyes wide open. Then he said, "You see, in the next few days, we'll be standing up to Japs. They'll be shooting at us and we at them. Let's hope all those hours on the loading machine will pay off and that we can knock them out first.

"But what if some fat cruiser hammers us with a lucky six or eight inch round? I don't know if any of you have seen what that can cause inside a gun mount, or in an engine room or in CIC. I have to tell you, I've seen it. And it's awful. People get ripped to shreds. Hamburger is what you see. Your best friend beside you may turn into a gushing blood fountain before he dies. The deck will be slippery with blood. You can't move about without something to soak it up and help you gain traction. That way, as terrible as it may look, you can still continue to fight the ship, and keep on giving it back to the Japs, making them suffer more than you are. Then, we win. It may be the only way. I hope we don't have to use it. But now, it's here, just in case.

"We have to get used to the idea that if we tangle with the Tokyo Express, that some of us may not make it through. That could be your best friend. It could be your worst friend. It could be me." He placed a hand over his heart. "But our job is to fight this ship. And to sink Japs. We have the means to do that. You guys have the equipment and the training and the men to get it accomplished. So all you have to do is to move ahead and let the cards fall where they may."

He paused and clasped his hands. "Any questions?"

Silence.

Ingram nodded, "Okay, until quarters tomorrow morning. By the way, we have a few old hands on board. They've seen this stuff. Let them talk it out. It'll help."

They didn't show a movie that night. Sailors spoke in small groups or wrote letters home. Some wrote a Last Will and Testament, signed it, had it witnessed and dropped it in the ship's mail box. Others walked the *Dunagan's* deck still hot from the day's blazing sun.

During the day, they had been standing off Choiseul, sometimes dashing in, seeking enemy strongpoints, or fuel or ammo dumps. But the Japanese had made good use of the jungle. Thus far nothing significant had been spotted.

It was quiet in the wardroom that night as they sat to a stale spaghetti. Just then, a messenger walked into the wardroom and stepped right up to

Ingram, duty belt, clipboard, and white hat. It was Henry Nichols, a second-class radioman with straw colored hair sticking out from under his hat. He didn't uncover and his duty belt meant he was on watch. Nichols was from radio central.

There was a frown on Nichols' face. "'scuse me, sir. This is operational immediate." Nichols handed over a clipboard.

Ingram accepted the clipboard and noted the messages' classification: **TOP SECRET.** He signed the message chit and handed it back to the radioman. "Thank you Nichols. No response."

"Yes, sir." Nichols walked off.

Ingram checked the message. Its cyphertext was arranged in five letter groups. But Ingram felt a jolt. He sat up directly when he spotted that the message was addressed directly to *Dunagan*. Info copies were directed to DESRON4, destroyers *Selfridge*, *Chevalier*, and *O'Bannon*. He muttered under his breath. "I'll be a sonofagun." He looked up. There were twelve men at this sitting. Most of them senor officers. All had stopped eating, their forks or knives poised. Quiet. The exhaust blowers seemed unusually loud.

Very loud. Almost deafening.

"Damn." He couldn't help it. The message was from COMSOUTH-WESTPAC: Admiral Halsey. Again he looked up.

They waited.

"Go on, go on. Eat, damnit. You're going to need every calorie before the night is over." He checked his watch. "Eat all you can. I'm not kidding. You'll need it all."

He looked off to his left finding lieutenant (j.g.) Eckert, the communications officer. "George, it looks like it's up to you. Take a last few bites then hustle this up to crypto and break the message. This is from Halsey. And I think we'll need to know what he wants chop, chop."

"Yes, sir." Eckert dabbed his lips with the napkin and made to push his chair away.

Ingram held up a hand. "I mean it, George. Finish your dinner. Pack it away." He looked down to his own plate and gave a thin smile. "Even this swill. Yes, pack it away. We might not be eating as well for a while."

33

5 October 1943
USS *Dunagan* (DD 504)
Standing off Choiseul Island, Solomon Islands

They finished their meals sporadically. But Ingram held them at the table. George Eckert, being the communications officer, was pretty fast on the crypto machine. It shouldn't take too long before they knew.

And it didn't. They heard footsteps outside the wardroom. By Ingram's watch, Eckert had been seventeen minutes breaking the message. Followed by the duty radioman, Eckert was nearly out of breath as he blasted into the wardroom and handed over a clipboard. It was a signature page. Ingram took out a pen and initialed it, acknowledging receipt of the message.

"Thank you." Ingram gave Eckert the quick smile usually rendered to duty messengers and handed the clipboard back to Eckert who passed it on to the duty radioman.

Ingram called to the duty radioman, "No reply at this time."

"Yes, sir." The radioman beat a hasty retreat back up the ladder to radio central.

Eckert handed Ingram a manila file folder.

Inside was a single flimsy message:

BT
FLASH
TOP SECRET
TO: HAYSTACK
KITTY KAT
FROM: BARN DOOR
REF: A,) OP ORD: SEVENTH INNING
1. HOODWINK PROC: 21.2.2(a
INFO: A) HEAVENS SAKE
B) BANGTAIL
TARANTULA
WASH BOWL
C) BRUTUS FOUR
RAT TRAP
CHART ROOM
FLAT TIRE
HAYSTACK DETACHED OPERATION BLISSFUL UPON RECEIPT.
HAYSTACK REPORT BANGTAIL ASAP IAW NAVI NWP 143 PARA 3 B, 16.1
REF A AND Λ(1)
IMPERATIVE HAYSTACK LEND ALL SUPPORT.
REPORTS ARE NINE JAP DDS ENROUTE FROM RABAUL PLUS
BARGES TO RESCUE TROOPS AREA 143
UNITS OF BRUTUS FOUR TO BEND ON ALL KNOTS TO JOIN
HEAVENS SAKE. ASAP.
GOD SPEED.
BT

Ingram passed the message to Tyler Childers on his right. To Jonathan Grout, the operations officer, he asked, "Jon, we have an op ord for something called SEVENTH INNING?"

To Ingram's surprise, Grout replied, "We do, captain. It's for what's going on now on Vella LaVella."

"Retaking the island?" replied Ingram.

"Exactly, Skipper. We're pushing the Japs out. The U.S. Army is driving up the East side—"

"I thought the Japs were out of there," Ingram interrupted.

"Yessir. Most of them, that is. This is supposed to be a mop up. Two, maybe three thousand are all the Japs have left. New Zealanders are pushing up the West side. They're all supposed to meet at the north end, shake hands with the Zealanders and sing *For Auld Lang Syne.*"

Childers handed him the message.

Grout scanned it quickly." Looks like we're putting it to them, except I don't think they'll take it lying down."

"Meaning?"

"Meaning, as I recall, our covering force is only three cans." Others groaned as Grout slapped the message with the back of his hand. "We make it four."

Eckert groaned with, "They're scraping the bottom of the barrel with us." He passed the message to the man next to him. Guy Huber, the gunnery officer, who would read, initial and pass it on until it went around the table.

There were a couple of snickers.

Ingram cut it short with a dark look. "We're outnumbered."

"We don't know," replied Grout.

"That's right, " said Ingram. "The message says nine destroyers. But we don't have size and shapes yet."

They both nodded. There were no coast watcher's reports yet. They came in about this time and were usually accurate. "We need the coasties," said Ingram.

He checked his watch. "Okay. Department heads meet here in ten minutes. The rest of you, check your GQ stations and equipment for readiness. No movie tonight. We'll rendezvous with HEAVEN'S SAKE in about two and a half hours. Snoopers may be about so let's go to GQ within the next half hour."

To Grout, Ingram said, "Jump over to CIC and get us a course to steer for area 143. Then pick up your op order and charts and let's figure this stuff out."

Grout quickly rose and headed out the door. "Yes, sir. Give me three minutes."

"Three minutes," Ingram said.

The others looked at him, some with mouths agape. Ingram said, "Welcome to World War Two, gentlemen. Get used to it. No movie tonight. Boo hoo." He clapped his hands. "Okay. Get to it. In case you didn't know it, you are dismissed."

"Yes, sir," they muttered in unison. Chairs scraped as they got up and crowded out the wardroom door.

Grout was back at the doorway. "Course to steer for area 143 is two-three-seven, skipper."

"Very well, thank you."

There was a telephone handset at the captain's place at the end of the wardroom table. Ingram grabbed and yanked it from its bracket and jabbed the button marked **BRIDGE**.

Childers, sitting next to him, cast a baleful eye.

The bridge phone squawked in Ingram's ear, "Bridge—Buckner speaking."

"Leon. This is the captain."

"Yessir."

"Course change to two-three-seven. Speed change to eighteen."

"Understand course two-three-seven, speed eighteen. Now sir?"

"Affirmative."

"Aye, aye, sir. Will do. Bridge out."

Ingram jammed the phone in its bracket. "I hope we're ready."

Childers said, "Nine Jap destroyers to four of us? Nice odds, huh?"

Ingram stood and looked out the port. "Rain squalls, twelve, maybe fifteen knots of wind, complete dark soon. They won't be able to see us until they get a lot closer. Meantime," he twirled a finger over his head and returned to his chair, "we got this thing called radar. So, we have the advantage."

Childers growled, "We had that advantage at Savo."

Ingram took his seat and sipped coffee. "Right. And we pissed it away. Not this time, and not on my watch."

Childers scooted back, his chair scraping, "Permission to lay below?" He stood.

"Where you going Tyler? I need you up here."

"Paperwork."

"Paperwork? Screw the paperwork. We're going into battle."

Childers rubbed his chin. "Helps me relax. I feel jumpy."

"You? The fleet boxing champion, jumpy?"

Childers planted his fists on his hips and threw a stare.

Ingram tried to fix a grin but did a bad job of it. "To tell the truth, I feel exactly the same. Always do at this point of the game. My hands shake." He held up his hands. Shaky, but not really noticeable.

Childers grunted and held out his hands, palms down. There was the slightest tremor.

They grinned.

"Okay, you got me," said Childers. "Just don't tell anybody."

Ingram said, "Your secret is safe with me."

"I wonder."

Ingram gave a quick laugh. "Go on. Do your stupid paperwork. But I want you in CIC when we join up with HEAVENS SAKE."

"Thanks, boss." Childers walked out.

34

6 October 1943
Operations Hut, First Marine Reconnaissance Squadron
Camp Crocodile. Henderson Field (CACTUS)
Guadalcanal, Solomon Islands.

Gilroy Hitchcock was not happy. Three days ago, he'd been officially retired from the United States Marine Corps, effective 3 October 1943. He'd sent a telegram to Lolli, had the other Lolli gassed and inspected, and marched out to perform his last official act: Fly his beloved TBF to Noumea, and sign it over to the USMC aircraft pool there for, presumably, further duties as a reconnaissance aircraft.

Not on your life, Hitchcock knew.

Lolli was temperamental. Even with a new engine she would be moody. No longer was she suited for combat or even long-range recon missions. Like the great old lady that she was, *Lolli* was just too unpredictable for all that. Thus, *Lolli's* last choice was in the recon pool of broken ships. Flying people and favors around the Solomons. Faithfully, she carried everything from captains and colonels to Lifebuoy soap, to Lucky Strike cigarettes, to Johnnie Walker Scotch, to Curries ice cream to whatever was required to keep the boys happy.

But now, she had this new Wright R-2600 Cyclone engine, the best kept secret at Cactus. Still, she would be like a drunken old lady. One had to know how to treat her right. All Hitchcock needed was clearance to Noumea.Then *Lolli* was somebody else's problem.

So Hitchcock fumed as he camped out in the operations hut, smoking cigars and the occasional cigarette, as rain pounded outside keeping everything grounded. The visibility was near zero. The airfield was closed. First it was fog and now, this damn rain.

He'd just about worn a path in the ancient wooden floor of the ops hut but they still wouldn't give him clearance to Noumea. The weather was terrible en route they told him. There probably wasn't enough gas to buck it all the way.

They'd given him a pass to have chow with the officers. But their food wasn't much better. And the officers looked at him, a stranger, with disdain. Hitchcock barely held off the impulse to give each and every one of them the finger when they cast a glance at him. They read Hitchcock's face which said: *The feeling is mutual you bastards. I'm retired. So go stick it.*

And now, it was early afternoon. A quick look outside told him the rain had moderated. It was more like a downpour than a fire hydrant out of control. He looked around. Maybe...

A tap on his shoulder.

It was major Alfred Nicholson, the base ops officer. One couldn't ignore big Al. With a large beer belly, bald, and a handlebar moustache, Nicholson was six three and was about two and a half pounds short of being classified hopelessly overweight. Yet Hitchcock knew him well; they'd gotten drunk together a few times. As base operations officer, Big Al was good at what he did.

"Huh?"

"Hitch, I gotta deal for you."

"Kiss my ass."

"You haven't heard me out."

"Go pound sand. I'm retired, in case you didn't know."

Nicholson waved a packet of papers. "Look, asshole. I can waive your retirement for seventy-two hours and give you a five-hundred-dollar bonus. It's all signed by General Vandergrift."

"Huh?"

"All you need to do is to fly a recon mission up to Bougainville."

"Five hundred bucks?"

"Look, the weather is clearing between here and Bougainville. But between here and Noumea it's still awful. It'll be a few more hours before we let anyone into that area. But, by the time you return, it will most likely have cleared and you will be on your way to Noumea."

"I dunno."

Nicholson scratched his head. "What the hell is in Noumea, by the way?"

"If you only knew." He paused. "What kind of mission?"

Nicholson walked him over to a wall of maps. He pointed. "Bougainville, east side. Nine Jap cans out of Rabaul coming down to interrupt our invasion of Vella LaVella. We need pictures."

"Why me? Where is everybody?"

"Out on assignment. This job belonged to Gordie Watson. But his engine conked on takeoff from Munda. He stacked it and—"

"Good God. Not Gordie. Is he...will he...?"

"Broken leg. He'll be okay. His photographer is one hundred percent. So...Nobody is left. We need..."

Hitchcock threw a thumb to his chest. "Me? You're scraping the bottom of the barrel."

Nicholson jammed his hands to his hips. "That's true, Hitch." The corners of his mouth turned up.

"I promised Lolli. I just sent her a telegram."

"Who's Lolli?"

"My girlfriend. She lives in Noumea."

"Oh, so this is all about nookie?"

Hitchcock snarled, "Back off Nick. She's my main event. I'm gonna be a Dad. I wanna do things right."

Nicholson nodded slightly and took a half step back. "I'm sorry. We really need this. Look, I'll throw in a couple hundred bucks. Cash. How 'bout it?"

Silence.

"Hitch?"

"Keep your cash and stick it up your ass."

"Aw fer—"

"I said keep your cash. I'll do it. Just make sure you have plenty of gas and a pot of coffee when I get back."

It's yours."

———————

Hitchcock was airborne thirty minutes later. According to orders, Hitchcock flew fifty feet off the deck. With him was Tommy Fowler, a six-three bean-pole with an enormous Adam's apple. But he was still a regular Marine with straight blond hair stuffed under a utility cap. He'd brought along three cameras and a large case of film magazines. They wore headphones but things were quiet. The kid was a corporal. He seemed to know his stuff but spoke in monosyllables.

Okay, figured Hitchcock. Not my job to entertain the little bastard. They reached Munda an hour later, refueled and then took off for Bougainville. It was then that Hitchcock discovered why Fowler had been so quiet.

The intercom buzzed with, "Wh...wh...ere, we...g-g-g-goin' sir?"

The kid stuttered, *How the hell did he get into the Marine Corps?* " Bougainville. Didn't they tell you?"

"Bougainville? That p...pla...place is full of Japs."

"We're lookin' for Jap ships, Tommy. Nine Jap cans coming down from Rabaul to intercept our guys off Vella LaVella. Meanwhile, that's why we are on the deck. Less chance of them spotting us down here. At the same time, they gave me a course to steer that should pretty much put us on target," Hitchcock checked the control panel clock, "Another twenty minutes or so. So keep a sharp eye out. Got your stuff ready?"

"You bet, Gunny."

Fowler sounded a little better. "What do you have there, anyway?"

"It...it...itsa lil sweet...sweetheart of a camera." Wind in the cockpit. The passenger compartment canopy had been modified so the passenger could crank it back.

"What's it do?"

"Everything ex...ex...goddamnit, except wash your underwear."

"Huh?"

"It's a F...F...Fairchild...F-1 rap...rapid action...semiauto...auto, goddammit...semi-automatic."

"No shit?" Hitchcock had no idea what Fowler was talking about. But he surely had seemed to come alive.

"Great for oblique photography."

"What is oblique photography?" He squinted. Something ahead. He pulled back on the stick to gain a little altitude. One hundred feet. There. He spotted it. Coming right at him. Good God. It couldn't be.

Fowler's voice sounded like an NBC radio announcer. Clearly he said, "An oblique photograph is one which has been taken with the camera axis directed at an inclination to the ground whereupon—"

"Uh, Fowler."

"Yes, Gunny?"

"There's a ship coming up on our port side."

"J...J...Japs, already?"

"Not so lucky, Fowler. This is one of ours. In fact, I've spent time on her."

They looked off their left wing. It was a destroyer, a bone in her teeth —making speed, maybe twenty-five knots. The numerals '504' stood out on her bow. "She looks p...p...pretty n...n...goddamit, new. A *Fletcher* class?"

"That she is, Fowler. That she is." *Lolli* swooped past and Hitchcock rolled into a left bank to circle the ship. "She's the U.S.S. *Dunagan*."

"D...D...Dunagan?"

"That Irish enough for you?"

"H...Hol...Godammit...Holland. My mother was Dutch. My dad was American as far as I know."

Hitchcock guessed, "He's gone now?"

"K..k...killed on an oil rig in Texas."

"I'm sorry."

"He was a drunk. I was only four."

"Oh."

"Lookit that." Fowler said. "White smoke coming out of the stack. What do you think is wrong?"

Hitchcock eased in some flap and cut the throttle back, dropping their speed to 105 knots. "Nothing wrong, Tommy."

"Sir?"

"That's steam coming out of the whistle mounted atop the forward stack. They're saluting us." Time to check in. He reached for the telegraph key and tapped out a quick position report. He added that they were flying over the *Dunagan* headed south at high speed.

They were abeam of the ship. Fowler was clicking off shots on his F-1. "N...n...goddammit, nice ship."

Hitchcock cranked back his canopy. "Think I'll give them the finger."

"Hold on, Hitchcock."

"I'm just kidding."

"I'm not so sure. You give them the finger and I'm getting off of this piece of shit."

Hitchcock grinned. This kid was going to be okay. He clamped the stick between his knees, raised his clasped hands over his head and waved. Passing slowly, he looked down to see sailors on the deck, the bridge, in gun tubs, and depth charge racks, waving and jumping up and down.

He called, "That better, Tommy?"

He'd seen it so many times. The southern tip of Bougainville Island with its jungle growing down to the water's edge. Hitchcock could almost smell it in the cockpit, so calming, so peaceful. And Bougainville was flanked off their left wing by Mono Island, a lonely volcanic throwaway twenty-five miles distant. Closer ahead were Shortland and Fauro Islands, sentinels to Bougainville, who thrust her volcanic peaks high into the waning afternoon. Off to the northeast was Choiseul Island, the one-time destination for *Dunagan*. Hitchcock wondered what happened to her, why she was headed south at such a high speed.

And yes. Up ahead, between Shortland and Fauro, he picked out a wisp of smoke; a column of ships steaming at high speed due south. He tapped out a quick contact report to Guadalcanal.

Target in sight. "Hey, Fowler. Get off your ass and load your camera. Target straight ahead."

"Oh, yeah? Where?"

"Your twelve 'o'clock. Straight ahead. Scoot up and look over my shoulder. Column of Jap ships. The Tokyo Express. Hurry up and get your shots. Looks like our boys are in for a hot time tonight. We're making one pass and then that's it. Then we blast on home. They'll need these pictures."

"Okay. Wait...uh, sheeeeyat. Lookee that. A bunch of 'em."

"Should be nine."

"Jeepers."

"All right. I'm going into a left bank and—"

Smoke. Chaos. Parts and shrapnel flew. The windscreen ahead blackened with oil. Hitchcock glanced off to his left to see them coming right at him. Out of the sun for a deflection shot. Three of them. Zeros. Their wings winking with 20 millimeter cannon fire.

A muffled scream back aft.

"Good God!" The stick was heavy. *Lolli* didn't respond.

Flames erupted from the engine. They'd been at fifty feet. Now, they were going in.

Hitchcock chopped the throttle. It didn't matter. The three-bladed prop jerked to a stop. The engine was dead. They were close to the water, maybe ten feet.

Hitchcock yelled, "Hang on, Tommy, we're going in." He held her off as long as he could. Fortunately, the water was smooth, slight white capping, maybe ten or twelve knots of wind.

I can do this. I love you, Lolli.

Her forward section afire, Lolli touched once, bounced, came back down where her right wing dug in, spinning the two men. Finally, the TBF jerked to a stop. Sizzling. Her flames extinguished.

Hitchcock blinked himself awake. The cockpit was flooding. Fast. He unbuckled and jumped out and onto the port wing. His fingers wouldn't follow his commands as he sobbed and yanked at the fasteners to the life raft locker. The little hatch became undone and the bright yellow life raft easily snaked out of the locker. Lolli's tail rose in the air. She prepared for her last plunge, this one down into the Solomon Sea. His fingers found the

CO^2 inflation cord. He yanked. Emitting a shrill whistle, the raft quickly inflated.

He had to look in there to see if...to see if Fowler was still alive...to maybe rescue whatever was left. It was his job. He turned and looked. A mass of redness coated the inside of the mid cockpit. What used to be corporal Tommy Fowler was something else. Completely unrecognizable. A gigantic lump of redness. Hamburger. For years, he would wish he hadn't looked.

The TBF slid under nose first. Hitchcock fell into the raft as the plane sank beneath him. He wished he hadn't looked.

35

6 October 1943
Operations Hut, First Marine Reconnaissance Squadron
Camp Crocodile. Henderson Field (CACTUS)
Guadalcanal, Solomon Islands

Beginning on 15 August, American and New Zealand ground forces had landed on the south coast of Vella LaVella Island. After fighting their way up, all that remained were about one thousand Japanese, initially squeezed into a mid-eastern cape called Lambu Lambu. But they had fought their way out of that and were now concentrated in the northern section of Vella LaVella in an area labeled Marquana Bay. Facing almost directly north, Marquana Bay looked more and more like it was going to be a pick-up point.

This was confirmed early this morning, when coast watchers on New Britain Island reported nine Japanese destroyers departing Rabaul Harbor and shaping course due south at high speed. Later, around mid-day, coast watchers overlooking Buin Harbor on Bougainville radioed in that sub-chaser type craft and the smaller *Daihatsu* one-hundred-foot barges were getting underway and heading south.

To planners on Admiral Halsey's staff, it became clear these ships comprised a relief column headed south to evacuate Vella LaVella.

From the trenches of newly won territory on Vella LaVella, to smoke-filled meeting rooms on Guadalcanal, Noumea, and Pearl Harbor, it was time to get serious.

———

"Anything from Hitchcock, Al?" It was General Vandergrift, on his way back to his office.

He'd caught Major Al Nicholson hunched over a Solomon Islands chart with two plotters. Coffee cups were scattered next to an ashtray, once the brass base of a five-inch powder case, now overflowing with cigarette butts. The temperature in the room was tolerable this day for a change. They'd had scattered thundershowers all afternoon. Windows were open helping to cool the place and disperse cigarette smoke.

They were getting ready for what was shaping up to be the main event off the northern coast of Vella LaVella Island.

Big Al bit the tip off the end of a cigarillo, spit it out, and faced General Vandergrift. "Wish I had better news on Hitchcock. Yes, it's been over an hour now."

"Busted radio?"

"Most likely, General. Something's always going wrong with that piece of junk."

"Maybe he ran out of booze," quipped Vandergrift.

"Or broads," Nicholson tossed back.

They laughed.

Vandergrift walked off, "Well, let me know when you hear."

Nicholsen got his cigarillo going and puffed smoke. "Yes, sir."

———

At 1645 that afternoon, *Dunagan* caught up with commander Frank Walker, commodore of Destroyer Squadron 4, who was riding in the USS *Selfridge*

(DD 357). Ingram stayed on the bridge taking dinner in his captain's chair on the starboard wing—junkyard spaghetti they called it. And yet, he knew there was plenty of protein and nutrients to keep him going.

Walker was pleased Ingram had shown up and displayed his pleasure by bombarding the *Dunagan* with lengthy messages by signal light.

Much of it was communications schedules and organizational blather. After paging through it all he signed off with the understanding Walker was saying, '*You are new to our group, are basically unaware of our squadron doctrine and procedures. So, just keep station 1000 yards astern of me and don't do anything unless I tell you to.*'

They were stepping from rain squall to rain squall with the temperature still in the high eighties. Each shower had given the ship a clean wash down, and also brought with it the smell of land with gardenia and other exotic flowers; in this case, those of Vella LaVella.

Tired. The spaghetti had done more than its job. He eased from the captain's chair on the starboard bridge wing intending to sneak a half-hour nap at his sea cabin, just steps away.

"Excuse me, captain."

"Huh"?

It was Chief Radioman Harry O'Toole, from radio central. He carried a clipboard. His face was dark, businesslike, not friendly. He handed over the clipboard.

"Very well." Ingram was in the process of bracing himself for bad news. But he hadn't got all the way there when he read:

BT
FLASH
TOP SECRET
TO: HAYSTACK
FROM: BARN DOOR
INFO: A) HEAVENS SAKE
RECON TBF TO BOUGAINVILLE FLOWN BY G HITCHCOCK
OVERDUE AND PRESUMED LOST.
DUMBO DISPATCHED TO LAST KNOWN POSIT.

HE WAS THE BEST.
BT

Ingram felt a cold sheet of ice wrap itself around him. He looked up to O'Toole's eyes.

The chief radioman's face reflected the news. *He's lost, nothing I can do.*

Ingram asked, "The exec seen this?"

"Not yet, captain."

"Okay. Chief. No reply. A sad trip for you. XO is next. Normal distribution after that. Then, go have a cup of coffee."

"Thank you. sir."

"You're welcome." Ingram raised his voice to Guy Huber, the OOD now on the open bridge. "Mr. Huber?"

"Yes, sir."

"I'll be in my sea cabin,"

"Aye, aye, captain."

It seemed to Ingram that a deathly calm had swept over the bridge crew. It was obvious the word had already circulated. Sound powered phones were the culprit. Huber knew about it. The bridge watch was connected to radio central.

Ingram toyed with announcing it on the PA system. But no, word would get around quickly. He'd let the jungle telegraph do its dirty work first. Then, in a half hour or so, he'd make the announcement. In the meantime, he called for another cup of coffee.

Hitchcock, gone. That crazy bastard. He'd just flown circles around the *Dunagan* just a few minutes ago. And now...

Gone.

––––––––––––

Hitchcock's stomach rumbled. Coffee. He yearned for it.

And out here, on the open ocean, with only the southern tip of Short-land Island off to the northwest, and Mono Island, shrouded in mist way off to the west. Mono was about twenty miles, he judged. Which way to paddle? Japs were most likely on Shortland Island. Nobody on Mono Island, so he'd heard. But so damned far.

Fowler. He was beginning to enjoy that kid. And then those Japs, three of them, poured all that twenty millimeter into *Lolli*. Target practice. She was a pin cushion. He didn't see them coming out of the late afternoon sun. Fowler torn to some unrecognizable glob of flesh mixed with patches of soaked uniform.

Hamburger.

Wish I hadn't looked.

And here I am, untouched. What the hell happened?

Why didn't he feel survivor's guilt? He didn't. Except for extreme sorrow for Fowler, he was happy to be alive. For Lolli. *That must be it. She's waiting. Don't screw around, Hitch. Gotta do this right.*

Inventory: He patted his pockets. Stiletto, a push of a button goes a long way. He fished it out and pushed the button. CLICK! The long sharp blade snapped out, seemingly at the speed of light, maybe a little slower. But yes, It was good. What else? Keys. Wallet, a photo of Lolli. She was gorgeous. A tin of rubbers. He always carried them. But since he'd met Lolli, he hadn't used them for anyone else. He kept them around from habit. A soaked handkerchief. A pair of sunglasses in his top pocket. Amazing. They were drenched, but he put them on,

He patted under his left arm. His M 1911 .45 caliber pistol was safely tucked there. Seven rounds were in the magazine and there were two more magazines on his belt.

The life raft: a three man. Plenty of room. In pockets, he found: two eight-ounce tins of water, a signaling mirror, some chocolate bars, a pack of dye markers, a flare gun, fishing kit, air pump and patching kit. Last, he found a pair of pliers, a light canvas shade and two aluminum oars in two parts each.

Ah. He assembled the oars, jammed them in the locks, and started rowing. Looking over his left shoulder, he found Mono Island. Maybe take me all night, he figured, but what other choices do I have? Plus, the Japs don't have me for target practice at night. Gotta get there.

Lots of time to think about Lolli. And maybe some names for the kid: Pierre? Jacques? Gabriel?

And for a girl? He liked Annette, Janine, and Marie. He rolled the names on his tongue. Breathing easily, he hummed *Frère Jacques* between strokes.

Jacques if a boy. But what if it's a girl?

Janine? He liked the name. It sounded wholesome, happy, playful. Working up a sweat he rowed toward Mono Island.

Janine.

That's who it'll be.

36

6 October 1943
S 7° 19.2' E 155° 54.6'
Mono Island to the West
Solomon Sea

As always in the tropics, that great door of sunlight slammed shut at 6:33 this evening, give or take a few minutes. A pale quarter moon clambered over the horizon to the east giving view to a flat, calm, sea for Hitchcock to row. Mono Island, barely outlined to the west, looked a little closer and he estimated he'd made two or three miles from where *Lolli* had sunk.

But shortly after sunset, he felt a vibration, then a low, muted rumble. Not knowing what it was, he rowed faster and faster.

The rumble rose a bit, then steadied. Soon, against the backdrop of Choiseul Island behind him, he saw ships...destroyers, yes, Japanese destroyers, two of them, with raked stacks, slipping past, about two miles directly astern, heading south.

Doing ten, maybe twelve knots.

But destroyers are powered by steam turbines and those don't rumble. What the hell is going on?

The source became apparent as smaller craft ghosted by: sub chasers, patrol boats, and landing craft, about four in each category.

That explained the rumble. They were driven by diesel engines, straining against the night, headed for Vella LaVella.

An hour later Hitchcock saw something else. Seven more Japanese destroyers with raked stacks, low to the water, creeping past. Their speed was also about the same: ten to twelve knots.

I'll be damned. It added up.

It was a relief column. That's why Halsey and Vandergrift wanted pictures. The Japanese objective was Vella LaVella and the American flag officers wanted photographs of what our people were up against. Nine destroyers all together. That's what the coast watchers had reported.

Those nine Jap cans got underway from Rabaul early this morning. And I was supposed to be there. A wave of remorse hit Hitchcock as he thought about his mission, and then Lolli, and then the other Lolli—the real one.

And then Fowler.

His shoulders slumped.

Should have been more vigilant. Too busy doping off and thinking of Lolli. My fault. Little bastards. They came right out of the sun. Should have known better.

Hitchcock called to the night. "The Tokyo Express srikes again."

Smart. These Japs knew their trade. Not a light was showing on those ships. It hit him that was what Ingram was doing this afternoon. It was obvious he'd been pulled off the Choiseul operation and sucked into that mess. Krulak would have to go it alone with just the *Conway* while Ingram headed south to help oppose the Japs.

God Speed, Todd.

Ingram was having similar thoughts. They cruised in a modified diamond formation

with *Selfridge* as formation guide, with captain Frank Walker, commodore of destroyer squadron 4, embarked in the center. *Chevalier* was on the left wing and *O'Bannon* steamed on the right. As Ingram anticipated,

Dunagan was assigned to a station 1,000 yards directly aft of the *Selfridge* as guide. With Vella LaVella ten miles to starboard, they cruised on a northerly course at a leisurely ten knots.

It struck Ingram that the crew had long since been fed and it was time to get

ready. He turned to Guy Huber, the OOD, "Okay, Guy. Set general quarters."

"Aye, aye, captain." It was 2235 when Huber called into the pilothouse to the boatswain mate of the watch. "Caldwell, sound general quarters."

"Yessir." Caldwell stepped to the 1 MC and flipped all the switches. His voice resonated throughout the ship and across the water. "Now general quarters. General quarters. All hands man your battle stations. This is not a drill. Set condition zebra. This is not a drill."

Yanking up their pants, men growled and ran down the decks, up ladders, and shoved aside hapless stragglers as they got their GQ station ready. Many didn't tie their shoes until they were on station and accounted for. The bridge watch was already on site and rapidly changed places with the helmsman, lee helmsman, and quartermaster of the watch. Caldwell was already GQ boatswain mate of the watch and took his place in the pilothouse against the aft bulkhead where a number of controls were positioned.

Ingram felt their urgency as Lutz, already beside him, donned his sound powered phones, and, with a grease pencil, began checking off ready reports on a bulkhead mounted status board.

But the crew was on top of it. Before GQ was sounded, many were at their stations, ready to jump in and take over.

And now, manned and ready reports buzzed into Lutz's earphones nearly at the speed of light. Furiously, he checked off stations, told others to slow down, but patiently got them sorted out and posted them on his chart.

The ship slithered through a rain squall. The water was warm, almost refreshing. And it ran down the bulkhead-mounted chart. Among the drops, Lutz crossed a 'T' with a flourish and announced, "All stations manned and ready, captain."

Ingram thumbed his stopwatch; three minutes and twenty-two seconds.

He held it up, looked at Lutz, and gave an appreciative nod. "Very well," he added.

And then, he looked out into the squall as if he could see what the evening offered. But he really couldn't. Weeks before, in Vella Gulf, he enjoyed the luxury of essentially being a bystander. Of not taking the consequences of his decisions, of not having to suffer what may happen to his ship and to his men if he bungled the job. Worse, if he just broke down and said nothing. Before, on Corregidor, he had seen such men. And they were terrible examples of command. Just poorly selected men who could not make up their mind. That was the worse thing, doing or saying nothing. Allowing the enemy to blast a ship from beneath their feet. He only hoped that if it came to that, that he would be killed so that he would not have to look anyone in the eye.

The bridge phone buzzed. Ingram yanked it from its bracket. "Captain."

It was Tyler Childers. "How you doin' boss?"

Ingram had been aboard the *Dunagan* long enough to understand Tyler's vulnerabilities. Childers sounded good. *What about me*, he thought. He hoped he would do the same. Yes, Childers sounded good. Ready to jump in the ring and start swinging. Like a prize fight. Tyler knows all about that.

"Hello?" Childers demanded.

Ingram said, "I said it's the Sailor's lament."

"Which is?"

"Can't stand all this damned waiting."

"I see. Well, we have something down here on the air search radar to get your juices going."

37

6 October 1943
USS *Dunagan* (DD 504)
S 7° 36.0' E 156° 14.0'
Ten miles north of Vella LaVella Island
Solomon Sea

Ingram's heart skipped a beat. In truth, he wondered if he was really ready for this. *Navy Cross winner my foot. Phony for sure. Relax, Todd.* "Life is a bitch," he said to Childers.

"What's wrong?"

"Popcorn machine is busted." Actually, after blowing out fuses, it had been on the fritz for the past two days."

"I'd let you use ours, but then my guys in here would kill me."

"Like I said, life is a bitch."

"You said it, boss."

Ingram felt a little bit better. Actually, he was glad the popcorn machine was out of use on the bridge. Too much of a distraction from some very important tasks. Ingram intended to leave it that way. He said, "Okay, whatcha got, Tyler?"

"We have fuzzy contacts off the air search radar. Looks like two groups of ships coming down from Bougainville. Estimated speed is twenty-two knots. Two columns. Side by side. One group of six and the other of three. Gotta be those Jap tin cans coming down to fish out their troops. Smart money says they are headed for Marquana Bay right behind us."

"Just about where we thought."

"Yes, sir. And now, some better news."

"Please proceed,"

A CIC loudspeaker blared. The phone screeched.

"Hey!" Ingram barked.

Childers rattled off a string of highly colored language at someone. The loud screeching and chatter stopped. Childers said, "Sorry, Boss. We're trying to bring up a secondary circuit."

"Uh-huh."

Childers continued. "Halsey and Vandergrift are sending up some players to help out."

"Who do you say?"

"You know. These are the guys who run the show down here in good old SoPac."

"Oh, those guys. What are they sending?"

"Four corsairs, two helldivers and two dumbos. All night if we need them."

"Great news, Tyler. Let's hope they put down a Jap or two."

Childers went on, "And it looks like the two Jap columns are beginning to paint on the surface search radar. You should see it on your repeater up there. Lots of little stuff swirling around, too."

"Maybe barges?"

"That would be my guess."

"Then, that's the main event."

"Right."

"Except we have to get by nine Jap cans to get at them."

"Could get ugly."

Just then the loudspeaker in CIC went loud again, louder than before. Ingram and the rest of the bridge watch heard it blast up from CIC two decks below. On top of that was Childers screaming.

The noise stopped. Childers stopped. With a wheeze, he said, "Sorry boss. That's the new kid, Pelligrino, a radarman striker. He's a genius with electronics. Really good on radar repeater maintenance. He'll go a long way."

"I can tell by the sound of it right now."

Childers laughed, "I hate yelling at him. Don't like to dampen his enthusiasm."

"Better keep him away from the radio gear for the time being."

"He was getting ahead of his game. Trying to patch in PriTac and SecTac and got it all screwed up."

"But you're all straightened out for now."

"Well, we're trying..."

"Talk to you later, Tyler." Ingram hung up.

He shouted into the pilot house for the boatswain's mate of the watch. "Griswold!"

"Sir."

"Please go on the 1 MC and tell the crew the captain will be speaking momentarily."

"Aye, aye, Captain."

Griswold stepped up to the 1 MC, flipped all the switches. His voice echoed throughout the ship as he announced, "Attention all hands. Stand by for an announcement from the captain." He stepped back just as Ingram walked up. He nodded to the mic and mouthed, It's all yours, captain."

Ingram stood close and said, "This is the captain. I want to belay some of the rumors flying around the ship and confirm others. With the other tin cans you see out there, the Selfridge, the Chevalier, and the O'Bannon, we are going to intercept a column of nine Jap destroyers who are steaming to Vella LaVella, the island you see on our starboard beam. They intend to relieve their troops there and bring them back to Rabaul. Yes, you heard me correctly. There are nine Jap destroyers who are screening a bunch of sub chasers and landing barges bent on evacuating their troops from the island. A couple of thousand people, we're told. Well, we're going to stop them. And don't worry about nine Jap destroyers. We have the advantage. Radar. We can see at night and in the fog where they can't. Thus we believe our chances are very good, their numerical superiority notwithstanding. So this is where all our drill and practice will pay off.

Just do your duty. Do what you have trained so well to do, and I can tell you, we have nothing to worry about. Most of all I want to tell you I'm proud to serve with you. Your improvement over the past few weeks has been most impressive. Now, it's our turn to meet those Japs and let them have it. That is all."

Ingram moved away and Griswold stepped in, gave a smile and a nod, and clicked off for him.

He stepped out to the starboard bridgewing, Lutz following closely. It was quiet, deadly quiet on the bridge. Everyone knew the basics. Four of us versus nine of them. But the nine were split into two groups: two Japanese destroyers were swarming around the ten or so small contacts. The landing barges intended to swoop in and rescue their contingent near Marquana Bay at Vella LaVella's north end. A side show was the Japanese Rufe float planes dropping navigation and illumination flares for their destroyers. Occasionally, light would flicker and one could momentarily see a silhouette at fifteen thousand yards or so, as the groups converged.

Walker kept the diamond formation intact. A thousand yards ahead was *Selfridge,* barely distinguishable by her wake. Likewise, the wakes of the *Cavalier* and *O'Bannon*, on either beam stood out, most of it visible by the eerier whitish green foam from plankton.

Suddenly, Lutz keyed his sound-powered mic and said, "Bridge aye." He turned to Ingram and reported. "Combat is telling us two Nips peeled off and are now on a westerly heading."

Walker came up on the primary net bridge loudspeaker, "*Toby, this is Santa Claus. X-ray peter three zero. I say again, X-ray peter three zero, standby, execute. Santa Claus, out.*" Ingram checked the radar; Walker was increasing formation speed to thirty knots. It looked like he wanted to chase down these two destroyers which looked like they were retiring.

Ingram felt better about things. If so, this was lining up to be an easy shot. He called to Jonathan Grout standing amidship on the open bridge, "Jon, you got that? Thirty knots."

"You bet captain, but I'd like to wait another half minute to make sure we have full superheat."

Ingram was incredulous. "It wasn't all the way up?"

"They finally kicked it in about three minutes ago."

"Okay, we'll have to work on that, meantime, give me turns for twenty-five knots.

We'll go up to thirty when the boys in the engineering department finish doing their fingernails."

"Aye, aye, captain." Grout called through the porthole to Rogers on the lee-helm, "All engines ahead full; make two-five-zero turns for twenty-five knots."

But then Walker called in a course change to the group—a change that would take them among the six Japanese destroyers. He followed that up with a signal to engage the enemy on the starboard side with torpedoes and gunfire. Ingram recalled the last reported course and speed for the six enemy destroyers was one-five-zero speed twenty. Wow! They would soon be closing at a rate of forty-five knots, soon to be fifty knots.

He called up to Guy Huber, the gunnery officer standing on the navigation bridge just above him. "Guy?"

"Captain." He raised his binoculars.

"Do you have any targets?'

"Bunch of them out there, sir. We're not wanting."

"How so?"

"Torpedo one has a solution for the lead Jap can."

"Amazing."

Huber continued, "The Japs are illuminating themselves with all those stupid navigation floats. Director 51 is locked on another Jap can at twelve thousand yards."

Ingram said, "Can you see any other Jap cans?"

His reply was, "Combat is giving us good information, but we have yet to lock one up. Still trying."

"Well, have at it. It's important."

"Don't I know it, skipper. We all do."

"Okay, Guy. Batteries released. Stand by to open up. I think that will come momentarily."

"I'll put a man right on it, captain." All the time his eyes were glued to his binoculars.

Ingram grinned. *Wise ass.*

Lutz stood close. "Combat reports torpedoes in the water."

Just then, the loudspeaker crackled stridently. *"Toby, this is Santa Claus. Turn nine. I say again, turn nine. Stand by, execute."*

Ingram called over, "You have that, Mr. Grout?"

Grout grabbed onto the pilothouse porthole ledges and called through, "Right fifteen degrees rudder. Steady up on course zero-one-zero."

Ingram was satisfied to hear the Bentley acknowledge the order and put his rudder over. At the high speed of thirty knots, *Dunagan* heeled sharply to port, her fantail beginning to slide around as she followed, the other destroyers in a ninety degree turn to starboard. Walker had put them into this turn to meet the Japanese torpedoes head-on. Thus they would 'comb their wakes' presenting far less of a target.

Ingram nodded. The Japanese had opened fire first by launching those deadly type 93 torpedoes: thirty feet long, capable of fifty knots, their warheads were packed with one thousand pounds of Torpex. How many? Who knows? With six destroyers, the Japs could have launched twenty to thirty torpedoes. He did some quick math, about four and a half minutes to get here. Anything could happen.

Huber yelled down, "What the hell happened? We had a perfect firing solution."

Ingram responded, "Sorry about that. The Japs have launched. Twenty plus torpedoes are headed toward us. We turned to comb the wakes. At the same time, we're closing the range. We'll be shooting pretty soon. Can you shift targets?"

"Yes, on torpedoes. Not so sure with the five-inch. In fact, we've lost visual contact."

Ingram looked about. Walker had taken them into a storm cell. Cooling rain splattered down to protect them from the enemy and to wash down her decks and her sailors. Ingram looked to the darkened sky. "Nice. They can't see us."

Huber said, "Good news. Directly ahead, we're still locked on a ship or two, desig mounts fifty-one, fifty-two, and fifty-three."

"Okay, Guy. Stay with it. I have a feeling we'll be shooting once we clear this rain squall."

"Sounds good to me."

"How about torpedo one? Still have a solution?"

"We have one based on dead reckoning. If Tojo stays on his same course and speed, then we should be okay."

"Let's hope that he does. Bridge out." Ingram picked up the phone and jabbed the buzzer for CIC.

"Childers."

"Tyler. We're still in this storm cell. Can't see a dammed thing. What do you have out there?"

"Sorry, Skipper. We're getting interference, too. About every three sweeps, the radar goes nuts. Don't know why. But our boys are working on it."

"What did your last good sweep tell you?"

"That we're in deep shit."

"Huh?"

"We have all these stupid torpedoes blasting toward us. We're at thirty knots for no good reason and our closing rate is about fifty-five knots."

Ingram said, "We have the best tracking equipment money can buy."

Childers gave a laugh, then said. "Don't know why I'm so happy. If one of those damn things hits us, it's lights out."

"We'll get through it."

"Do me a favor, boss?"

"Sure."

"I left a letter on my desk. If I don't make it through this mess, please make sure it gets to my Mom and Dad."

Ingram said, "I was thinking of the same thing. But I forgot to write the letter."

"I'll tell your wife you were a dumb shit but that you still love her. How's that?"

Ingram laughed.

Just then the lookout on the port side of the bridge pointed and shouted, "Jeeeez. Lookit that."

Ingram followed and saw a white foaming wake streaking toward them. It would pass clear of their port side by about twenty yards.

It zipped on by. There was a collective sigh of relief in the pilot house.

"Shiiiit. No." The lookout pointed directly ahead.

Another torpedo was streaking straight toward them.

Ingram yelled, "I have the conn. Left standard rudder."

The *Dunagan* healed over in a turn to port. The torpedo now headed directly for the ship's starboard side as she continued her turn.

Ingram watched closely and counted silently. Soon, he barked, "Shift your rudder."

Life or death. A wide-eyed Bentley hung on every syllable his skipper ordered. He knew exactly what was happening. "Shift my rudder, aye captain. With a grunt he spun the wheel. The rudder dug into the opposite setting and corrected their turn.

Seven seconds later, Ingram called, "Rudder amidships!"

Bentley crisply wheeled his rudder to zero degrees. "My rudder is amidships, captain."

"Very well," replied Ingram.

It took four seconds for the *Dunagan* to stand straight up and down and assume a straight course. The torpedo arrowed right at them.

Lutz crossed himself.

Huber at the highest vantage point on the weather decks mumbled, "Dear God."

The torpedo reached them three seconds later. And screamed down the starboard side. With eight feet to spare.

Childers came up on the 1 MC intercom. "Ingram. What the hell is going on up there?"

Ingram jabbed the switch, "Trying to fix the popcorn machine."

38

6 October 1943
USS *Dunagan* (DD 504)
S 7° 36.0' E 156° 14.0'
Ten miles north of Vella LaVella Island
Solomon Sea

Commodore Walker quickly organized his four destroyers into a column, formation course three-five-zero. With a separation of 1,000 yards, *Selfridge* was in the lead, *Chevalier* next, *O'Bannon* in third place, and *Dunagan* in the fourth slot.

Onboard *Dunagan*, it was a perfect setup. Guy Huber had his targets lined up. At 12,000 yards, he had torpedo mounts one and two trained out to starboard, ten Mark 15 torpedoes in all, ready to launch. With the column movement, all Dunagan's five-inch guns were trained to starboard and had selected Japanese destroyers out to 9,000 yards.

Ingram braced his elbows on the bulwark, binoculars in hand. The bridge was silent. The entire ship was silent. *It's our turn*, they urged.

The primary tactical loudspeaker crackled with, "Heaven's Sake, this is Hood Wink. Execute William. I say again, execute William. Out."

Ingram called up the navigation bridge. "You may launch torpedoes, Mr. Huber. Mounts one and two."

Huber called, "Gun Control aye." He turned to his talker and gave the order. The order was relayed to each of the torpedo mount captains who pulled the firing pins. Soon, each tube's impulse charge ejected a bright, silvery, mark 15 torpedo. Smoke belched from the exhaust port in the torpedoes' tail as the little turbine engine spun up to drive the deadly piece. Beneath a half-moon, sailors on the weather decks watched ten of them go, streaking toward the enemy.

Ingram stood back for a moment to catch his breath.

But the primary tactical circuit blasted again, "Heaven's Sake, this is Hood Wink. Execute Dog. I say again, execute Dog. Out."

Ingram spun and looked up to his gunnery officer. "Mr. Huber."

"Sir?"

"Are you still with me?"

"Yes, sir."

"Very well. Take the enemy under fire, Mr. Huber."

"You mean now, captain?"

"Not tomorrow, damnit, Mr. Huber. Of course I mean now. Right now. Commence fire."

Huber keyed his mic, gave the order to director 51 atop the ship. Seconds later the five, five-inch thirty-eight cannons loosed their fifty-four-pound projectiles at the enemy in ragged sequence, mount 52, its muzzle within fifteen feet of Ingram's ear got its round off first. Its CRACK nearly blew him over.

This was followed by mount 55 and mount 54 all the way back aft. Mounts 51 and 53 belched almost simultaneously after that.

"Continuous fire," Ingram called.

"Gun control aye" answered Huber. Suddenly, he looked forward and pointed. "Woah, Captain!"

Ingram raised his binoculars. A streaking wake on calm waters gave away the presence of another Japanese type 93 fifty knot torpedo heading right toward them. "I have it, Mr. Grout, I have the conn. Right standard rudder."

Bentley was ready this time. "My rudder is right standard," he answered.

"Very well."

Again, the ship leaned to port as she turned right, her fantail sliding around. In eight seconds she snapped around almost ninety degrees.

As the ship turned, the forward pointing five-inch guns kept blasting away. To Ingram and the people on the bridge, it was a world of choking cordite and incredible noise and overpressure.

Ingram called, "Rudder amidships!" He pointed to Bentley, who mouthed something back Ingram couldn't understand. But Bentley understood the order, for he whipped the rudder to zero degrees.

Nearly completing a ninety-degree turn, the *Dunagan* stood straight up and down.

In the gloom they saw the torpedo's wake as it zipped down their starboard side missing by fifteen yards.

Ingram began to think again. "Mr. Grout. You have the—"

An enormous explosion ripped the air. The sky lit up to port for two seconds as the thunderclap rolled over them. Flames and smoke billowed into the nighttime sky.

Ingram sucked in a lungful of cordite drenched air. Good God. It was the *Chevalier*. Her bow section up to her forward superstructure was gone, entirely. Fires were breaking out amidships as the hideous hulk with no bow, still under power, ploughed ahead, digging into the ocean, interior bulkheads collapsing.

Men scrambling. Men screaming. Men on fire.

Ingram rose to his feet to see fuel oil rise to the surface. Immediately, it caught fire, overwhelming the few men who had saved themselves from the conflagration aboard ship by jumping overboard. They were now swallowed up in it.

Shell splashes scattered all around the *Dunagan*. The *Chevalier's* flames were illuminating them. Making them a target.

Come on, Todd. Move it!

"Mr. Grout. Take the conn and resume formation course."

Grout didn't reply. White knuckled, his hands had a death grip on the bulwark.

A round landed thirty yards to starboard. It exploded; shrapnel showered the decks.

Ingram crawled over to a supine form. It was Ensign Anthony Hill, junior officer of the deck, unconscious. Blood flowed from a vicious cut running across his forehead.

My people are falling like ten pins. He yelled into the pilothouse, "Get a medic out here."

Chief Griswold answered, "Yes, sir."

Lutz lay on the deck, eyes blinking, looking up into darkness. Blood ran from an ear. Ingram yanked at his arm.

Lutz groaned.

"Up, come on up, son. I need you up here with me."

Lutz nodded but had trouble getting his feet beneath him.

Ingram yanked him up and braced him to the pilothouse bulkhead. "Hold on to the rail," he shouted. "You'll be okay."

Lutz said, "Gsssstuniinn."

"That's the spirit." Ingram clapped Lutz' shoulders then stepped over to Grout. He still had a steel grip on the bulwark.

Damnit. Ingram leaned in the pilothouse. "I have the conn. Left standard rudder."

"Huh?" The helmsman looked through him.

"Bentley. Get with it!"

Bently's eyes snapped into focus. "Left standard rudder, aye, captain. My rudder is left standard." He glanced down to the rudder angle indicator to double check.

Atta boy. "Very well."

He looked up to see Huber trying to stay on his feet. Ingram yelled up to him, "Guy! Mr. Huber."

"Yo."

"Cease fire."

"Huh? Now? We got 'em where we want 'em." Huber looked up. Blood ran down his face. It was obvious he couldn't see.

"Guy. We're shooting at nothing. Cease fire."

Huber wiped at his eyes and drew back a bloody hand. "Somebody got a towel? I have a bad cold."

Ingram caught the attention of Huber's talker, a tall blond-haired bean-pole. "Call cease fire, damn it. Do you understand me?"

"Y...Y...Yes, sir." The talker keyed his mic and spoke. The ship's main battery stopped shooting.

Something yanked on his sleeve. It was Grout. "I'm here, captain."

Damnit. Ingram remembered; they were in a left turn. "Rudder amid-ships," he yelled.

"My rudder is amidships," replied Bentley. Ingram looked into Grout's face. It must have been a mirror image of his own. Blackened, grease-smeared, bloody, awful.

Grout opened an eye. "I got it. I'm here captain."

Ingram reached the pilothouse and grabbed a rag off the chart table. He handed it to Grout. "Blood on your face, get rid of it, then resume formation course, three-five-zero."

"Got it, captain." Grout grabbed the rag and then dabbed at his face. He smiled at Ingram. Then his eyes rolled into the back of his head. With a groan, his knees buckled and Lieutenant Jonathon J. Grout of San Juan Capistrano, California, collapsed into a heap. That's when Ingram saw Grout's back. A nasty wound up near his right shoulder blade was bleeding heavily. A dark piece of shrapnel protruded.

"Medic!" Ingram shouted. With Griswold's help, they rolled a groaning Grout to his left shoulder and braced him to the bulkhead. Ingram looked to Griswold, "You got it, Chief?"

"You bet, captain. I'll keep with him until Tony shows up. Now you better get with it."

"Thanks, chief." Ingram rose, dashed for the handset, and jabbed CIC.

Childers was right there. "That you, captain?"

Ingram gasped, "Right Tyler. Get up here. Grout is wounded and unconscious. The JOOD is likewise out like a light. I need you to take over OOD."

"Me? What about CIC? Whose gonna do that?"

"Jack Taylor. Now get with it."

"Taylor doesn't know shit."

"They say he's qualified for command, Mr. Childers. As far as what he knows, we'll just have to find out, won't we?"

"He doesn't know shit, I said."

"Mr. Childers, I'm giving you a direct order. Come to the bridge right now and take over as officer of the deck."

Childers waited two seconds. Then, he said, "Of course. How stupid of me. I'll be right there."

"Thank you."

"Wait one, sir." Ingram heard a mumbled conversation.

"Captain?"

"What? Jack?"

Apparently, Jack Taylor had grabbed the handset. "That's right, captain. Don't worry, I'll take good care of you."

"I know you will, Jack. Now, tell Childers to get up here."

"He's gone. Faster than a speeding bullet."

"All right. And good luck, Jack. Bridge out." He jammed the phone in its bracket.

Ascending the two decks quickly, Childers rushed up, tipped a salute to Ingram with two fingers and strapped on his headphones. He said, "I have the conn, sir."

"Very well." Ingram looked out, seeing nothing but a jumble of masts and smoke and broken ships, among them, a heavily listing *Chevalier* in her death throes. He sliced a hand toward the northwest, "Formation course is supposed to be three-five-zero, but I'll be damned if anyone knows what they're doing.Tell you what. Head over to the *Chevalier* and pick up those people in the water."

"Yes, sir."

WHACK! Another flash lit up the night. Ingram looked to port. The *Selfridge*. She had just taken a Type 93 torpedo also at her starboard bow. What remained was a crumpled, tangled mess, once called a bow, now hanging off the forward part of the ship. Fires erupted amidships as men scurried about her decks. Some were on fire, a few jumped overboard.

On the *Dunagan*, a hatch clanged open on the foredeck. In the gloom, men erupted through the hatch of mount 51. They ran aft and took shelter behind the superstructure. Last one out was Benedek, the mount captain, a hulking, dark haired Hungarian, still wearing his headphones, now disconnected.

Ingram yelled down to him, "What is it?"

"Huh?" Benedek looked up and cupped his hand to his ear. Even though they had stopped shooting on the *Dunagan*, other ships were still blasting away, wildly. "Was?"

"What's wrong?" shouted Ingram.

Another stood alongside Benedek. A thin blond curly-haired gunner nodded and shouted. "Hang fire, captain. And that damned barrel is really hot. Breach block won't open. It's stuck. We can't extract."

Hot barrel. They'd been firing like crazy—as rapidly as possible, the barrel temperature notwithstanding. Something had jammed the gun's breech block. The projectile's main explosive charge, now awaiting the boosting charge to kick it out of the barrel, could 'cook off' due to the barrel's heat. The explosion would be very serious, the barrel ripping open like a giant toy cigar spewing fine shrapnel everywhere. Many could perish.

"Hang on." Ingram waved and said to Lutz. "Get Chief Dotson up to mount 51 on the double." Chief gunners mate Charley Dotson was the senior gun technician on board *Dunagan* and was assigned to main battery plot during battle stations.

Ingram yelled to Benedek, "Move your men further aft. Chief Dotson is on the way.

Benedek looked up with a toothless smile, "Yeah, yeah. Will do. Thank you, captain. "

Just then, a man in khakis blazed past Benedek, jumped onto mount 51's ladder rung and scrambled inside.

Ingram shouted, "Who was that?"

Benedek shrugged. "An officer, I dunno."

Childers jumped beside Ingram, "You're not gonna believe this."

"What?"

"That's Jack Taylor who just went into mount 51."

Incredible. Ingram stared at Childers for two seconds. This was not the same Jack Taylor who reported aboard with an unzipped fly.

Childers keyed his mic, "Conn aye." He looked over, "Beside all that, we just got a report on sectac. *O'Bannon* collided with the *Chevalier*. Hit her in the aft engine room. As if that's all she needed to stay afloat."

"No kidding." Ingram raised his binoculars to the *Chevalier*. But the smoke was so thick from the fires and the gunfire that he could only make out masts, radars twirling, and other topside clutter of two tangled ships. "It's horrible. Can't see a thing."

Just then, there was a bright flash, followed by a loud, ripping thunder-clap, from among the Japanese destroyers ten thousand yards to the north. Smoke, flames, parts, and people twirled hundreds of feet in the air.

Childers said, "Holy shit."

Ingram said, "One of ours for one of theirs. Maybe—"

He heard it coming. A round ripped through mount 51 with a 'clang'. The ship shuddered. A flash of light, smoke, cordite, parts flying, shrapnel.

Childers said. "Holy cow. Taylor was in there."

39

6 October 1943
USS *Dunagan* (DD 504)
S 7° 36.0' E 156° 14.0'
Ten miles north of Vella LaVella Island
Solomon Sea

Not so.

From main battery plot, Chief Charley Dotson had to squeeze through two small hatches to get to the main deck. He finally arrived out of breath. He dashed up behind Jack Taylor, now half dazed and sitting on the deck, legs askew. Having successfully extracted the twenty-four-pound powder case, Taylor had just jumped from the mount and, with the shell still cradled in his arms, had been blown to his butt.

A blinking Taylor looked up to Dotson and, with a lopsided grin, handed up the gleaming brass-bound powder case.

Dotson grabbed it, stepped onto the rail and flipped the powder case into the Solomon Sea. Then he reached down and pulled Taylor to his feet and patted him on the back.

They spoke for a moment, then trudged back into the gun mount knowing they still had to get the projectile.

Childers pointed to a group of men in the water up ahead. "Gotta go get these guys. Good luck, skipper." He walked to the other side of the pilot house and began rescue operations,

Chief Dotson appeared at the hatch of mount 51 and shouted at Benedek. The gunner's mate walked forward and handed over his sound-powered headset. Dotson jammed it on and leaned inside to connect it. Benedek lingered at the hatchway talking to Dotson.

Lutz, beside Ingram, was watching, too. Fully conscious, he said, "Those three guys are a crazy bunch of brave bastards."

Then he said, "Woah! Bridge aye. Mount 51 is on the line. They report the mount is all screwed up inside. It's a yard job for sure. Also, there's no firing circuit. They did get the breech block to open and pull the powder case. But the projectile is stuck in the barrel. They're gonna jury-rig a firing circuit and see if they can kick it out with a short round. They estimate twenty minutes to let the barrel cool and to rig a firing circuit."

Ingram said, "Nice. Make it so."

"Sorry sir. What was that?"

Ingram stood close. He had to shout. "I said yes go ahead. That sounds good." He clapped Lutz on the shoulders. "Got that?"

"Yes, sir." Lutz relayed the message exactly as Ingram said.

Childers was beside Ingram. "We got about fifteen guys to haul in. Not in bad shape after all they went through."

"Well, that's something."

Lutz said, "CIC reports, sir."

Ingram looked at Childers, "Speaking of CIC, since Mr. Taylor is absent without leave, who is minding the store down there?"

Childers cleared his throat, "Lieutenant junior grade Travis Allread. The CIC officer. Damn good man."

Ingram gave a half grin. "Very well." To Lutz he said, "Yes, what is CIC telling us Lutz?"

"What?"

"Can you hear me Lutz?"

"My left ear is kind of screwed up."

"Better have the Doc look at it." He looked down. Tony Laws, the pharmacist mate first class was putting the finishing touches on a large pressure bandage on Jonathan Grout, now awake and flashing a thumbs up. Laws stood and spoke to two stretcher carriers. Then he turned to Ingram, "That should hold it." He pulled a jagged piece of metal from his pocket. "Hideous looking thing, huh?"

"Good God," said Ingram.

Laws said. "We'll put him in his rack down below. Keep him quiet. Assign someone to watch him for four hours. But I think he'll be okay."

Ingram said, "Okay Tony, can you check Lutz' ear? Something might have blown out an eardrum?"

Laws asked, "Which one?"

"Left."

"Okay." He was already on Lutz' left side. Laws cupped a hand and shouted, "Hey, Norman, you stupid shit. Can you hear me?"

Lutz was watching the rescue activities as the last few men alongside crawled up the cargo net. He didn't respond.

Laws turned to Ingram and said, "Yes, sir, I'd say something is wrong with his left ear. Maybe both. Send him down to sick bay in about an hour. Right now, I have a bunch of guys who need attention."

"Go, Tony. Thank you."

"Yessir." Laws bolted down the ladder.

"Skipper." It was Childers. "Just spoke with Allread in CIC. Message for us on sectac. Commodore is going to pack it up and go home. They'll torpedo *Chevalier* soon and put her out of her misery. Then *Selfridge* and *O'Bannon* will limp for Purvis Bay while they still have some nighttime to hide in. They want us to stick around until mid-morning and make sure we have all the survivors. We'll have air cover, it says. After that, we can come back."

"Okay. What's for breakfast?"

"Damned if I know."

Twenty minutes passed. Taylor called on the dot.

Lutz cupped his right ear. "Bridge aye." He said, "They're ready, captain."

Ingram checked the barrel of mount 51. It was frozen in place but pointed in a safe direction off to starboard. "Okay, Lutz. Tell them to go ahead."

"What?"

Ingram shouted at him to say, 'go ahead.'

Lutz' eyes crossed a bit then he keyed his mic. "Mount 51 Bridge. Permission granted."

Fifteen torturous seconds passed. Then, COUGH. With a puff of smoke, the round wobbled into the night. Moonlight glinted as it traveled about a hundred and fifty yards and plopped into the water.

They had a quiet meal under red lights in the wardroom: Ingram, Childers and Jack Taylor. The others had already eaten. Canned spaghetti. But nothing ever tasted so wonderful. They were hungry and ate like cavemen.

Finally, they pushed back and poured coffee. Ingram asked, "Okay Jack, let us in on your secret. Where did you learn all that stuff?"

Taylor nodded, "Glad I could do this."

"What are you talking about?" asked Childers.

"Payback time. My Uncle Bob. He and my dad were both chief gunners' mates. That's all they ever talked about. Drove my mom and Aunt Alice nuts at dinner time. But yeah, my brother and I both learned some of the finer points of the five-inch thirty-eight from those two. They would drill us. Get out stopwatches. Make bets.Take us on tours. We got to be better than some of those gunners' mates."

"Wow," said Ingram. "And they're retired now?"

Taylor looked in the distance. "Dad is. He's doing fine. Uncle Bob bought it at Pearl Habor. He was on the *Oklahoma*." He slowly shook his head. "Six months short of retirement."

Again, profound silence. Ingram sipped coffee and said, "I'm sure your Uncle Bob is up there now, looking down and pleased as all get-out. Yeah, it was payback time. And you did it up very well."

"For sure. For damned sure," added Childers.

Taylor snorted, "But you should have heard us in the gun mount, trying to work out a firing circuit. We argued like thirteen-year-olds, screaming at each other. It almost came to blows. Benedek got between us. Jeez, he's a strong little bastard."

Childers said, "What the hell? We couldn't hear up on the bridge."

"Nobody could, thank God," said Ingram. "How'd it play out?"

Taylor shrugged, "I wanted it wired B to A and Dotson wanted it A to B."

"What happened?" asked Ingram

"Benedek. He wanted B to C. He said we were both full of shit. Now, we're all yelling at each other. But it was Benedek's mount so we figured he knew the firing circuit better than anybody."

"So, he was right?" asked Childers.

"It was his mount and he is the gun captain so we wired it that way," chuckled Taylor. "But I checked later. All three wiring schemes worked."

Childers slapped the table. "Damn. Ain't that one for the books?"

Ingram said, "Nevertheless, it worked."

Taylor grinned, "Glad I could do it. Never thought I'd have this kind of chance."

Ingram steepled his fingers, "Maybe I make you gun boss rather than CO?"

"Worse things have happened to me."

They laughed.

More silence followed. Air rushed from the blowers. Childers mused, "How do you think we did today? Was it worth it?"

Ingram drummed his fingers for a moment. "Well, when you think of it, four destroyers against nine: not bad. We sunk one of theirs. They sank one of ours. But I think they got away with their troops. We were too busy getting our butts kicked to stop them from getting out."

"Yeah, but four to nine; that ain't bad," said Childers.

"Not bad," agreed Ingram. "But the party isn't over. Those guys are still intact and full of fight. It's not going to be easy."

"That's for sure," Childers pushed his chair back. "Permission to secure, captain?"

Ingram nodded. "Last one to hit the sack is a rotten egg."

Their air cover was two Marine F4F Wildcats. They showed up at 0600 and they laid down a search pattern beginning about ten miles off Marquana Bay. The planes buzzed back and forth at 5,000 feet as the search expanded below them. They ran across seven Japanese sailors hanging on to the remnant of a wooden platform. They refused to surrender. After pleading with them for twenty minutes in pigeon-Japanese, Ingram had the storekeepers toss over three quart-sized tins of fresh water and a gallon can of tomatoes. Then they rolled on to the north and called off the search about 1030 and dispatched the Wildcats which flew north.

They were back in ten minutes and flying low. The leader called in on the sectac circuit patched into CIC. Ingram listened on the bridge.

"Haystack, this is Calamity one zero. Over. "

"Go ahead Calamity." It was George Eckert, the officer on watch.

In echelon, the two wildcats growled over the *Dunagan* as they came back on the circuit. "Be advised there is a Marine in a raft about twenty miles northwest of Haystack. Over."

"That's great, Calamity. How do we find him? Over."

"We'll loop around and fly over you. Our direction will be your vector. Over."

Eckert responded with, "Very nice, Calamity. Thank you. Uh, interrogative. How do you know he is a Marine? Over."

"Haystack, this is Calamity one zero. He identified himself properly."

Ingram sighted the two wildcats approaching the pelorus. "Looks to be three-zero-five," he said to the bridge talker. The talker relayed it to Eckert in CIC .

"Say again," demanded Eckert, forgetting proper radio procedure.

"Because he gave us the finger, Calamity one zero, out."

At that moment, the two wildcats again roared over the top heading northwest. The leader came up again with, "Haystack. Concur: course three-zero-five is good enough for government work."

Ingram nodded to Leon Buckner, the OOD, who ordered, "Steer three-zero-five."

Then he said, "Crank it up, Mr. Buckner. Thirty knots, please."

Buckner grinned from ear to ear and called, "All engines ahead flank. Indicate three-zero-five turns for thirty knots."

40

31 August 1943
Solomon Sea
S 7° 21.3' E 155° 34.1
Eighteen Miles east of Mono Island

Morning. The sun's upper limb blasted above the horizon. Bright. It nearly
blinded Hitchcock with the new day as it shone directly on him. Afraid
of good news or bad news, he hadn't looked all night. But now, he was
beyond exhaustion, far beyond the limits of his endurance. He needed a
pick-me-up. A bit of encouragement. With a massive groan, he shipped his
oars and turned.

Sheeeeyat.

Mono Island was still out there miles away. Maybe eighteen to twenty
miles. What the hell was going on? Maybe he should—

VROOM, VROOM. Two planes blasted overhead. He looked up in time
to see green paint and the meatball on their fuselages.

Japs.

They were turning. Yes, coming back. Maybe to strafe him. He took off
his shirt and boots and waited. On they came, slower. He laid out on the

raft, arms, and feet askew, as if he were dead. They flashed overhead. He opened an eye and peeked. One had his canopy cranked back, looking him over. They zipped on past, their engines howling louder as they gained speed and flew...yes, directly north, soon out of sight.

He waited and checked the oar blade dangling in the water. For the first time, he

saw it.

Current. Swirling around the oar blade. In the wrong direction dragging him

away from Mono Island and back toward Vella LaVella. All that time wasted. That rowing, all for nothing.

Sleep. Suddenly it all drained from him. He felt tired. The inside of his mouth: pasty. And full of salt. He needed food, water...and sleep. Think of something.

But he had been pulling most of the night and was tired, dog tired. He slouched over the oars. At times, he couldn't figure out which way was west.

And a good deal of the night had been occupied by the thunder of naval gunfire. A couple of times he heard the sharp crack of a big explosion, like a ship going up, or at least a torpedo hit. The sky would light up, too. Light flashes danced to the southeast, from where those ships were duking it out. It was the hideous sound of men dying, he knew. At times the whole southeast sky was illuminated by gun fire, five inch, he guessed.

Hitchcock remembered we were going up against those nine Jap cans. And as far as Hitchcock knew, three destroyers were all that the U.S. Navy had nearby. A tin can war. Three of ours against nine of theirs. Todd Ingram and his *Dunagan* would have been there for sure duking it out with the Japs. *Go gettum, Todd.*

Little wavelets slapped the life raft. He looked back over his shoulder. Mono Island stood way back there, laughing at him. Mono beckoned like an ancient siren, *I'm right here, you stupid Jarhead. Come and get me.*

The gunfire confused him at times. He'd just stopped rowing and gaped at the explosions as one watches a Fourth of July Fireworks show.

At length, things slowed down, then eventually fizzled out. He couldn't tell who did what to whom.

He found strength to wiggle back into his shirt. He left his boots off. Water slopping in the bottom of the raft felt good on his feet...his eyes kept closing...he couldn't...except her face. She raised a hand...

41

31 August 1943
U.S.S. *Dunagan* (DD 504)
Solomon Sea
S 7° 21.3' E 155° 34.1
Eighteen Miles east of Mono Island

Dunagan dug in. As she approached thirty knots, she actually squatted down low in the water, her powerful screws driving hard. Her decks vibrated and her uptakes screamed as blowers packed air down to the boilers. Wind whistled through the standing rigging, and her bow cut an enormous wave as she cut through the calm, mirror-smooth, waters of the Solomon Sea. Once at thirty knots she threw an enormous stern wake which stood above her fantail by about ten to twelve feet.

The word traveled fast. Childers, Taylor, and half the wardroom cascaded up to the bridge.

Hitchcock? They mused. It can't be. They were afraid to say his name. Only that the stupid jarhead must have lived ten lives. How could he survive all this? But then they figured, it's only been a couple of days. Piece of cake.

Harry O'Toole, a chief radioman, saw it first. He pointed a bit off to his left. Buckner picked it up with his binoculars. Ingram saw it with the rest. A man lay in a bright yellow life raft. Ingram slowed to ten knots lest they swamp the poor man. Then he had the cargo net thrown over and men ready to scramble down and lift him aboard.

They still didn't know who or what it was in the raft. Just that it was an amorphous mess of canvas and gear and rumpled clothes. They stopped engines and coasted the last two ship lengths.

With fifty feet to go, they heard a hoarse voice, "Ingraaaaam. You sorry son-of-a-bitch. What took you so long?"

Ingram sent Jack Taylor to bunk with Childers. Hitchcock got the best the *Dunagan* could offer. The bunk in the captain's in-port cabin; the stateroom with its own bathroom and shower, the stateroom where he excommunicated Jack Taylor when he reported with his fly unzipped.

And it turned out Hitchcock needed the solace. He didn't realize he'd been wounded. There was a nasty deep gash on the back of his left thigh. He'd been hit by something. A piece of flying shrapnel maybe. Hitchcock never discovered what hit him, only that he'd lost a lot of blood.

Hitchcock growled when Tony Laws refused medicinal booze. He also grumbled when Laws allowed only a light portion of solid food and water. Laws was afraid Hitchcock would vomit it all during the first few hours. But Laws and one of his corpsmen stood him in the shower and sudsed him up. Then, they sewed up the wound in his thigh. With that, they dried him and put him between clean sheets in the bunk while the ship raced for Purvis Bay in Tulagi. With the four superheaters still lighted, the ship thundered through The Slot at thirty-five knots throwing an enormous rooster tail above the fantail.

And so, a semi-delirious Gunnery Sergeant Gilroy Hitchcock cried as the ship vibrated and shook. Ingram sat alone with Hitchcock while he got it all out. He bawled like a baby. Cried about Fowler. Cried about getting married.

He cried about the night he got Lolli pregnant; it was a balmy evening, Hitchcock was in town on a delivery. They'd had dinner then walked along the beach under a delicious half moon. Blind woman or not, that was all it took. It seemed she was more after him than he was after her.

Then he cried about bungling the mission and Fowler getting all chopped up with twenty millimeter cannon fire. He started all over again.

It wasn't until they were abeam of New Georgia Island that he calmed down. One could tell Gunnery Sergeant Gilroy Hitchcock was headed for the sleep he needed so much. But, just before, his eyes blinked and then popped open: fully awake. He looked up at Ingram.

He grinned, "Yeah, you're still here."

"Just trying to help a stupid Marine."

Hitchcock extended his hand. His eyes were intense, like embers. "Do me a favor?"

Ingram grabbed it. His grip was firm. "Anything you want, Jarhead."

"Be the best man at my wedding?"

42

9 September 1943
USS *Wahoo* (SS 238)
La Pérouse Strait
Sea of Japan

It was 9 September 1943 when *Wahoo* left Pearl Harbor on her seventh war patrol. With a refueling stop at Midway, she was bound for the Sea of Japan with a load of twenty-four mark 18 torpedoes. During her time in her assigned patrol area, records show that five Japanese cargo ships were lost due to torpedo attacks. *Wahoo* was then scheduled to exit the Sea of Japan via the La Pérouse Strait between Hokkaido Japan and Karafuto Islands on 11 October 1943. From there, she was to sail through the Etorofu Strait in the Kurils en route to Midway for fuel, and on to Pearl Harbor.

There is no doubt that Morton and his crew were well prepared on this trip. A number of modifications had been made to the *Wahoo* after her previous patrol, her sixth. This time, far more attention had been paid to torpedoes and tactics. They were itching, almost vengeful. For after nearly two years of frustration, Morton, in particular, believed he was on top of something and was anxious to try it out. She was also scheduled to share the Sea of Japan with the USS *Sawfish* (SS 276): Wahoo in the Southern half, *Sawfish* well to the north. A close examination of Sawfish's records indicate there was no infringement by either vessel in their assigned areas.

And five cargo ships if that was it, was not a bad record.

But the *Wahoo* didn't make it beyond the La Pérouse Strait on her homeward trip. She was caught on the surface by gun batteries on Hokkaido's Northern shores, later by aircraft with depth charges, and after that, by anti-submarine vessels with more depth charges.

Thus, the *Wahoo* came to rest in 213 feet of water, not to be discovered for sixty-three years until 28 July 2006. Lost were one hundred brave souls including her captain, Commander Dudley W. Morton and her executive officer, Lieutenant Commander Verne l. Skjonsby.

RIP.

EPILOGUE

M. AND Mme ANDRÉ LAPRESSE
REQUEST THE HONOR OF YOUR PRESENCE
AT THE NUPTUAL MASS UNITING THEIR DAUGHTER

CHARLOTTE MARIE CARLEEN
AND
GILROY HITCHCOCK, GUNNERY SERGEANT,
UNITED STATES MARINE CORPS, (RETIRED)

SATURDAY, THE TWENTIETH OF NOVEMBER, 1943
Cathédrale Saint-Joseph de Nouméa
3 RUE FREDERICK SURLEAU
NOUMEA, NEW CALEDONIA
AT SIX O'CLOCK IN THE EVENING

20 November 1943
Room 216, Phillipe Auberge Hotel
Baie des Citrons (Lemon Bay)
Noumea, New Caledonia

Cathédrale Saint-Joseph de Nouméa was high on a hill with a spectacular view of the harbor. The church was a sprawling Romanesque revival building built between 1887 and 1897. One could not have picked a more beautiful setting.

Ingram was happy for the whole family who he enjoyed meeting. And Lolli was everything Hitchcock had said she was. Indeed, Hitchcock had, this time, snagged the right woman.

The night before they had a little celebration with dinner and a hosted bar. They'd all shared: Hitchcock, the Lapresse family, Ingram, Childers, Taylor, Jon McGovern, and Marine buddies Hitchcock never knew he had, even General Vandergrift showed up. Add to that, more people from Chanel and many more friends Andre and Charlotte Lapresse never knew they had. It was as if the war never existed. Andre had the staff pull some of that fantastic French wine from the cellars. The cares and sorrows of the Pacific and the Atlantic theaters were dashed and buried somewhere else. Temporarily, at least. All enjoyed themselves and looked forward to the wedding and reception.

Hitchcock had just wanted a small wedding. But Andre and Charlotte Lapresse opened the floodgates. Coco Chanel helped financially with the wedding, reception, and the honeymoon.

The little phone rang. Strident. Penetrating. It wouldn't stop. Hitchcock cranked open a single bloodstained eye. It found his wristwatch stretched across the nightstand. Moonlight glimmered on the face: 0215.

A dream began. The telephone crashed into that. "Damnit." The night before his wedding and that thing was destroying his sleep.

Last night's activities were taking their revenge. A non-scheduled pre-party. The worst kind and too much fun. Marines and sailors. An uproar.

This evening would be more sedate. Hopefully. The wedding would begin at six o'clock: eighteen hours away. Then a reception. Yes, today was the main event.

His head swam.

"Shit!" Hitchcock grappled with the phone and brought it to his ear. "Hullo?"

"Darling! It's me."

Good God. He sat up. "Lolli?" His voice was hoarse.

"You sound terrible."

"Baby, are you all right?"

"Well, there is one small problem."

"What is it?" Hitchcock was wide-awake.

"I'm pregnant."

He grinned. "You're telling me, babe. You're beginning to show." He settled back. He heard voices in the background. Her folks. "No. I didn't mean that. You're not showing at all. I thought about it when we danced. Very nice. Say, is that Mom and Dad?"

"*Oui, monsieur.* And they are very happy as am I."

He heard Andre and Charlotte singing out "*Vive la Gilroy. Vive la Gilroy.*"

Hitchcock said, "Tell them thanks, but they don't know me that well yet."

Lolli said, "But, I do. You see, I can see. My sight has returned. Vive la Sergeant Hitchcock," she nearly shouted.

Astounding. She can see. He jumped out of bed. "You mean..."

"Yes."

"My God, really, see?"

"Yes, about fifteen minutes ago. I woke up. Like in a dream. A strange light. It was the first thing I saw. The moon. Just outside my window. It's beautiful."

Hitchcock stepped to the window and was bathed in full moonlight. "Amazing, you're right. It is a full moon. Maybe I should come up and celebrate."

There was a hurried conversation. Lolli came back with, "Mama and Papa say not a good idea. Not on the day of the wedding."

"Aw shucks." He exhaled. "I wanted you to see me in moonlight rather than discover how ugly I am in broad daylight."

"Not to worry. I can see you anyway."

"Of course, baby. Sure you can."

"No, I mean it. Up here, on the sixth floor. You're not so bad after all."

"No kidding?" The building was 'U' shaped. He looked across and up to see a lone figure in white. Waving.

"My God, is that you?" Glad he was in shorts, he waved back. "Never seen anything so beautiful." Good God. She has a set of—"Binoculars. That's cheating."

She laughed, a deep laugh of mirth and good health. "No, my love. You are better looking than Mama said. I can't wait."

Hitchcock said half seriously, "Well, hell. If that's the case I'm coming up there right now. Kick the friggin' door in." Like a wolf he went "Oooooowwwooooo."

"No, you are the—" The light went on in the room. Suddenly, Lolli was gorgeously backlit. She screeched, "Papa!"

Laughter. Charlotte yelled at her husband. The light went off.

"You are handsome, like Mama said," Lolli repeated almost reverently.

Lolli came back to the window, a blue-green apparition that Hitchcock would never forget. "I must go, now. Good night, dear love," she said.

"Sweet dreams to you, too."

They hung up.

———

A fully awake Hitchcock didn't waste time. A watch messenger roused Ingram from his bunk to let him know there was phone call for him. The *Dunagan* was in Noumea Harbor, undergoing the installation of a new five-inch gun on the foredeck. While Hitchcock blabbered from the warmth of his hotel room, a shivering Ingram took the call on the quarterdeck in a misty rain.

"Yes, Lolli was beautiful. Thank you so much for letting me be there."

"It was a hell of a party, yes?" Hitchcock roared.

Ingram's teeth chattered while Hitchcock, snug in his snazzy hotel room, slopped up scotch. Yes, Ingram agreed. A hell of a party. And Lolli's father, Andre, was a bigger screw-off than his son-in-law-to-be. After a couple of drinks, the two started horsing around with everybody roaring, including General Vandergrift.

Jack Taylor, it turned out, played the piano and they all started singing.

Later on, Ingram discovered after a long conversation with Charlotte senior, that Andre may have gotten out of France just in time. A two-page handwritten letter from Coco Chanel let on that things had become a bit tepid. But that she, with the help of Dinklage, had suppressed it. However, Coco had added, Andre was to be on good behavior henceforth.

Hitchcock blasted into his reverie, "And the best news?"

Ingram checked his watch: 0252. He was about ready to hang up. "What's that?"

"Her sight returned. She can see." Hitchcock blasted.

"She what? You mean...?"

"Hell yes, I mean exactly that. She can see. She's already seen me from her hotel room and approves. I think. I gotta tell you. I was sweating that one. I really think she approves of me. Can you believe it?"

"I told her to watch out, that you're ugly."

"Well, somehow, she tuned you out, old buddy. She approves of me. And her folks do too." Hitchcock went on with the excitement that his bride's sight had returned. That she would be fully aware of everything in the church. Something she would remember for the rest of her life.

"And it's dress whites, you stupid squid," Hitchcock went on. "Medals, swords, everything. You still have all that shit?"

"I think so."

"You ever done a crossed swords ceremony?"

"No."

"Never mind. We'll teach you."

"Okay."

"Don't forget your Navy Cross."

NOTES

Chapter 1

1. Swissair had suspended its regular commercial operations during World War II.

Chapter 8

1. ONI – Office of Naval Intelligence
2. Dumbo – PBY twin engine sea plane famous for air rescue and bombing missions.

Chapter 14

1. DCA = Damage Control Assistant
2. Able Able Common projectile (AAC) A medium penetrating shell with a mechanical time fuse and a base detonating fuse. Designed to be used on either aircraft or lightly armored ships. For aircraft, the time fuse is set to explode the shell just before it reaches the target. The detonation shock wave and the expanding cone of shrapnel increases the chance of target destruction. For vessels, the time fuse is left on safe, and the base detonating fuse will explode the shell 25 milliseconds after impact.
3. DIW – dead in the water

Chapter 24

1. The Walrus and the Carpenter", Partially adopted from a narrative poem by Lewis Carroll that appears in his book *Through the Looking glass.*

Chapter 27

1. Brow - large gangplank leading from a ship to a pier, wharf, or float; usually equipped with handrails.

Chapter 32

1. Brig – Originally referred to as a brig, a sailing ship. The Navy conveniently used two masted ships., i.e. brigs, as a prison to confine offenders.

A Call to Colors
By John J. Gobbell

General Douglas MacArthur's promise to the Filipinos was "I shall return."

But it will take 165,000 troops and 700 ships in the bloody battle of Leyte Gulf to do it.

Among them is the destroyer USS Matthew and her skipper, Commander Mike Donovan, a veteran haunted by earlier battles. What Donovan doesn't know is that a Japanese admiral has laid an ingenious trap in the Leyte Gulf.

But Donovan faces something even deadlier than Japanese battleships: explosives secretly slipped on board by saboteurs, set to detonate at any time.

Now the ship's survival hinges on the ability of Donovan and his men to dismantle a bomb in the midst of the panic...and the chaos of history's greatest naval battle.

Get your copy today at
severnriverbooks.com

ABOUT THE AUTHOR

JOHN J. GOBBELL is a former Navy Lieutenant who saw duty as a destroyer weapons officer. His ship served in the South China Sea, granting him membership in the exclusive *Tonkin Gulf Yacht Club*. As an executive recruiter, his clients included military/commercial aerospace companies giving him insight into character development under a historical thriller format. An award-winning author, John has published eight novels. The books in his popular Todd Ingram series are based on the U.S Navy in the Pacific theater of World War II. John and his wife Janine live in Newport Beach, California.

Sign up for John J. Gobbell's newsletter at
severnriverbooks.com
johnjgobbell@severnriverbooks.com